The Money Tree

The Money Tree

By

Sam Mills

About the Book

Set in the wilds of Western North Carolina, the story turns on two brothers' chance discovery of a marijuana dealers-growers money "drop" in the knothole of a tree. The impoverished boys enjoy the "fruits" of "the money tree" until they are caught in *flagrante* by the drug dealers, whose money it is. (At the same point, they witness the murder of a pot grower wrongly thought by the dealers of being the one who's ripping them off.)

The boys escape by the skin of their teeth, setting off a wild, downriver chase through the trackless Green River Wilderness, a chase that pits unarmed country boys and armed-to-the-teeth city men in a "guerilla" war to the death. (Shades of *Deliverance* meets *The Client* meets *Home Alone*!)

The Money Tree's cliffhanger storyline delivers a fast and furious read with cinematic vividness. On a deeper level, as a rite of passage-coming of age story, it charts the initiation of the brothers, while examining the related, universal themes of love vs. money, greed-generosity, crime-honesty, courage-cowardice.

A BOY. COMING ALONG THE RIVER ROAD. Orange sun tangled in the treetops. End of an endless summer's day. He carried a fishing rod in one hand and a long stringer of rainbow trout in the other. (Some of the fish were still alive, flopping, red gills fluking, rattling the rusty stringer.) Sagging knapsack on his back. Red baseball cap with a white W pulled low over his eyes against the slatting sun. He was shirtless, and from time to time, the X-shaped tan-lines the suspenders had left on his brown back were visible.

Now, stumbling, he scuffed his feet in the gravel. Kicked up—then picked up—a big piece of road rock. Putting down rod and trout, he hefted the stone for weight. Slowly, he wound up like a big-league pitcher. Taking a stretch, he held the runner close at first, then winged the rock at the yellow-and-black HOMELITE CHAINSAWS sign. Connected with a loud gong.

Whirling, he sank to his knees, right arm pumping. "Steeee-riker!"

Picking up rod and trout, he continued up the road. In the rutted wheelways, hot sand up to his ankles. On the washboard inclines, the road eroded to its sandstone ribs.

The boy, Mitchell Rainey, age twelve, trudged happily along, fatigue evident in his dragging footfalls. Clothes ragged hand-me-downs. Patched denim overalls—Oshkosh b'gosh!—watermarked at mid-thigh from wading. His little toes stuck through the sides of his black, high-top tennis shoes.

Two dogs, Mica and Suellen—blooded Walker coonhounds with woebegone, bloodhound faces—followed at his heels, lop-ears dragging in the dust. (The young male, Mica, barked halfheartedly at the squirming fish.)

Now, shrugging into his pack, bouncing it higher on his thin shoulders, Mitch left the gravelled state road. Fell off the steep embankment toward the river below. Toward the sound of white water. Toward the shuddering roar of Mine Falls above.

THE FALLS WERE IN SIGHT—sunstruck and glittering in the westward-flowing river; spray rising like woodsmoke from the base behind the trees—as Mitch waded up a wide shallow stretch of green river. Water up to his thighs. Overalls two-tone now, new-looking and old-looking, a line of wet and dry.

On either shore, moss turfed the banks like a golf-course water hazard. Sawlogs that had escaped the loggers in the log drive bobbed against them, held fast by the current. Mitch saw the deep gouges the climbing spikes had made ascending, and the deeper gouges of the canthooks where the logs had been turned and graded. Long corkscrew shavings like potato curls still clung to the climbers' descending gouges. Mitch could see the millmarks burned into the resinous end-grains. He couldn't read them at this distance, but knew they said STILSON PULP & PAPER. He recognized the logo. In the logo, the P's were rendered as axes; the ampersand was a spruce tree.

Mitch took a worm from the red tobacco tin in his back pocket and looped it on the hook. (Threading it, he knew, killed them too fast.) He spat on the wiggler for luck and cast upstream toward the deep green water along the left bank. Reeling, he took up slack as the current tumbled the bait back to him.

Overhead, the steep, westering light streamed through the cathedral spruce in dust-defined rays as through high yellow skylights. Crows cawed. Appeared above the sheer-walled canyon of spruce, flying to roost. Mitch watched them over the river, glinting black as fresh-cracked anthracite.

After three casts, he reeled in. He swung the line in and, gripping it above the hook, waded toward the thundering falls. There was a long pool below the falls, and logs had jammed up across the tailrace. At the base of the falls, one log had buried up endwise in the sandbar and stood in the falling water like a telephone pole. The long curling slivers gouged out by the climbers made it look even more like a phone pole.

Mitch crouched to lower his silhouette and walked like a lumberjack burler out onto the rafted logs. They rocked in the current and water broke over the upstream end. Already, the bark was slippery with algae. He knew it was dangerous. Loggers who fell between the logs during a drive often had their skulls crushed, or were held down until they drowned.

Now Mitch felt them shift under his feet and went into a three-point stance. He cast into the sudsy, green-water tailout just where the white water ended. Though there were three splitshot above the number-six hook, the current swept the bait quickly back to him. Mitch reeled steadily, taking up line.

There was an eddy behind a boulder near the right bank, twirling a suds of fir needles, green and brown. When the line reached it, it stopped. Mitch took up the slack and lifted the rod tip, and there came a jolting strike. He set the hook, and the rod bent over steeply.

Mitch ran across the logs, and spinning, they sank beneath him like piano keys. Near the bank, he leaped off into the shallows, splashed ashore and landed the trout by swinging it into the undergrowth. There, it bounced around in the dry leaves, then lay still, gills working.

Mitch put his foot on the fish and reeled up the line. He unhooked the fish—this one a brookie, metallic blue with red and tan spots—and clipped it on the stringer. He held the stringer high, smiling wide, rotating it, admiring the day's catch. Out of the water, the living fish began to flurry, sprinkling him, and Mica danced around them, barking.

The trout had made seven, his limit. Mitch reeled in. He cleaned the mangled worm from the hook and buried the hook deep in the cork grip of the flyrod.

Whistling up the dogs, he took the riverbank footpath toward the falls. This near the cataract, the roar was more concussion than sound, and his eardrums popped again and again. Mist rose into the streaming sunlight dense as smoke from a forest fire. Mitch felt the ground quaking through the thin soles of his shoes. Felt the cold wet wind that gusted down the pool, exhilarating after the heat of day.

THE FOOTPATH ENDED ON THE SANDBAR AT THE BASE of the falls. Mitch looked up the cascade and saw the river bending green and solid as a flying buttress; as though blown from molten Coca-Cola glass, barely an arm's length distant.

Now a tree limb flashed by, breaking the illusion.

Mitch put the trout in the pack to free his hands and, with a weary sigh, began to climb. (Once they divined his intention, the dogs disappeared downstream to circle through the woods.)

Hand over hand, he worked his way up one green-algaed side. The granite quaked from the force of falling water, and ice-water spray beaded on rod and reel, blown into his face and lungs as from a mister. The mossy, musty smell as of a springhouse was strong. Straining against backpack and trout, slipping and sliding, he knocked loose slates that floated into the gorge light-seeming as Frisbees.

Finally, Mitch stood high atop the falls and looked down at the river a hundred feet below. He watched the white water fanning out, foaming out to green; then let his eyes follow the river, noting each hole where he'd taken trout.

Mitch looked far downstream, beyond the road—visible as a band of dust-dulled leaves in the unbroken canopy of waxy hardwoods—and saw the white water disappear into the spruce forest as into a green-painted tunnel. He had never been down there before, and someday soon, he would pack a knapsack and fish it all the way through to the Interstate bridge. In the fantasy, Mitch caught the state-record brown trout and released it. He sighed happily at the prospect. Mitchell Rainey inhabited a world altogether perfect in its seamless simplicity. Within the half-hour that was to be changed forever.

Now he spat and watched his spittle float out into the void. Spreading like a silvery spider's web. Vanishing in the white water.

THE TRAIL CONTINUED ABOVE THE FALLS, boggy at first, the high-heeled wader tracks filled with black water; then rose, dusty and rooty, into the riverbank trees. Dark was falling, the gnats had begun to bite and a river-mist chill was in the air as Mitchell trudged through the trees.

Now the trail dipped down, following the fishermen who made it, and came back to the river at the next good pool, deep and green, sudsy where the river broke around two boulders in midstream and sluiced against the undercut bank. The rhododendron canopy trembled from the current and dripped with spray. Faintly, Mitch smelled a skunk.

Mitch followed the path, boggy again with the springhead that entered there. Where the spring boiled up above the path—set in the mossy staves of an old barrel; the surface pulsing convex, deep and clear and achingly cold; a tiny tornado of sand spurting in the bottom—he stopped to give the fish a final bath. All of the trout were dead, sand in their rigid red gills, the vivid, crimson rainbows gone from their sides. Wrinkled, covered with sand and peanut shells from the knapsack, the lone brookie had lost its metallic sheen.

Briefly, Mitch considered cleaning them, but a look at the pinkening sky dissuaded him. It was deep dusk beneath the trees. He stood and slipped his suspenders—his overalls falling at his feet; his underpants muddy in the seat—and pulled on the teeshirt he had taken from his hip pocket.

There was a clearing ahead where the footpath left the river and started by steep switchbacks up the mountain. Mitch stopped in the clearing, breathing hard, and leaned against a tree. He used the pack for a cushion, and through it felt the cylindrical hardness of his thermos. In the clearing, the skunk smell was stronger.

Head back, he saw evening above the moving treetops, the color draining from the salmon sky. Whistling up the dogs, he shrugged into his pack, bounced it higher on his shoulders and started up the mountainside with a quickened step.

Above, where the road curved back and crossed the river at the first falls, there was an old millhouse below the shake-covered bridge. Mitch didn't want to pass the old mill after dark. Years before, terrible things had happened there. A love triangle had been surgically separated with a double-bitted axe, and according to legend, the ghost of the cuckolded husband continued his practice on a freelance basis.

Leaning into the pack, Mitch climbed the mountain. Here, the path was steep and strenuous-going, especially with the backpack and trout, and he was quickly winded.

At the fifth switchback, he stopped, chest heaving, and

leaned against a tree. He looked down at the river, roaring faintly in the valley below. The sound of white water filtered up, softened by distance, hardened by echo. Looking up, he saw the first bats cutting didoes in the dusk. An owl hooted on the mountain across the river, and another answered from down the valley. At the sound of the owls, Mitch remembered the mill.

He stood with a sigh and started off. Leaning into the steep grade. Leaning into the heavy pack. Using trailside saplings to pull himself along. Hands up to knock down the spiders webs, invisible as the path began to tunnel through the dark rhododendrons. Mica and Suellen were coursing out on either side—when with a yelp, the dogs happened on a squirrel—Mitchell's first startled thought was a snake—and it scurried down the mountainside in a flurry of dry leaves.

Mica bolted after it, barking.

Mitch leaped to collar him but missed. Now he screamed after the dog, "Mica, here, boy! Heel, Mica! Mica, *heel!* Dammit, Mica, *come here!*"

But though he screamed himself hoarse, the dog paid him no heed – even when he searched the gullied footpath for rocks and winged a couple after him. Far below, Mitch could hear dog and squirrel crashing through the undergrowth. Mica sang out in his deep, melodious, trailing voice.

The other dog, Suellen, made no move to follow. Instead, she looked at Mitchell with a wrinkled, funereal face and wagged her tail. What's a mother to do? her long-suffering expression seemed to say.

"Mica, you son-of-a-bitch!" His voice echoed off the facing mountain. Now he looked at Suellen and laughed. "No offense, Suellen."

With a sigh, Mitchell slipped his pack. Turned and went after Mica. Went toward the sound of the rich, throaty baying in the river valley below.

DOG AND SQUIRREL HAD LEFT THE FOOTPATH, and Mitch crashed after them, breaking a trail through the heavy underbrush. Limbs took him full in the face. Tendrils of Turkey Paw sent him headlong. Spider webs enclosed him in a dewy embrace that he backed out of, sputtering, his skin crawling at the image of the big yellow-and-black spiders that inhabited them. Back down the mountain he went, muttering all the way. Impugning Mica's pedigree back ten generations. Suellen followed dutifully at his heels, letting Mitchell break the trail.

Though it was nearly dark in the undergrowth, when boy and dog broke out near the river—green and wide, creaming around the mossed boulders of midstream; glimmering in the twilight, casting liquid reflections on the underside of the rhododendron canopy—it was daylight again.

Mitchell knelt and splashed water on his face. Absently, he studied the mink tracks in the sandbar there—like cat tracks but with pointed toes—then lay in a prolonged pushup as he drank. Tannic acid leached from the log bark gave the water a faintly acidic taste and smell. Suellen snuffled at the cold tracks without interest, then joined Mitch for a drink.

Following the river, easy going now in the thinned growth of the sandy floodplain—the big sycamores and spruce floodwater-marked; a rib-splintered piece of a red canoe wedged in a crotch high overhead—working toward the sound of the barking, Mitchell found Mica in the clearing on the riverbank. The dog stood with both front feet up on an immense oak, barking at a knothole high above him. The tree, Mitch noted as he came up, was only fifty feet from the base of the trail.

He sighed and shook his head in disgust; then collared the dog and jerked him roughly down. He jerked Mica by one long ear until he yelped.

"Bad dog!" he told him, punctuating his remarks with jerks on the ear. "Bad dog! Dammit, Mica! *Bad!*"

The dog yelped pitifully at each painless jerk.

There was a small maple next to the oak, and with Mica collected, Mitchell leaned back against it to catch his breath. With the pack off, he rubbed against the tree like a bear cub, scratching a mosquito bite high between his shoulders. (Chastened, Mica lay at his master's feet, regarding him warily. He thumped the ground with his tail, and dust rose into the streaming sunlight; hard side-light that bisected the trees in a sharp line of illumination.) Mitch sighed at the thought of the long climb wasted. Chest heaving, he put back his head and rested it on the tree.

Now, opening his eyes, he looked up at the oak and saw— where the nearly horizontal rays struck the tree ten feet above the ground—a glint in Mica's knothole. His eyes narrowed, and squinting in the bad light, he studied the hole in puzzlement.

"What in the world?" he asked Mica, who stood, whining, tail wagging, at the sound of his voice. Suellen crowded in too, now that the danger was past. The dogs could read him like a book.

Mitch kneed them aside and shinnied up the tree. Carefully, he reached in the knothole. As he reached to his elbow upward in the trunk, his hand touched something that stopped his groping.

Slowly, his arm trembling from the exertion of holding him there, he withdrew a large plastic bag—the kind with a Ziploc top—and hanging by one arm, he lifted it and saw that incredibly, improbably, it was full of money! A thick wad held in a roll with a red rubber band! Looking closer, Mitch saw that what he first took to be a $5 bill was in fact a $50!

He dropped to the ground with a shout of delight, scattering the startled dogs. "Aw-right! I ain't believing this! This ain't happening!"

Mitchell's hands trembled as he unsealed the top. He took out the roll, slipped the rubber band over his wrist and began to count.

"Fifty, one-hundred, fifty, two-hundred, fifty, three-hundred" His jaw had slackened when he was done; his eyes glazed. "A thousand dollars! *A thousand dollars!* Ain't no way!"

As he recounted the money, he saw that the bills looked new, crisp $10's and $20's and $50's of unfaded, Uncle Sam green.

8

Mitch held a $50 up to the last light and noted the gold thread. He rubbed the bill between sweaty fingers and smiled at the green smudge on his fingertips.

He counted the money a third time. That his find was not lost Confederate treasure had already occurred to him. This might be stealing, his momentarily troubled expression seemed to say. Furtively, he looked over his shoulder, up the river and down then dismissed his misgivings with a wild yell of animal joy!

Mitch knelt beside Mica and gave the dog a big hug. He kissed him and rubbed his head with such vigor, he set the long ears flapping.

"Good dog, Mica! Good dog! *Good dog!*"

Mica whined and rewarded Mitchell with a sloppy kiss of his own.

Mitch embraced him again and kissed his wet snout, and Mica snorted and shook his head. He looked at his master uncertainly and gave him a tentative wag of the tail.

Then he went to tree and, front feet up on the trunk, standing taller than Mitchell beside him, he put back his head and let go a mournful howl. Echoing down the darkling river. Silencing the duelling owls.

THE BASEBALL SAILED ACROSS THE ROOM and smacked into Lee Rainey's first baseman's mitt. Mitchell's big brother reclined on his bed, propped up by half a dozen leaking, feather pillows. He was still in his baseball uniform—he was number 8—and still wore his cap. (Like Mitchell's, it was red with a white W for Waycross.) His shoes were off, and his white athletic socks were orange-stained in the shape of his spikes.

Lee took the ball from the glove and fingered it nervously. Two fingers along the seam for the curve ball. Two fingers across the seam for a knuckler. But he looked tense as he fidgeted with the grass-stained ball, not at all like a kid playing with a baseball.

Now, without warning, he told his brother—

"Think fast!"

—and fired the ball back at Mitch, sitting kicked back in a chair across the room.

Mitch caught the ball with a smack and went over backwards, tail over tea kettle, crashing into a laden table, bringing it down on top of him. His flying, tennis-shod feet were the last thing Lee saw as he disappeared behind the foot of the bed.

At the sound of the crash, there came a piercing whistle from their father downstairs. The boys froze, listening for their father's heavy footsteps.

When it was apparent that the noise was being ignored—that they'd won a reprieve—Lee began to laugh. Rolling on the bed. Holding his stomach. Barking, Mica jumped up on the bed with him; then jumped down and danced around Mitchell's prostrate body. Growling. Tugging at his pants legs. Licking his face.

Lying near the door, Suellen cracked one wrinkled eye, sighed and went back to sleep.

When Mitch sat up—his big-eyed face appearing over the foot of the bed; the bill of his cap over one ear; Mica licking his goofy, Gomer face—Lee began to laugh all over again.

Mitch grinned, and Lee told him, still giggling, "Nice catch, hotdog—for a fat boy."

"Thanks, coach."

In an earlier life, Lee had been a correspondence-school taxidermist, and the walls and shelves of his bedroom still supported lumpily mounted mammals, birds and fish. His masterpiece, a red fox with evil amber eyes, watched from atop the gun rack. Sawdust escaped his black-painted nostrils.

Elsewhere, the room was a wreck, the objects positioned by entropy—or a head-on collision. (Lee could apply for—and receive—Federal disaster aid.) Dusty shelves were piled with fishing tackle. An Army-surplus knapsack and a splintered wicker creel hung from nails in the wall. A flyrod, its guides held in place with black, electrical tape, shared a cobwebby corner with an old, single-barrelled shotgun, its cracked forearm held in place by wrappings of the same tape.

Yet the room possessed the schizoid quality of blooming adolescence. In with the field-and-stream clutter, the new Lee's tattered "wish-books"—*Car & Driver, Consumer Reports, Stereo Review, Gentlemen's Quarterly*—lay scattered on the floor near the side of his bed. A broken boom-box, its gate also held in place with electrical tape, shared the bedstand with a model NASCAR racer. Bootleg tapes lay around it. Schoolbooks and baseball paraphernalia were obviously jettisoned as soon after entry as would permit closure of the door. (The biology book lay open to a green diagram of the photosynthetic chain.)

There was, however, one note of order in the polyester wilderness. An ironing board and iron were set up in a corner near the window. Above it, Lee's faded shirts and scrubby jeans hung impeccably starched and pressed.

Now Mitch stood and righted the chair. Sitting, he fingered the ball, imitating his big brother. He cocked and rolled his wrist, putting English on the slider, down and in. Beyond his shoulder, the moon touched the dewy window like neon.

"Hey, Lee," he said, tossing the ball back. "You still wanna take Jenny Holt out Saturday night? After the Rosman game?"

Mitch smiled to himself as at some secret joke.

With a scowl, Lee threw the ball into the glove, and it

11

smacked loudly on the oiled leather. He smacked the ball again and again.

"That's a stupid question. 'Course I do. I done told you, didn't I? I ain't got the money. How come you keep bringing it up for?" He sighed. "Anyways, she's probably going with Andy Carver."

Mitchell gagged. "Andy Carver? That nerd? Oh man, he'd gag a maggot! I wouldn't go to a dog fight with him if he was top seed." Mitch looked at Mica, stretched out belly-up by his chair. "No offense, Mica."

At the sound of his name, Mica looked at Mitchell and thumped his tail.

Mitch shook his head in utter wonderment. "Wow, girls is sure weird, ain't they? How come she to go with him for? He ain't but maybe five foot tall. Zits all over his face. Probably picks his nose … or wets the bed … or …"

"For one thing," Lee said wistfully, "he has a car. A Mustang. Convertible."

"So? Daddy said he'd lend you the truck."

Lee gave his brother a look of utter disgust. "You are such a moron," he told him, smacking the ball with renewed fury. "You are such a total idiot. Don't you know nothing? A girl like Jenny Holt ain't gone ride in no truck what smells like cow doo."

"How come? We do."

"Jist shut up for once, okay?"

"She could ride in the back. It's plenty air-ish back there."

"Shut up, I said!" Violently, he smacked the ball. "Frigging townies! Frigging townies! I hate 'em! I hate 'em all!"

"Me too, Lee!"

"Shut up! You don't know nothing about it."

"Yeh, I do! You said they wudn't nothing like us. You said they never had to work after school like us, jist sit in the booths down at Worley's and drink Cokes and eat french fries with ketchup, and they always got new clothes, and they wear they good school clothes even after they get home—"

"Shut up," Lee told him with quiet menace, "or die."

Mitchell opted for the former. He crossed the room and flopped on the other twin bed. Mica jumped up beside him and

12

lay down with a sigh. On his back, Mitch took off his shoes by pushing down on the heel of one with the toe of the other.

"Hey, cut it out!" Lee said, baseball poised over the mitt. "Them's your good school shoes. Mama told you not to take 'em off like that, didn't she? You're ruining 'em. You're running 'em all down at the heel."

When Mitchell took off the other shoe the same way, his brother sat up. There was real menace in his face. "Dammit, are you deaf too?"

Mitchell grinned. "I got some money, Lee."

Lee fell back with a sign. "Nah, squirt ... My share of gas is five dollars. Plus I gotta pay for two movie tickets. Plus Cokes and candy." He smacked the ball harder and harder. "And she'll want burgers after the game. I appreciate it, okay? But jist forget it."

Lee's look was troubled. With a final smack, he put the ball in the webbing of the glove and lay it on the bed beside him. He picked up a copy of *GQ* and flipped through it. (The tweedy, young New Yorkers on the cover looked into the room from a seeming million miles away.) Seconds later, he pitched the magazine into the floor and lay back, hands behind his head. Again, he sighed deeply.

Mitch watched his brother with concern. "What's wrong, Lee?"

"Nothing ain't wrong."

"Yeh, they is. Come on. What is it?"

Lee rolled over with a groan and faced the wall.

"You flunk geometry again?"

"I got another ticket today."

"Oh, no! How bad?"

"Sixty-five in a forty-five."

"Oh, God, Lee! What's that? Three?"

"Four. I'll probably lose my license." Lee winced. "Eighty-eight dollars."

"You are *screwed.* The old man'll kill you this time. He had to scrape to pay the last one."

Lee sat up. "And I'll kill *you* if you tell."

"I ain't gone tell, Lee -- you know that -- but he'll find out

13

anyways, sooner or later. I mean, if you don't pay the fine, they'll pick you up. Right?"

Again, Lee groaned and rolled back to face the wall.

Mitch rose and crossed to his brother's bed. He sat beside him and put a hand on his arm. "I got some money, Lee. I'll give you ten dollars. No—twenty."

"Where'd you get twenty bucks from? Have you been in mama's pocketbook?"

Mitch gave his brother a meaningful look. "I ain't the one what goes in mama's pocketbook."

"Then where—you're lying."

"Scout's Honor, I ain't." He gave Lee the three-fingered sign. "I found it, Lee. Truly I did. A thousand dollars!"

"You are lying like an egg-sucking dog." He looked at Mica, belly-up on the other bed, and laughed. "No offense, Mica."

Without opening his eyes, Mica thumped his tail.

"Nah, I ain't, Lee. I swear I ain't."

"Yeh, right, you're lying. Daddy's right, you are such a liar. Always was."

"He never said I was a liar. He said I had an overactive imagination."

"Same difference. Liar!"

"Come on if you don't believe me."

Lee sat up and gave Mitch a big-brotherly cuff, a body-shot to the shoulder that knocked him off the bed and into the floor. It was done in fun, and Mitchell managed to laugh, but it was a painful shot.

Now he sat up, rubbing his shoulder, cap again askew, as Lee stood, towering over him.

"Okay, but if you're lying, swear to God, I'm gone beat the living dog doo outta you. Understand?"

The brothers looked at Mica, still stretched out on the bed, and told him in unison, "No offense, Mica."

Mica lifted his head and wagged his tail.

4

SOCK-FOOTED, THE BOYS MOVED QUIETLY down the upstairs hallway. The dogs padded softly after them, toenails clicking on the heart-of-pine floor. They paused at the head of the stairs. The TV—*The Real McCoys,* their father's favorite program—came softly up from the living room below. (Grandpappy Amos and Little Luke were having it out over a report card.) Their father snored, exhausted, having spent another fruitless day in search of "painter-work." These days, supper conversation in the Rainey house revolved around Recession. Now, in a pause in the laugh track, they heard the soft clicking of their mother's knitting needles. (Her friend, Mrs. Talbot, was expecting in June.) At length, Lee elbowed Mitch, and they tiptoed toward a closed door at the end of the hall.

Mitchell's bedroom was a loving approximation of his big brother's, another horror-movie menagerie of clumsily stuffed fauna. (The only thing missing, it seemed, was Norman Bates's mom.) One ensemble of birds and rodents sat in a glass terrarium, pressed into service as a science-fair exhibit. The poster-board read, ECOSYSTEM - AREA FAUNA - MITCHELL RAINEY, 6TH GRADE. A gold-crested blue ribbon was affixed to it.

But one difference was immediately apparent: Mitchell's room was neat as a barracks. Everything had its place and was in it. Guns were in gun racks; rods were in rod racks. Every article of clothing was on a hanger or in a dresser drawer. Four pairs of shoes were lined neatly beside his tautly made bed. His magazines—*Field & Stream, Outdoor Life, National Geographic, Scholastic, Boy's Life*—were carefully stacked on his battered dresser, separated by title like at the library.

A *Holy Bible* with a gilt cross sat on his rough-cut nightstand, and there was a second gold cross on the wall over his bed. Photos of his family sat framed on the other bedstand, beside snapshots of Mica and Suellen as pups.

On his desk, his schoolbooks were neatly stacked. Beside

them, his geography book was open to an Amazon-veined map of Brazil. The reading lamp was on; a notebook was open; a ballpoint pen was uncapped and at the ready. (For the record, Mitchell Rainey had never made a B.)

There was a SAVAGE ARMS calendar on the wall over his desk, turned to June, and on it, a slavering grizzly bear, rearing on his hind legs, hopelessly charged a red-garbed hunter equipped with a Savage 99. Near it, a map of the world showed Waycross, North Carolina, with a blue stickpin.

Inside, Mitchell closed the door and locked it. As Lee watched skeptically, arms folded, Mitch went to the mirrored dresser. Kneeling in front of it, he looked up at his brother and smiled, milking the moment—

"Come on, come on!"

—and reaching to the shoulder, Mitch retrieved the baggie and stood. He handed it to Lee—who took it with an open mouth.

"Holy - cow! Ain't no way!"

"I told you!"

"You sure did!"

Lee unsealed the baggie and dumped the contents on the patchwork quilt. His hands shook as he picked up the money and began to count.

"Fifty, one-hundred, fifty, two-hundred ..." Halfway through, he looked up at Mitch with an open mouth. "Fifty, three-hundred, fifty, four-hundred ..." He stared at the money when he was done. "Jesus, Mitchell, they's over a thousand dollars here!"

"One-thousand-seven-dollars-and-eighty-one-cents.   And change. I done already had seven-eighty-one. From my birthday."

"Unreal!"

"Nah, it's real all right. Ink ain't dry. I checked her jist like you showed me."

Lee smiled and nodded and counted the money again—crisp $10's and $20's and $50 of mint-fresh green—then fanned it out like playing cards. There was a rapt, excited look as he counted it a third time.

Finally, he looked up in utter wonderment. "Mitchell … where…?"

Mitch smiled. "I'll kill you if you tell."

"Come on."

"In this old big knotty oak. On the river. Right above Mine Falls."

"No lie?" Lee eyes glittered as he licked his lips. "When did you find it?"

"Today. Coming out. Actually, Mica found it."

At the sound of his name, Mica looked up and wagged his tail.

"Huh?"

"He denned up a squirrel in it. In the hole where the money was at. Like to never of found him. Son-of-a-bitch."

Lee put the money back in the bag and resealed the top. He tumbled it, watching raptly as all his favorite presidents floated by, distorted by the creased plastic.

"Mitch, was you serious? Can I borrow twenty?"

Mitch feigned consideration; then told him, smiling, "You can have … half."

"No way! I couldn't do that."

But Mitch put out his hand, and they shook on it.

"You mean it? No lie?"

"Yeh—but you gotta take me to the high-school games, okay? Away games too. And you gotta take me deer-hunting with you, okay? And—"

"Aw-right, *Mitchell!* Thanks a lot! Thanks a whole bunch! *Really!* You're helping me outta a major jam. I owe you, baby bro. Big time!"

Mitch smiled at his brother, and Lee rewarded him another shot to the shoulder that knocked him to the floor.

Again, Lee looked at the bag with love, devotion and surrender. He turned the baggie over and over, watching with patriotic pride as all those big-nosed faces tumbled by … Washington and Jackson … Grant and Honest Abe.

Finally, he looked at Mitch, still sprawled in the floor, rubbing his charley horse, and told him, "Hey, act your age. Get outta the floor." Dreamily, Lee took in the bag again, then smiled at his kid brother. "Mitchell? Where 'bouts exactly is this here tree?"

Mitch grinned. "You got practice tomorrow?"

5

AN ENDLESS STRAIGHTAWAY, A COUNTRY MILE of gleaming rails—on white-ballasted railbed and creosote-blackened crossties—converging toward a vanishing point in the next county. Beneath a sky of unvapored blue, the tracks stretched through a tableland of mast-straight pines in rows like corn.

The brothers were far down the tracks, running toward the river-road crossing. In the heat waves, they seemed to float above the rails, and faintly, there came excited chatter. Today, as part of their cover, they carried fishing rods and wore backpacks that gave them from a distance, in the heat, a bulbous shape.

The dogs were with them, fanned out on either side, noses to the ground. Hunting the weedy right-of-ways and brushy embankments. Snuffling at the steel-banded bundles of discarded crossties. Rolling in the stinking, skeletal remains of raccoons and opossums run down between the rails. Half a dozen times, Mica hiked and watermarked bundles. Like his masters, his sphere of influence was ever-widening.

That afternoon, Lee was in old clothes too—overalls patched in seat and knees, and holey, high-top sneakers with bean-twine laces. It was the hayseed image he was trying so desperately to shed, and he would have been mortified had any of his classmates seen him. Toward that end, he kept to the pines, running, as now the rails paralleled the highway.

As for Mitch, he was walking on air. It had been more than a year since his brother had taken him fishing. Mitch was aware of Lee's sudden discomfort with who he was, but didn't understand it. To Mitch, unafflicted by teenage, a life of hunting and fishing seemed the best of all possible worlds, and he wouldn't have traded places with anyone.

With the highway safely behind them, the boys slowed to a walk, breathing hard. Lee sang breathily while Mitch played along on air guitar. (Lee had illusions of rock stardom, and Mitch was working it as part of the new connection.) Fretting the unjointed flyrod, he whirled like Hendrix. Duck-walked like

Chuck Berry. Swung his arm in great circles like Pete Townshend. You just can't beat those summertime blues.

AN HOUR LATER, THE BROTHERS WENT THROUGH the shake-covered bridge, footsteps booming, and passed the old millhouse. It sat on the river below the road, post-and-beam settled out of plumb, the shake roof fallen in, the few unbroken windows dulled by road dust. Just beyond the mill, the trail to the river began as a rocky wash at a broken culvert pipe. With Lee in the lead, the boys stepped into the trees as through a green door and took the mossy footpath toward the sound of white water.

From the first switchback, they saw the river far below. The rapids flashed like ice in the afternoon sun, and sunstruck spray steamed from beyond the molten lip of Mine Falls. Now the trail switched back into the twilight of the cavernous rhododendrons, and the sight and sound of the big river vanished.

There was a sandy wash in the third curve, and Mitch noted the fresh footprints there. He observed with unease that they were not wader tracks. City shoes with pointed toes. Workboots with a faded cat's paw on the heels. Peculiar footwear for mountain trout.

IT WAS NEARLY SIX WHEN THE BOYS BROKE from the rhododendrons, crossed the dusty clearing and came up to the hollow oak. Mitch leaned his rod against a tree and slipped his pack. He grinned at his brother and pointed to the knothole. "Yonder it is."

"That it?" Lee asked. He leaned against a tree, his knapsack cushioning his back. It was the same maple Mitch had used the day before. "You sure?"

Mitch nodded, and Lee studied the knothole with shining eyes. Mica put both paws up on the trunk and began to bark. Wagging his tail, he looked at his masters for approval, but Lee pulled him down and kneed him away.

"Shh! Shut up, Mica. Good dog." Lee slipped his pack and

motioned Mitch to the tree. "Come here. I'll give you a boost up."

With his hands locked together for a step, he boosted Mitchell shakily up, and stretching, Mitch reached into the knothole, arm to the elbow, feeling down, feeling up, teetering ... and smiled at the touch of cool plastic.

He grinned at Lee as he pulled the baggie out. When he held it aloft, the boys saw that again, it was full of greenbacks! Another roll, this one wrapped with a green rubber band!

With a yell, Mitch dropped to the ground, and the boys whooped with delight. Like prospectors of old who had struck a motherlode.

Lee took the baggie and hugged it to his chest, then planted a couple of passionate kisses on it. The brothers hugged each other, and singing, danced a two-step with the bag sandwiched between them. Now they danced a jig, arms hooked together at the elbow. Lee held the bag under his other arm like a football.

"We rich, Mitchell! We rich! I don't believe it! This ain't happening! This is not *happening!*"

Mitchell beamed. "I told you! Didn't I, Lee? I told you! I never told no lies."

"You sure did! You're a genius, Mitch." To the sky, Lee proclaimed, "My brother, Mitchell C. Rainey, is a genius!"

"I am? But you said I was a moron. And an idiot."

"You *were.* People can change, Mitch—if they want to bad enough."

Lee turned the baggie over, and the banded wad bounced in the thick plastic. His hands trembled as he unsealed the top and withdrew the roll.

"Fifty, one-hundred, fifty, two-hundred, fifty, three-hundred ..." His grin widened as he counted. "Another thousand!" he said when he was done. "You hear me, Mitchell? *A thousand dollars!*"

Lee loved the parchment feel of new money, and he fanned out the bills as he counted them again. His hands flashed like a casino cashier's. As he counted, Mitch noted again that the bills looked new.

"What you gone do with your share?" Lee said finally.

21

"I gotta couple ideas."

"No lie, me too! Right now, staying outta jail's at the top of my list—not to mention the woodshed."

Mitch regarded his brother hopefully. "I'll need a deer rifle ... right?"

"Then there's the small matter of a letter jacket, size—huh? Oh, yeh. *Yeh!* What the hell—get two—get three! Tomorrow's Saturday. We'll go to Goldstein's."

But Mitchell's face was dark with misgiving. "Lee? Reckon whose it is?"

Lee looked at his brother intently, entertaining the question; then examined the money again, fanning out the bills, turning them over, holding them up to the sun, as though he might find the answer to the riddle there, in the serial numbers and Roman numerals and quaint Latin phrases.

Finally, after a thoughtful, analytical pause, he looked at Mitchell and told him factually, simply, with a straight face, *"Ours."*

And the brothers broke into crazy laughter! Beaming, grinning, dirt-streaked faces! Rolling on the ground! Whooping and yelling! Legs kicking the air! Dogs barking in confusion! Jumping into the free-for-all! Tugging the boys' pants legs with growls and mock-savage shakes of the head!

At length, Lee lay breathlessly back, happily staring through the summer-lush foliage at the blue sky.

"Finders keepers!" he screamed to the heavens. His sneaker-shod feet pounded the ground and dust rose in the air. Yellow sunbeams palpable as columns hung in the rays of the westering sun. "Losers weepers!"

6

BEYOND THE PLATE-GLASS WINDOW—gilt-lettered GOLDSTEIN'S SPORTING GOODS—a deer rifle to end all deer rifles: a 'scope-sighted .300 Weatherby Magnum. A hundred bird's-eyes stared back at the boys from the lustrous stock. Mitchell stood with his face to the glass, drooling. He knew without looking that the red pricetag on the trigger guard said $1500. (He'd priced it in *The Shooter's Bible* at home.) Standing closer, his breath fogged the glass, and he gripped the cuff of his new UNIVERSITY OF NORTH CAROLINA sweatshirt and wiped it clean with his forearm.

Lee stood beside him, a head taller, polishing a window of his own. Beneath their red caps, the brothers wore identical new clothes, head to toe—new jeans, new sweatshirts, new sneakers—and Lee sported a new letter jacket. (There was a big red W on the right pocket boasting four brass sport bars.) Their hair had been freshly mowed, and the handle of a styling brush stuck from Lee's back pocket. (The victim's black-and-blue copy of a speeding ticket peeked from the other. Lee had paid it at the courthouse first thing that morning.)

Now he elbowed Mitch. "Mitch, that it? Mitchell, we ain't got but maybe—"

Mitch shook his head. "Unh-unh," he said, grinning. "*There.*"

And with his chin, he indicated another rifle leaning against the woodpile of the deer camp-themed window display—a classic Winchester 30/30. A side-mounted, telescopic sight accommodated the gun's outdated top ejection. Mitchell loved it anyway. For him, the Winchester had been the quintessential prop in every fantasy he'd had since his blood pressure was first raised by the sight of fresh deer tracks in a red-clay roadbed, cut to the dewclaws by the weight of autumn fat; by the sight of a young pine running resin where a rutting buck had killed it with his antlers to stake his claim. His was no cowboy fantasy of saddle scabbards and home on the range. Mitchell was an

Eastern deer hunter. He wrote fan mail to Erwin A. Bauer and L.L. Bean. They answered.

Lee smiled at the choice. "The old man'll freak."

"He ain't gone know. You're gone take me. Remember?"

"I get to use it too."

"Sure, Lee, halvers on everything, but you gotta—"

"It'll near about clean us out."

"Well, easy come, easy go."

"I hear that!"

Still giggling, the boys pushed through the glass door, and inside, they went through all the motions of empty comparison shopping. No two suburban housewives with credit cards over the limit ever made a better day of it. Over the course of the next hour, Mitch hefted every rifle on fifty feet of rack, all to prolong the ecstasy of his final selection.

At the end of the hour, they stood at the glass counter with a balding salesman, Mr. Goldstein's son, Mordecai, who handed Mitch, his eyes bugging with excitement, a clone of the Weatherby in the window. Other rifles were on the counter, seduced and abandoned. Little red pricetags fluttered from their trigger guards. They had all been culled as second choices from an even three dozen that were back in the rack, wiped clean as a crime scene by Mr. Mordecai's oiled chamois.

Now, hefting the Weatherby, Mitch took aim at the whitetail buck on the WINCHESTER calendar across the store. He tried to align the crosshairs behind the ten-pointer's shoulder, but his hands shook so violently in the grip of buck ague that he had to lower the gun.

Finally, he could stand the charade, the suspense, no longer. He shook his head, handed the Weatherby back and pointed to the window. With a nod, Mr. Mordecai turned and took down one of the Winchesters, racked ten in a row like a movie-set sheriff's office. Mitch levered the silken action, and his face broke into a wide smile. He was fairly shivering with excitement.

At the rod rack in back of the store, Lee selected a graphite flyrod and cast expertly down the aisle, while Mr. Ira Goldstein himself, a sixtyish, silver-haired man who wore a hearing aid, smiled his approval.

Back at the counter, the trio looked through the glass flycase, making a selection of colorful trout flies. Heads bent over the box, Mr. Ira squinting through the big square magnifying glass, gingerly stirring the flies with their fingertips, they looked like beekeepers searching for the queen.

At length, the brothers were brought to account at the ancient, chuttering cash register. Gun, fleece-lined case, cleaning kit, a box of ammunition, flyrod, reel, weight-forward line, 12X tippets, and a dozen weighted nymphs came to $548.68—"plus something for the Democrats," Mr. Ira noted sadly.

Lee was chancellor of the exchequer, and in the faithful prosecution of that high office, he had purchased a brass money clip. When he withdrew it from his jacket pocket—the clip already sprung by the buffalo-choking dimensions of their roll—the Goldsteins raised their eyebrows and exchanged a look over the boys' heads that said "drugs."

FROM GOLDSTEIN'S, THE BROTHERS DROVE ACROSS TOWN. They took a window booth at BurgerBarn with a classic shot of the parking lot. (The Rainey pickup didn't lock—technically, it *did* lock, but a window vent had been broken out during pulp-wooding—and the boys wanted to keep an eye on their merchandise.) Burgers were stacked four high in front of them on the knife-endorsed Formica. Milk shakes stood beside their paper plates, frothing yellow and brown, pink and white.

It was Saturday, and The Barn was full of its teenage clientele: country kids in a country place; testosterone the drug of choice. From the ancient Wurlitzer in the corner, The Eagles counseled taking it easy, a message that would go largely unregarded.

"I could learn to like this," Lee said, biting back a belch with a signal lack of success. Heads turned all across the diner. Boys grinned. Girls registered obligatory scowls of disgust.

"Not me," Mitch told him. "I took to it natural-like."

Lee giggled. "You and me both."

A plump teenage waitress came up to them then with two bags of fries. She gave Lee an amorous smile as she placed the fries in front of them.

"Hey, Lee."

Lee returned an ambiguous grin and looked down. "Hey, Vanessa."

When she was gone, the brothers broke into hysterics. Mitchell gagged and ran a finger down his throat.

It was at this point—as Lee lifted a ketchup-laden fry to his mustard-stained mouth—that a group of tray-carrying teenage boys passed the booth and stopped to speak.

One boy—in a letter jacket like Lee's but with only one sports bar—asked, "You babysitting today, Rainey? Or did you finally go homo on us?"

Lee grinned, and the other boys cackled dutifully. Passing on, the boy told Lee, "Well, dude, see you in summer school. C equals pi r square."

"Nah, man, pie are round. That's how come you flunked."

The boy laughed and slapped Lee on his leather shoulder. "Nice jacket."

THAT AFTERNOON, OUT ON THE BACKPORCH, Mitch took two new collars from a paper bag. (Mica's was red and studded like a badass bulldog's; Suellen's was "Fifi" blue.) Kneeling, he buckled them around the dogs' necks and kissed them on their wet snouts. Mica snorted and licked away the kiss. Like Mitch, he had an aversion to displays of affection.

LEE WASN'T HAVING THAT PROBLEM. That night, a red-and-white activity bus whined down a steep, switchback highway. (WAYCROSS HIGH SCHOOL was painted on the side and, above it, a banner—BEAT ROSMAN!—flapped and cracked in the slipstream.) Now the bus entered a curve, Coach Frankhausen downshifted, and the headlights swung through the tops of the great spruce like a lighthouse beacon.

In the back of the dark bus, Lee in his baseball uniform shared a seat with a pretty teenage girl in a red-and-white cheerleader's outfit. (His arm was around her over the seatback.)

From his jacket pocket, he produced a birthstone ring, and Jennifer Holt smiled as she took it. She tried it on, and it fit perfectly. Looking into each other's eyes, they kissed for the first time.

Applause broke out around them. Shortstop Keith Markham gave them a standing ovation.

"Go for it, Rainey!"

Coach Frankhausen smiled as he watched the kissing couple in the mirror.

7

AND SO, IN THIS FASHION, OVER THE COURSE of the next two weeks—the last two of the school year—the brothers bartered with the fruit of The Money Tree. It was a funny thing about money; how it made you feel; how subtly it seduced you. Suddenly, there was nothing wishful about Lee's "wish books." They were now simply consumer guides acquainting him with the goods and services of the crowded marketplace. And with something like alarm one night, Mitch, thumbing through his dog-eared *Shooter's Bible*, realized he could buy near about anything in there. The world was suddenly one of infinite possibilities.

Now Lee scanned the newspaper for clothing sales, and his clothes rack grew accordingly. And shortly, Mitchell possessed the best-stocked tacklebox in the tri-county, and new binoculars joined the new sheath knife and new deer call in a drawer beneath his underwear. A hundred rounds of 30/30 ammunition—enough, he hoped, for a hundred seasons—were now secreted beneath his socks.

A pattern soon developed with respect to "withdrawals." Money was rarely there every day. (It would take several dry runs to establish this lamentable reality; later, off-days were spent with shopping and their sadly neglected chores.) The brothers quickly determined there was something like a two-day rotation.

Sunday was a dry run, but Monday they were back at the tree. (Lee carried the new flyrod.) This time, when Mitch withdrew the bag, it was full of green. The boys whooped joyously and gave each other a high five. But by Friday, they were almost blase as Lee broke the rubber band, counted the wad and divided it—giving Mitch a single $20 and pocketing the rest. (Lee had developed a masterplan for wheels of their own, and to date, the tree had yielded $5,000—less expenses—toward the car.)

Tail wagging, Mica watched from over their shoulders.

Transaction complete, he followed the now-familiar ritual. Front feet up on the trunk, he put back his head and let go a mournful howl.

Nervously, Lee pulled him down and looked long and hard up the dark trail. Mitchell had misgivings of his own, better concealed.

THAT FIRST SUNDAY, AS HE AND HIS MOTHER SAT in the front-row pew at Gethsemane Baptist Church—Mr. Rainey and Lee rarely accompanied them—Preacher Stevens took his text from the Ten Commandments. Mitch was sure the good reverend was looking right at him as fulminated on the wages of sin—death and damnation.

Afternoons and nights now, as he lovingly ran the oily rag over the new Winchester, the walnut stock darkening almost to black, the sermon came back to him, and he put the gun aside. Under the cloud of theft, the joy of ownership had lost its luster. (The jangling tags on Mica's and Suellen's new collars were a constant reminder.) He thought about it always, lost as in a daydream, and already his schoolwork was suffering. Though he slid a full letter grade on his final exams, after a year of hard work, it was too late for it to affect the straight A's.

Likewise, the change in Lee was nothing short of phenomenal. He moved in his new clothes as in armor; walked with his shoulders back and his head held high. The sullen moodiness that had descended on him like a cloud a year before dissipated, and the old smiling Lee was back as from a trip. (Everyone noticed, his parents too, and all put it down to love—which was surely part of the equation.)

At school, for the first time, armed with his money clip and letter jacket—a fitting uniform finally for his athletic prowess—Lee sought out company he had heretofore avoided—for his shyness and feelings of inferiority had made him too uncomfortable in their presence. (He didn't know he was much admired, but considered stuck-up and aloof.) In Jennifer's wide orbit, his star rose and his circle of friends grew accordingly.

Now, with Jennifer running interference, he lunched at the

in-crowd's power table in the school cafeteria and hung with them after school. And back home in the boonies, he lived on the telephone. He considered having a line put in his room, but didn't want the hassle of explaining it to his mother. (Already, she was sniffing around the trappings of the new lifestyle.) All he lacked was the appropriate set of wheels. The Rainey pickup, dinged and rusted and redolent of manure, was totally at odds with the new Lee's burgeoning self-concept.

CHARLIE SHIPLEY HIMSELF WAS ON DUTY that Saturday morning when the two boys appeared on the lot. He watched through the window with an appraising squint as they sauntered down a row of cars with SALE prices soaped on the windshields. Coffee cup in hand, he came to the door of the little concrete-block office— SHIPLEY'S USED CARS painted on the window—and sized them up. They were from the same litter all right, he could see that; carbon copies right down to their clothes—though one was a foot taller than the other.

But shortly, he went back inside: They weren't ready yet. He could tell by the way they wandered aimlessly about the lot. He didn't see them stop before the candy-apple-red '87 Corvette, exchange a smile and slap hands.

LEE WAS IN BY MIDNIGHT—HE AND JENNIFER were a nightly item now—and the whole family was abed. From downstairs, there came the ticking of the big wall clock in the kitchen. From the upstairs hallway came the sound of Mica getting at a pesky flea. His hind leg hammered the hardwood like granny's old washer going through the spin cycle, and the dogtags on his collar jingled like pinchbeck bells. Now the racket subsided as, snuffling, he slurped at the mangy hot spot beside his tail.

Upstairs, Mitchell tossed in the grip of another nightmare. (He'd had the same one three nights running.) In the dream, he climbed the tree to fetch the bag when suddenly the knotty oak embraced him—like the apple trees in *The Wizard of Oz*—and he woke in a sweat, yelling. (He had wakened Suellen, and she lay

30

at the foot of the bed, head up, whining, watching him intently.)

Mitch lay awake a long time, fearfully looking around his room. The moon shone through the windows, and the moonshadows of mullions and trees turned the room into an arbor of black and evil roses that enclosed him in a thorny embrace. Tonight, the deer-hunting fantasy—through the black trees, the ten-point buck materializing in the dawn mist; the crosshairs rock-steady low behind his front leg—couldn't exorcise his demons.

He was a thief, and the Eighth Commandment was quite clear on the subject: *Thou Shalt Not Steal.* Lee said they found the money, but you didn't *find* anything in a bag hidden in a tree—'specially not $7,000. What made it worse was that he liked it—the new clothes, the flyrod, the movies and, most of all, the new rifle. But someday soon, they'd be brought to account. Meanness always caught up with you. With a sigh, Mitch folded his hands and began to pray. *Our Father, Who art in Heaven, hallowed be Thy Name ...*

Downstairs, his mother woke in the darkness and stared long and hard at the ceiling. Three nights running, Mitchell's nightmares had wakened her. In her weekly cleaning and twice weekly washing, she had seen the new things in their rooms. She'd taken Lee aside and questioned him, but he swore they earned it, mounting fish and such for the teachers at school. She hadn't seen any fish, except for the ones she cooked—though, God knew, Lee didn't spend his nights at homework.

And speaking of fish, the boys were suddenly gone three afternoons a week and had yet to return with the first trout. Why the sudden interest in fishing anyhow? Lee hadn't cared a thing about it since he'd discovered girls.

She'd kept her suspicions from her husband for fear of what he'd do. He'd always over-reacted; always been too hard on them since they were little. She hated to see them whipped— especially Mitch since, often as not, it was Lee who got him into things. And Mitchell had grown so tense: Every night near about these nightmares. It was funny how her boys were flip-sides of the same coin. As Mitch became more and more withdrawn, Lee, for the first time in a year, was his old happy-go-lucky self.

She shook her head. It didn't do no good to worry. Whoever said that was like as not a man. All mothers did was worry, seemed like. They'd tried to raise 'em right, God knew, but these days, what with drugs and all, you never knowed how they'd turn out or what they'd get theirselves into. Still staring at the ceiling, Mrs. Rainey folded her hands and began to pray. *Our Father Who art in Heaven, hallowed be Thy Name ...*

Beside her, her husband lay awake, worried sick about money. It had been his preoccupation for so long, it seemed he thought of little else. Gladys suspected, he was sure, though not just how bad things really were; how close they'd come. It was important that the boys not know—though, if they had to move, summer with school out was the best time for it. Get it over with; get them settled in a new place. Thank God they were picking up a little extra cash with their taxidermy. Lee had always had a real talent for mounting birds and fish and such.

Rolling away from her, fighting the tangled quilt, he ran the numbers again and came up with the same ruinous bottom-line. How could they lose the farm? It had been in the Rainey family for three generations. Why had he used it to secure the loan for the new van and air compressors, only to watch the damn work dry up? It had been a terrible mistake. And what with the recession and those bastard Republicans down at the bank licking their chops, he'd be lucky to keep it through the summer.

If only he could get the contract to paint the old school. He'd low-balled the bid until, after paint, he was barely making five dollars an hour. But with the boys to help, he might just swing it. Marvin at the hardware would carry him ninety days—leastways, he oughta. Must of bought a thousand gallons of paint from the sumbitch over the last ten years. That would get the bank off his back—for awhile anyways. On that happier note, he rolled back to his wife and saw her blink ...

Up in his bedroom, Lee lay awake too, also thinking about money -- though not about who the money in the tree belonged to. Unlike Mitch, he was careful never to think of that—except to wonder when it might dry up. By flashlight, he turned the pages of *Stereo Review* as he assembled the ultimate component setup. After the car, he—they—would get the Bang & Olafson

32

system. Like the ads said, it was the most "bang for the buck," and he loved the look of all that blond wood. (Also, he had seen it featured in several *GQ* fashion plates, so it had to be cool.)

Tonight, before dinner, as he caught a little of *The Beverly Hillbillies*, he had watched his father snoring in his sweat-stained easy chair—a strand of drool yo-yoing from the corner of his mouth—and had felt such a wave of shame and pity it stunned him. It terrified him to think that that was where his future lay. He wasn't like Mitch; wasn't good at books, so college was out. Jennifer would go, her family insisted, and already she was sending away for catalogs and such. But he would cross that bridge when he came to it. There was always the chance of a scholarship—though no scouts had ever approached him. (Maybe they waited till your senior year.)

Thinking of Jennifer, he turned off the flashlight and, stretching, yawning, let the magazine slide off into the floor. (Mica woke with a start and growled, half-asleep.) There was an image of her he carried like a photo: Jennifer spinning in her cheerleader's outfit, the pleated, red skirt swirling out to reveal petal-like panels of white; the perfect pale legs; the fit of the ridden-up, red tights from behind. Lee watched her spin and spin until he carried the image into untroubled sleep …

THE NEXT NIGHT, TRUE TO HIS WORD, LEE TOOK MITCHELL on his date with Jennifer. They parked in the last row at the Tarheel Drive-In Theatre in a line with other necking couples. All around them, car windows were steamed to translucence by the body heat trapped within, and Mitch noticed, a couple of the cars bounced on their mushy old shocks in tempo with some strangely syncopated music from inside. The movie was Mitchell's favorite, *Deliverance*, and for the dozenth time, he watched as the three city-slickers in the red canoe negotiated the rapids.

It was toward the end, the best part, where the men ran the waterfall, that Mitchell's view was suddenly eclipsed by two gigantic heads, male and female, that joined in a kiss; black silhouettes against the roaring white water.

33

After what seemed an interminable exchange of saliva, Lee and Jennifer parted, revealing Mitch in the backseat of the Holt family car, arms over the seatback, exasperated at the amorous interruption, ignoring the lovers with manifest distaste, as again, he fixed excited eyes on the darting, dipping, leaping canoe.

THE FOLLOWING AFTERNOON, THEY WERE BACK AT THE TREE. It was Wednesday, the last, Lee noted happily, of the school year. But this time, the bag was empty, and when Lee inverted it, a single green shotgun shell fell in the dust at their feet. For the first time, the brothers exchanged a look full of ominous misgiving.

FRIDAY WAS THE LAST DAY OF SCHOOL, a half-day actually, and that afternoon, up in Mitchell's bedroom, Mr. Rainey, dressed in his spattered painter's coveralls, examined the new flyrod with concern. Stepping around the bed, he looked across the room and saw the new deer rifle in the back of the closet. His frown deepened.

For a week now, he had kept his suspicions from his wife— no need to upset her—but something wasn't altogether right. When the boys came in tonight—back from these supposed fishing trips they were on instead of at their chores—he would talk to them. Tonight, he would get to the bottom of it, once and for all …

8

THE BUZZARDS ROSE WITH LABORIOUS WINGBEAT far down the tracks, struggling into the heavy summer air. Mitch watched the pair ride the updraft above the rowed pines, against the glimmering, cobalt sky—turning as though tied together, wings rocking—until, squinting, he had to look away. Magenta blobs floated on his downward ken, a vision of white rock, black crossties and silver rails.

"Must be something is dead," he said, sniffing. "Hey, Lee?"

"Huh?"

"Reckon how long it'll be 'fore we can get the car?"

"Dunno. Purty soon, I guess. We got nearly five-thousand saved up."

Mitch frowned. "This is great, ain't it?"

"What's that?"

"You know—the money."

"Beats working for a living." Lee laughed. "Never knowed anybody to turn this here kinda profit from trout fishing—and never wet a line."

Mitch frowned. "Yeh, I guess so."

"I know so. What the hell's eating you?"

Fifty feet farther on, a watermarked *Sears* catalog appeared between the rails. As Mitch approached, the wind riffled the catalog to facing pages of farm implements. At the image of hoes and cultivators, Mitch remembered his forgotten chores with a wince.

He looked up. Far away, the gleaming rails converged in a needle-bright vanishing point. (He knew from science class that this was something called an optical illusion.) Nearer, nearly a mile away, the town of Waycross was an oasis of green trees and red brick on the heat-shimmer of the ballasted railbed.

As always, the dogs were with them, noses to the ground. Left of the tracks, only Suellen's crooked tail was visible, moving above the sumac and sawbriars like a periscope. On the right, Mica hiked to pee on a bundle of crossties. He hadn't missed them once in two weeks. Now he paused to roll between the rails.

"Mica, no!" Lee screamed. "Mica! *No!*"

When Lee stooped for a rock, Mica took off, afterburners aflame.

Thus, the boys discovered the buzzards' banquet: A dead opossum so bloated it looked like a Mexican *piñata*.

Beyond the possum, downwind, the stench was terrific, and Mitch pinched his nose. He sounded like Donald Duck as he told Lee, "I'm sure glad it's Friday." He frowned. "I'm gone buy me that hunting coat tomorrow."

"Me too! No more school! We out, Mitchell!" Lee whooped and threw his cap in the air. He tried to catch it on his head but missed. Now he picked it up and examined it critically for grease stains. "Oh, man, I'm gone have me some fun this summer. Me and Jenny … and you!"

"You gotta take me to all the away games. Plus, you gotta—"

"I said I would, didn't I? Jesus! Jist shut up about it, okay? Give it a rest. I remember what I said."

"Let's run."

"Nah, too hot."

Since acquiring the new letter jacket, Lee had lost all concern with being seen from the highway. He practically sauntered now.

"I got practice at six." He grinned lustily. "Then me and Jenny's going to the drive-in. Cain't take you this time, Mitch," he hastened to add. "Sorry, it's an R. The old lady would freak."

"Come on. I'll beat you to the crossing."

"Uh-huh, you and who else? Carl Lewis?"

"Betcha."

"How much?"

"Five dollars."

"Twenty."

"Ten."

"Hate to take your money."

"You ain't got it yet."

"Count it down."

"On your mark—get set—GOOOO!"

And off they went, knapsacks clanging, running toward the river-road crossing.

Mica and Suellen joined the race, running circles around the boys. Many times before, Mitch had noted sadly that the dogs had four legs while he had only two. He considered arms and hands small compensation for Mica's greyhound speed.

TWO HOURS LATER, DOWN AT THE TREE, the brothers went through the motions with practiced nonchalance. (They might have been rich kids at the mall making a withdrawal from a 24-hour teller.) Lee slipped his pack and boosted Mitchell up. Mitch reached into the knothole and withdrew the bag. With barely a smile, they regarded the roll of money. Dropping down, Mitch handed it over, and Lee unsealed the baggie and began to count.

"Fifty, one-hundred, fifty, two-hundred, fifty, three-hundred, fifty—"

Suddenly, Lee's hands stopped. Frowning, he looked intently up the mountainside.

Mitchell followed his gaze with palpable unease. "What, Lee? What is it?"

After a time, Lee shook his head. "Dunno. Nothing, I reckon. Thought I heard something. Guess I'm getting—*Shh!*"

And clearly now, Mitch could hear it too! Men's voices coming toward them down the trail! And already, they could hear that the voices were loud-pitched and argumentative!

"Dammit!" Lee said.

He looked up the tunneling footpath to where it turned out of sight at the first switchback. The sounds of stumbling, cursing, of tree limbs slapping twilled pants legs were louder now, closer; and now there was a flash of motion through the trees a turn or two above them.

"Somebody's coming!"

Lee looked frantically around and saw the log at the edge of the clearing. He stuffed the baggie in his jacket pocket, and on the run, grabbed the packs, grabbed Mitch by the suspenders, and pulling him along, scrambled to the log and leaped behind it.

He took off his cap, then knocked Mitchell's off and pushed his head down.

And pressed to the ground, the boys watched big-eyed from behind the log, as seconds later, two gun-bearing men and an unarmed third stumbled out of the trailhead into the clearing.

9

THE UNARMED MAN WAS BETWEEN THE OTHER TWO, and they each gripped a red-flannel arm, sweat-stained at the armpit. He was older than the others, sixty or more, unshaven and white-haired. He wore baggy, gallused overalls over red longjohns, stagged at mid-calf, so that Mitch could see -- with the kind of pointless, indelible detail that comes of perfect fear—there were no socks under the ankle-high workboots.

The men who escorted him were a study in contrasts—North and South; city and country; thick and thin; short and tall. The long-legged countryman carried a rifle under one arm, a long, octagon-barrelled squirrel gun. The other man, the sunglassed city-slicker, had a snubnose revolver that hung from a ring-encrusted hand. The boys recognized the country fellow as Eggar Mosely from in town, a painter who sometimes worked with their father, but his companion was a stranger.

Now, as the men came up to the tree, they gave the old man a shove, and he landed with a groan in the dust at the base of the oak.

Quickly, he sat up and raised his arms defensively. His fear and his lion's mane of white hair gave him the look of a wild man, a Ben Gunn.

"Tony, now please!" he told the city man. "I never took no money. I swear on my mother's grave. Wunt none *to* take. I'm telling you'uns the truth."

"Bull!" said Eggar, training the rifle on him. His thumb drew back the hammer with a *click* the boys heard across the clearing. "Put it there myself."

"Eggar, I swear to you'uns! I ain't took nothing what weren't mine. Wunt no money since end of May. The hole was allus empty. Jist like I told you."

"And I say you're a lying sumbitch."

The man called Tony scaled the tree, felt the empty knothole and dropped to the ground. He crossed to the old man, cursing, his face flushed with anger.

"Ante up, pops—*now*—and we'll be friends again. Else me

and Eggar's gone take it outta your hide. Ain't we, Eggar?"

Eggar nodded and gave the old man an evil, orange grin. He was about thirty-five, dressed like the old man in overalls and half-laced workboots. He wore a red, Massey-Ferguson cap, and like his overalls and boots, it was paint-spattered. (Of the dozen or so colors, white seemed to predominate.) He was three days from his last shave and three decades from his last visit to the dentist. His remaining teeth bespoke a fondness for Red Man, and right on cue, he spat in the dust, and his quid beaded up, inches from the old man's liver-spotted hand.

Of about the same age, Tony was a New Yorker with a heavy Bronx or Brooklyn accent, nasal as Eggar's but full of "dems," "deeze" and "doze." He was well-dressed, dandified, if your taste ran to polyester—wide-lapelled, white suit, tasseled loafers and a loud, Hawaiian-print shirt like some kind of bizarre, jungle camouflage. The top three buttons were undone, revealing black chest hair and a yard of gold chain.

Now, without warning, he kicked the old man in the side, and he rolled away with a groan.

"You are one lying mother, you know that? Now where the hell is it? Ain't got all day."

Behind the log, Mitch gulped, eyes wide in his bloodless face. Beads of sweat stood out on Lee's ashen forehead, and dead leaves clung to his cheek.

"I swear to you, Tony!" the old man cried, holding his side, gritting his teeth. He had the perfect dentition of toothlessness. "I ain't took nothing! I swear on my mother's grave!"

"I heard enough bull 'bout your old lady's grave. Hear me? It's your grave we talking here. Where's my money at? No pot, no money. That's the way it works, ain't it, Eggar?"

Eggar nodded.

"Ain't no bull, Tony!" the old man sobbed. To Eggar, talking fast, he said, "Eggar, now please! Tell him! You ain't never knowed me to steal afore!"

Eggar spat, again just missing the man. "First time for ever'thing, I reckon."

"Eggar ain't gone help you none, pops. Eggar's pissed off too. Ain't you, Eggar?"

Eggar nodded.

The old man turned back to Tony and his words fairly tumbled out.

"How come me to steal from you'uns? Huh? How come? We had us a good thing going, right? Pardners!"

Tony took a silver flask from his inside coat pocket and took a drink. He capped it one-handed and wiped his mouth with the palm of his hand.

"Till you went and got greedy on us."

"Tony, I swear to you! Swear to God!" The old man was on his knees now, his hands clasped prayerfully before him. "I ain't took *nothing!* Eggar, tell him! He'll listen to you."

"I ain't gone tell him squat. You're the one what needs to tell him."

"Okay," Tony said. "Take him down to the river. Maybe a little cold water'll refresh his memory."

"No, no! Please, God! Eggar, don't! Y'all listen to me now! Wunt no money!"

With the old man backwards between them, kicking and screaming, they half-dragged, half-walked him to the river.

Lips trembling, the boys watched from the edge of the clearing.

"We'll baptize his cracker ass," Tony said. He raised his free arm—the one with the pistol—heavenward in a parody of televangelism. "Gone wash away them sins of deceit! Evil spirit come out!"

As part of the headrace above the high falls, the river ran deep and green here with a sandy beach along the near shore. Eggar dropped his rifle on the mossy bank, and the men waded into the river.

Waist-deep, with the old man between them, they did indeed look like fundamentalist preachers preparing for a baptism, a complete immersion. Tony had his revolver, and he pressed the muzzle to the old man's silver temple.

"Now I'm a reasonable man—ain't I, Eggar?"—Eggar nodded—"and I'm gone axe you just once more. *Nice.* Where's my damn money at?"

Again, the old man clasped his hands. "Tony, I ain't took

nothing!" He looked from one to the other, walling his eyes with fear. "I swear it, swear to *God!* Eggar, please! Tell him!"

"Somebody took our money. Wudn't inflation, was it, Eggar?"

Eggar shook his head sadly and spat. "Not hardly."

The oily quid strung out in the current, and downstream of the men, a trout struck at it, rolling, white belly flashing in the afternoon sun.

"Well, hit weren't me!" Desperate, talking fast, he grabbed the tobacco-stained bib of Eggar's overalls. "Tell you what! Tell you what! I seed kid tracks all 'round 'at 'ere tree! I *did!* Dog too! Look fer yourself!"

Across the clearing, the boys tasted an ammonia wash of fear. Mitch shivered as from a chill. Lee licked his lips and swallowed.

"Kid tracks, huh?" Tony shook the man by the suspenders till his uppers flew out. "How 'bout tire tracks? Huh? Maybe some woman-tracks"—Tony snorted—"wid high heels? Hey, Egg, maybe Bigfoot got our bread." Tony shook his head sadly. "Nah, pops, you gotta do better'n that. You have a nice swim."

And they pushed him under the swirling water and held him there a long moment ... legs flailing, arms waving, arthritic fingers clutching at the blue sky ... until finally, they pulled him up, dripping, and held him by the suspenders between them.

He coughed and sputtered, gasping for breath. Water poured from his nose and mouth. His wild white hair was plastered down now, revealing a pink, hypertense bald spot.

"That cold water clear your head?" Tony hit him in the stomach with the pistol, then together, he and Eggar straightened him up. "One more time: Where the hell's my money at? Talk to me, dammit."

"I swear to you'uns!" the old man said in a spasm of coughing, his face scarlet. "I ain't took it! Swear to God I ain't! Wunt nothing to—"

Again, they pushed him under, and again, his sticklike arms waved, his legs thrashed, his hands plucked weakly at Tony's gaudy shirtfront, Eggar standing at arm's length to avoid the lunging legs--when suddenly, his exertions ceased.

42

Quickly, they pulled him up and looked into the staring blue eyes. Water poured from his mouth, and now his nose began to bleed.

At the sight of the corpse, Mitch whimpered and covered his mouth. Tears leaked from Lee's crimped eyes.

"Christ!" Tony said. "Well, this here sumbitch ain't telling nobody nothing now. Dammit! Dammit to *hell!*"

They dropped the old man back in the river with a big-bodied splash, and he floated away, face-down. Out in midstream, the current caught the body, turned it gently around and swept it downriver, head-first. As the boys watched in horror, it sank. Moments later, the corpse appeared again when it slipped through the shallow tailout and swan-dove over the high falls, the pale calves visible to the knees.

Eggar shook his head. "Well, I reckon he never had it."

"Looks like it. Well, somebody's got it. It didn't climb down that tree and go to town." Tony looked toward the oak. "You ever see any tracks around that tree?"

"Nah, never looked. Hit was allus nighttime."

"Well, *hit* ain't nighttime now. Come on."

10

THE MEN WADED OUT OF THE RIVER—Tony fussing with his ruined shoes—and climbed the bank. Eggar stooped to pick up his rifle, and standing, he withdrew his foil tobacco pouch. He watched sadly as brown water ran from it. He tossed the pouch away, and when Tony came abreast, they started for the oak. Tony's shoes *squilched* with each step. They were coming directly for the boys, and Mitch and Lee pressed their faces to the ground, eyes shut tight and trembling.

But eyes fixed on the tree, the men walked right past them and on across the clearing to the oak.

There, they crouched and began to comb the ground. At length, Eggar saw a waffle-soled track and called to Tony across the clearing.

"Yo. Here we go."

The men knelt beside the track. As Tony studied it, he drank from the silver flask. With a nudge, he offered it to Eggar, who declined with a faint shake of the head. Tony smiled at the Bible-belt rebuff and helped himself to another, longer swallow.

"Well, whadaya make of it, Tonto?" he asked, capping the flask one-handed. The cap was attached to the neck by a short silver chain.

Eggar spat. "Kid track. Looks to be two of 'em. Big un and lit'l'un. Dog too." He spat. "Big dog."

"Yeh? So? Gimme the short version."

Eggar shrugged. "Could be fishermen. Warden stocked this here crick Tuesday. School's out now. Near about it."

Abruptly, Tony stood. "Screw it! Come on, let's go. We falling behind. Frigging farmers!"

Eggar stood, and with a final look around the clearing, the men turned toward the trailhead.

The brothers pressed themselves to the ground, relief already in their faces, the beginnings of a smile—when Mica and Suellen bounded into the clearing, back from the hunt. At the sight of the strange men, they began to bark.

Eggar knelt and called to them, and the barks gave way to low growls. Mica came up to him then, tail wagging, and licked his outstretched hand. Eggar began to gently fondle his ears, talking to him in a low, crooning voice.

"Well now, looky here. Who belongs to y'all? Huh? Whose is yourn? Whose is yourn?"

While Eggar looked at the tags on Mica's red collar, Tony began to inspect the clearing again. Kneeling, he examined the track; standing, his eyes scanned the clearing and the woods on either side.

Mitchell's whimpers were audible now, and Lee's eyes were shut tight, teeth clenched. Both boys trembled violently.

Suddenly, Eggar stood and clapped his hands. "Hunt 'em up, boy! Hunt 'em up!"

And nose to the ground, Mica ran straight to his masters and began to bark, dancing around, tail wagging. When Mitch screamed, the men whirled and saw them. The brothers jumped up to run—but quickly, Tony and Eggar brought their guns to bear.

"Hold her right there!" Eggar walked toward them, gun up. "Stand, I said! Move and I'll—hold it, I said! I ain't joking neither!"

The boys froze. Fearfully, they watched the men's approach. Mitch was crying openly now, mouth open, silent tears. Lee's clothes clung to his bony frame. There were red twig marks on one pale cheek where he'd pressed his face to the ground.

As the men came up, Eggar recognized the boys.

"Well, I'll be," he told Tony, lowering the rifle. "I thought so. Hit's 'em Rainey boys from in town." He nodded neighborly to the boys. "Mitch, Lee."

With the momentary reprieve, the brothers managed a nod. Mitch sniffled and wiped his nose with the back of his hand, smearing his tear-streaked face.

"Hey, M-Mr. Mosely," Lee said, his voice trembling.

"How's yer daddy? Staying busy?"

Lee gulped. "N-nah, no sir, cain't find much work these days."

"Know the feeling, son. Painter-work been real scarce here

lately. Past year or so." Eggar spat. "I give it up."

"Wh-what's Lon up to these d-days?"

Eggar smiled. "Well, he best be hoeing corn this evening—if'n he knows what's good fer him."

Tony couldn't believe his ears. "Who the hell's Lon?"

"My oldest young'un. Him and Lee come up together."

"You are *breaking* my heart." Tony lowered his gun and smiled at the boys. "What's up, fellas?"

"N-nothing much," Lee said. He could see his big-nosed reflection in Tony's sunglasses. "J-jist a little trout f-fishing 'fore dark." He wiped his face with a trembling hand. "Ain't b-biting though."

"That so?" Tony said, eyebrows raised, the mirthless grin a frozen rictus on his suntanned face. "Fish ain't biting but the mosquitoes sure is? That about it?"

"Yes s-sir."

Tony saluted. "'Yes sir.' We know how that is, don't we, Egg? What you boys using for bait—tens or twenties?"

"S-sir?"

"Search 'em," he told Eggar.

"Ah, Tony, they ain't got no—"

"Search 'em, I said!"

Eggar patted Mitch down and found a pack of gum; but when he frisked Lee, his groping—and chewing—suddenly stopped. Looking Lee in the eye, he reached in the pocket of the letter jacket and withdrew the baggie. Eggar paled under his summer tan.

As Tony counted the money, the color rose in his face. "Ain't biting, huh? Why you thieving little punks!"

"You boys is in a world of hurt!" Eggar trembled in his agitation. "You hear me? How come you'uns to do a thing like this?"

Tony snatched Mitch by the suspender and motioned to Lee. "Bring him down to the river."

"*Huh!*"

"You heard me. These here boys is gone have a little fishing accident. Them orange rocks is slick. They gone fall and hit they heads."

46

Eggar grabbed Lee but told Tony, "Nah, Tony, we cain't do it. Them's Cleve Rainey's boys. They be hell to pay fer this."

"It's gotta be done. Hear me? They seen us. You wanna end up in the gas chamber?"

"Dammit!" Eggar cried. He shook Lee. "How come you boys didn't tend to yer own bidness? Huh? How come you to get mixed up in a thing like this here?"

By the suspenders, the men dragged the brothers, kicking and screaming, to the river. Lee dug in his heels, and Eggar's backhand knocked him to the ground. Mitchell screamed, and Tony slapped him to silence. The boys sat up groggily. Blood was coming from Mitchell's nose.

Out in the river, the roiled silt made brown clouds in the green water.

"I don't like this, Tony. Not one little bit, I don't."

"Well, it ain't my idea of a good time. Shut up your crying and do it. Do it, dammit! *Do it!*"

And they forced the brothers under the icy water!

And underwater, bubbles streamed from Mitchell's mouth as he kicked and lunged, but Tony was just too strong for him. And underwater, bubbles streamed from Lee's mouth and nose as he clawed and scratched at Eggar's thick wrist, but he couldn't loosen the viselike grip. And topside, Tony and Eggar bore down, dodging their thrashing legs and sneaker-shod feet.

At that moment, the men heard a growl and looked up in time to see the airborne dogs. Arms up, they took the full force of their weight, and with a splash, men and dogs went into water so cold it burned.

When they felt the hands release, the boys kicked free and swam for it underwater.

11

THEY SURFACED, COUGHING AND GASPING, a hundred feet from shore. Out of the trees, the boys could hear the full volume of the falls. They were being swept rapidly toward it. Mitch thrashed, trying to keep his head above the stiffening current. Lee swam for the far shore with all his strength. In the sodden jacket his arms were leaden. Though numb with cold, Lee could feel all along his body the river shudder from the force of falling water. As he neared midstream, he glanced toward the falls. Beyond the green-glass lip, sunstruck spray boiled upward like smoke.

Tony and Eggar had regained their feet and splashed toward the bank. Lee saw them reach Eggar's rifle, just as the current swept him out of sight.

Now gunshots roared, and Lee heard a dog yelp in pain.

Moments later, he saw the men running through the trees along the bank, firing. He ducked as bullets *spanged* into the water on either side of him. Quickly, he dove, and surfacing, he saw a log drift by in the current, already quickening as it approached the falls.

"Mitchell! The log!"

Lee gripped his brother's suspenders, and tuggng him along, side-stroking, they made the sawlog and ducked behind it. Eggar had the range now, and bullets *thudded* into the wood with explosions of bark. Straining, they swung the log around to shield them from the bank. Furiously, they kicked their legs in an effort to make the far shore—but the log was just too heavy; the current just too strong—and before they could reach midstream, the glassy green water bent as though molten, and the brothers were swept into the headrace of the falls.

Over the falls they went, boys and log, end over end, arms and legs windmilling, freefalling as in a nightmare.

They landed feet-first in the great pool at the base of the falls, their screams lost in the thundering monolith of falling water. The roar was suddenly silenced as they went deep, deep in a column of bubbles.

Underwater, the whole river shuddered from the sheer

tonnage of falling water. Rocketed along by the murky current, the boys fought to right themselves; to fight off the looming rocks and splintered, spearlike logs. Finning trout shot away at their approach. A Coke can, sand-filled, bounced in place. Deeper in the pool, a rusty bicycle lay on its side, half-buried in the sand, front wheel spinning.

TONY AND EGGAR STOOD HIGH ATOP THE FALLS. Tony smiled as he regarded the thundering white water a hundred feet below. Through the soles of his shoes, he felt the granite tremble. Now he looked toward the tail of the pool and saw the great sawlogs becalmed in the eddies, their ends white-splintered. He pocketed the snubnose and turned away.

"Tony! *Look!*"

LEE SURFACED, LUNGS BURSTING, GULPING IN AIR, and looked frantically around for his brother.

"Mitch! Mitch!"

He was at the center of the cyclone, just downstream of the falls, buoyed by the upwelling. The roar was thunderous; the air so thick with driven spray he gasped for breath. In the creaming froth of white water, the piling current broke over him like surf. He screamed to be heard as he turned left and right, trying to see through the spray.

"Mitch! Mitch!"

Finally, Mitchell broke the surface, coughing up water, gasping for air. Lee swam to him and took him by the suspenders. The boys were trapped in the upwelling, and Lee struggled in the heavy current as he pulled his brother toward the near shore.

Now bullets pocked the water around them and glanced, whistling, through the riverbank trees. Limbs fell, bullet-lopped, and shredded leaves pinwheeled to earth.

Lee looked up and saw the men atop the falls. He saw Tony's revolver leap as he pulled off another round. The bullet missed widely. Now Eggar fired, and Lee's ears rang from the near miss. Driven water stung his cheek.

The boys changed directions then and were kicking toward the far shore when the log popped up. Taller, Lee saw it first and swam for it. Mitch followed, arm-weary. Bullets *whocked* into the water around them, geysering.

Finally, they reached the log and ducked behind it.

"Help me, Mitchell! Swing it around! Kick your feet!"

The boys strained to turn the log against the current; across the current to make a shield. Though Tony's snubnose was useless at that range, bark and sap flew as rounds from Eggar's rifle struck the log again and again. The Christmasy smell of pine resin filled the air. Now Lee winced as a splinter was driven under his scalp. He ducked and pushed Mitchell down.

"Dammit, Mitchell! Keep your head down!"

Now, out in midstream, the current grabbed the log, swung it around and swept it rapidly downriver. The brothers were soon out of range.

FROM THEIR VANTAGE HIGH ATOP THE FALLS, high above boys and log, Tony and Eggar watched their escape. Watched the black log, bucking and veering, down the glittering river. The boys hung from either side with just their heads above water, and their sleek seal-heads bobbed like on a roller coaster. Now the log went out of sight around a bend in the river.

"Dammit!" Tony and Eggar stared hard downriver. Tony stared at the riverbend, mouth working. The men were just refracted silhouettes now, sticklike against the declining sun, as they stood immobile, watching the empty river. "Dammit to *hell!*"

"What we gone do, Tony?"

Abruptly, Tony turned away. "Let's get the others."

12

IT WAS LATE AFTERNOON WHEN THE LOG finally grounded far downriver. The boys looked up, lips purple, faces pale from the icy water. They had drifted ashore on a sandspit, a long low island that stretched out into the now slow-moving river.

Here, the river had once meandered, and where the new channel cut through on the right—slow and straight as a barge canal—it had created a daisy-chain of crescent-shaped, willow-canopied, oxbow islands left of the new rivercourse. Behind the islands, the old riverbends were deep, algae-green backwaters of matching curvature. A fine dusting of pollen gave the moveless water a look of solidity. Cattails fringed the shores, and white-blooming lilypads the size of dinner plates blanketed water too deep for cattails.

Across the backwater was the riverbank. Lee could see the old settlers footpath running faintly along the flank of the mountain. Far from Civilization now, only the whitetails maintained it.

On the side of the island against the river—the side where the boys had grounded—the current kept it clear of cattails, and the island sloped down to the river in a wide sand beach. Dozens of sawlogs, becalmed by this first slack water, floated in the river or lay half-submerged on the shore. With knothole-eyes at the waterline, they looked to Mitch like alligators closing a circle.

Across the river, a vast floodplain extended half a mile to the very foot of the mountain. It had come up in a thousand acres of cattails, and muskrat lodges, made of cattails and mud, stood up across the treeless marsh like brown igloos on a green ice-floe. Muskrats foraged through the flooded reeds, their zigzag paths marked by waving, sausage-shaped tassels.

Now, near the end of one such path, there came a harsh cackle, and a redwing blackbird rose into the air. Seconds later, the rest of the flock got up and followed the first bird across the marsh, settling on banked wings near the center. Downstream, a water moccasin glided across the river, its heart-shaped head the apex of a widening wake, and disappeared into the cattails.

Regarding the snake, the trembling reeds, Mitch moved closer to his brother and hooked an index finger through the tool loop on his overalls. His eyes followed the snake's path back through the cattails—where another blackbird got stridently up and flew toward the middle of the marsh.

"Where you reckon we at, Lee?" he said. His teeth chattered and his voice trembled. His other hand, pruned from hours of immersion, still gripped the log.

"Dunno for sure." Lee looked around, waist-deep in the river. "Ain't never been down this far before. Looks to be Yeller Banks Island."

They stood then with difficulty, shivering, exhausted, sore, stiff from the fall, numb from the icy water, and staggered ashore.

There, they collapsed on the sandbar, a pair of sodden puppies. Over the past two miles, they had managed to stay with the log through three sets of rapids and a small waterfall. Submerged rocks had split their knees and elbows, and limb stubs on the log had bruised and raked their ribs. Beneath the shriveled letter jacket, the tail of Lee's teeshirt was a tatter. A mile upriver, they had floated within fifty feet of a ten-point buck, his antlers in swollen velvet, and Mitch had watched him—snorting, whirling away, wet hooves clattering on the bedrock; snorting again, stamping in the riverbank trees—without interest. Deer-hunting figured marginally in the new scheme-of- things.

Abruptly, Lee stood and waded back into the river. "Gimme a hand."

Straining, they set the log afloat and pushed it out into the current. Ponderously, it swung around, and they stood waist-deep, watching it float away. The dozen bullet holes oozed sap. Mitch looked at them with a sense of unreality. Except for the bullet holes, he might have imagined it all. In the perfect, purple silence of eventide, the events of the afternoon seemed far away. Like something he'd seen on television.

"It mighta give us away," Lee said.

"You reckon they still after us?"

"Yeh."

"Me too."

Their eyes rose from the log then, and looking far downriver, they saw the Interstate bridge, its threadlike arches leaping the gorge, leaping the cathedral spruce. From this distance, the bridge was tiny, a spider's-web tracery of tower, arch and undertruss. The river flowed west, and the bridge's spires and parabolas were silhouetted high and black against the orange wafer of the setting sun. From atop the central tower, an aviation beacon blinked red as the sky around it.

It might have been the spires of the Emerald City—its significance was the same—for the expressions it inspired on the boys' faces. Mitch regarded the bridge wistfully, lips trembling, tears welling. Lee's pale face, as he bit his lower lip, was tense with longing.

Lee sighed. "Well … yonder it is."

"It's a long ways off, Lee."

"You got that right. Ever' bit of five mile--six maybe--and seem like sixty 'fore we there."

Now, as they stood staring, there came a sudden, shuddering roar, and seconds later, a helicopter—STILSON PULP & PAPER painted in green on the white underbelly, bearing the same logo burned into the logs—thundered over the willows, low enough to make them whip in the propwash; landing lights flashing; UFO-looking in the coming night—and the boys staggered to turn, waving, screaming, splashing, falling—but the chopper was gone almost before they could react.

They looked after it, listening to the fading throb of rotors. Mitch struggled to hold back his tears. "Who was it, Lee? Highway patrol?"

But Lee had glimpsed the logo and already turned back to the bridge. "Nah, Stilson Paper. They counting the logs."

Finally, Lee could look at the bridge no longer. With a sigh, he turned and took in the sodden sandbar behind them, surveying their dismal situation. Beneath the willow canopy, an evening chill had settled on the island. A hatch was on, and all across the backwater, trout dimpled the water like the onset of rain. Across the river, a cold mist rose from the marsh.

A lone crow flew over the cattails then, cawing to roost, and the boys watched it out of sight over the mountain. It was black as a Halloween cut-out as it crossed the pumpkin face of the sun.

Lee shook his head. "We be okay here—for awhile anyways. Be dark soon. They gotta go all the way 'round to get acrost. Nearest bridge is Old Mill Road. They got cars—but we gotta good jump on 'em. Most likely they won't start out till morning."

"I don't know, Lee. Old Eggar knows this here river purty good."

"That's how come they ain't gone start out till morning. Eggar don't want no broke leg."

Now the weight of their situation descended on Mitchell. He looked around in desperation. "Lee, I'm so hungry! I'm *starvin!*"

"You ain't the only one. Maybe we can kill us a trout or somelike." Lee pointed. "They's some cattails yonder on the backside of the island. We can roast up some of 'em."

But Mitch hardly listened. "I'm so *cold,* Lee!"

On a single sob, the tears began to flow.

Lee snatched Mitch by the suspenders and gave him a shake. "*Hey!* Don't start your crying on me now. Hear me? I ain't gone listen to one second." He released him. "I'll build a fire. I reckon them matches is all wet."

Sniffling, Mitch reached into his pocket and took out the cylindrical, silver matchcase. He unscrewed it and poured the matches into his palm—along with several ounces of river. He handed the matches—a sodden, red-flecked mass—to Lee -- who slapped it out of his hand, scowling.

As Mitch watched, shivering, Lee removed the lace from his tennis shoe. On the island's rocky high ground, he cut a green willow switch and with the lace bent it into a bow. Next, he kicked through the driftwood until he found a piece of weathered planking. With the point of his pocketknife, he drilled a crude hole halfway through the board—as he did in a second, smaller piece he broke from the large one. It would serve as the handpiece. Finally, digging through the driftwood, he found a small straight stick. It was the thickness of his thumb and a foot in length.

His excavations had unearthed a Coke can, a candy bar wrapper, a Hardee's hamburger wrapper and a red-white-and-blue Eagle Claw fishhook card. Mitch looked longingly at these icons of Civilization. He recalled that a Hardee's Whopper featured two quarter-pound patties, cheese, lettuce, tomato, pickle, ketchup and onion. The image of melted cheese unloosed his salivary glands.

"Fetch me some of that driftwood, Mitchell," Lee said, rudely intruding on the fantasy. He was pointing with the knife. "Reach in deep where she's dry. And hurry up. Ain't got all day. Be dark soon."

Mitch returned with a double-handful of marsh grass and twigs. (A second trip produced the bleached bones of hardwood.) Lee shredded the grass and rubbed it rapidly between his hands, producing a short rope of punk. Kneeling, he arranged it on the board around the hole. Now he looped the stick through the bowstring and placed one end of the stick in the hole, the other in the handpiece.

Rapidly now, he began to bow the fire-drill. Rhythmically, the drill creaking like an unoiled pulley, he sawed at the punk. He shivered in the misty river-chill that lay on the island.

While Lee sawed away, Mitch stared at the candy bar wrapper, a Three Musketeers, and recalled the old television commercial: "Big enough to share with a friend!" Under the circumstances, he knew of no such friends.

Mitch had already given up on the whole enterprise when, after a frozen eternity, a pencil-thin column of smoke began to drift up from the drill-board and a fragile spark appeared in the punk. Tenderly, Lee lifted the board and began to blow. Mitch knelt to help, his face right over the punk, blowing like a bellows, and Lee thrust him roughly away.

"Take it easy! You'll blow it out."

"I was jist barely blowing, Lee. I was blowing jist like you."

"Hell you was!"

"I was too!"

"Shut up!"

55

With a crackle, the punk burst into flame. Lee placed the board on the ground and covered the punk with marsh grass, and the little flame leaped up, searing. Still blowing, he fed the fire pencils of driftwood, stacking them in a teepee, and the flames crackled higher. The yellow light illumined his pale, intense face.

Carefully, Lee slid the fire off the board onto the sand. There, he began to feed it ever-larger sticks of wood. Overhead, the willow canopy stirred in the updraft, and smoke eddied as though trapped in a small green room.

With the fire finally popping and cracking through sizeable driftwood logs, Lee sat back with a sigh.

"Now all we gotta do is kill us a trout."

A BIG BROWN TROUT FINNED IN THE SANDBAR SHALLOWS. Thumping in bits of wood fiber, Lee managed to coax it within a few feet of shore. There, the fish struck halfheartedly at the splinters, its nose breaking the pane of green water. The trout hung in the current, facing upstream, finning, as Lee stalked it at a crouch.

Finally, he stood poised over the fish. In his upraised hand was an orange river rock the size and shape of a dinosaur's egg. With all his strength, he threw the rock, and a geyser of water leaped up, soaking him.

When he could finally see past the falling water, he saw the trout holding in the current, deeper in the river, safely out of range. Lee cursed and shot the fish a bird.

"I think you missed, Lee."

"Shut up!"

Shivering, Lee cursed and picked up another rock.

13

THE LINE OF CORVETTES AND LINCOLN CONTINENTALS followed a green Ford pickup down the steep switchbacks of a gravelled state road. Headlights on in the coming night gave the cars the look of a funeral cortege. Now, down in the valley, the road straightened, and the procession crossed the river, small here near its headwaters, on a shake-covered bridge. The cars rumbled through the bridge, loose planks booming. On one of the 'Vettes, Cherry Bomb sidepipes crackled.

Emerging from the bridge, they crossed long river-bottom fields, corn on the left, pasturage on the right—where John Thompson's Brahma bull watched, chewing his cud, his eyes like phosphor in the headlights. In among the Herefords and Guernseys and whitetail deer, with his huge hump and wicked horns, he looked like a Cape buffalo.

Inside the lead pickup, Tony and Eggar sat without talking. In the green of the dashlights, their unshaven faces were grim. Eggar's rifle was racked in the window behind them. (A long-handled paint roller and a carpenter's level occupied the other racks.) They stared straight ahead as the lights picked out the road. Beyond the fields, the forest recommenced, and in the high beams, the dust-whitened trees formed a glimmering cavern vault over the sandy roadbed so that they seemed to be travelling through an endless tunnel.

Tony fidgeted, drinking again and again from the silver flask. Though the night was cool, his face, as he regarded the dark woods, shone with sweat. He was dressed in Army surplus now but, Eggar noticed, Tony's name, VENDETTI, was over the chest pocket of the olive field jacket. Eggar found that somehow worrisome.

"I figger we can get attar 'em at first light," Eggar said, downshifting as the road began to climb.

He pressed the washer on the new pickup, and the wipers cleared two arcs in the dust-floured windshield. His ownership of a working washer made him absurdly proud, and he pressed it again.

Tony took no notice. "First light, my lily ass!"

"Tony, 'at river ain't no place to be attar dark."

"Wimp!"

"You'll think wimp when you find your tail hanging offa one of 'em ivy bluffs. Long ways to the bottom."

"That's your job, Tonto. You're the fait'ful Indian guide."

"I still don't like it."

"Hey, nobody *likes* it, okay. But them kids go to the cops and we go to the chair. The *both* of us. No ifs, ands or buts. Hear me? I don't like it no better'n you. I got kids. It's somethin's gotta be done."

Eggar looked back at the road. He was trying to keep his mind off of just what the successful termination of the mission entailed. He had painted alongside the boys' father since before they were born. Though both were teetotalers, he had gotten roaring drunk with Cleve Rainey the night of Lee's birth. His wife had warned him—weekly—about Tony and his Italian friends. Yet she happily spent every dime the lucrative new arrangement earned them. (Well, not every dime, he noted wryly, eyeing the spotless interior of the new pickup—the first new anything he'd ever owned.) No doubt about it, the Moselys had never before lived so high on the hog.

Eggar sighed and shook his head. There was a Campbell's soup can on the seat between them, and he used it to relieve himself of tobacco juice. Tony watched him with disgust, and looking back at the road, he cracked the dusty window vent. Eggar, he now knew, could no longer be trusted.

14

WHILE LEE WAS EXHAUSTING HIMSELF WITH THE ROCKS, Mitch wandered away down the island. The water moccasin had spooked him—like all reasonable people, Mitch was terrified of snakes—and as he walked, pushing through the willow tapestries and head-high tussocks of marsh grass, he tapped the rocky ground ahead of him with a stick.

Where the island began to climb, Mitch stopped, breathing hard, and let his eyes travel across the river. The sun was down now, the light rapidly fading, and the whole floodplain lay in purple shadow.

Leaning on his staff, Mitch looked up. Far above where it was still day, a jet's vapor trail caught the sunset, a crimson chalk line on a blue blackboard. Mitch watched it wishfully. Though Mitch had never been on a jet—on any plane, for that matter—he'd read about it in novels. On jet-planes, they ate dinner and watched movies. For a moment, as he watched the jet streak behind the mountain—the contrail dissipating, joining the high pink cirrus—he felt hot tears burn against the backs of his eyes. He blinked them away though—crying was for babies and girls—and with a sigh, continued on, tapping the ground ahead of him like a little blind man.

Climbing up, Mitch made the high ground of the boomerang-shaped island. This part of the original riverbend still supported sizeable hardwood trees. The oaks and maples stood in sandy washes above the willows, driftwood banked around them, paper streaming from their lower branches.

Mitch looked toward the riverbank and his eyes took in the moat of black water that separated them. Above the yellow-clay embankment, he could see the footpath running through the trees. Looking downriver, he saw the Interstate bridge and eyed it wistfully. With another sigh, Mitch continued on.

He was halfway down the island, at the bend of the boomerang, when he first noticed the water marks on the trunks of the island's hardwoods. The rings were a good ten or twelve feet above the ground. Mitch studied them closely; then shook his head and moved on.

He had taken hardly a dozen steps when he stopped again and looked at the riverbank. He frowned at the silty line ten feet up on the marly, yellow clay. Slowly, Mitchell's eyes followed the floodline downstream until they came to rest on a wall of banked driftwood. Still intent on the floodline, it took a moment for the object to register—red-and-white, half-buried in the silt-matted leaves. Now Mitchell's eyes lit up. Floodlines and snakes were forgotten as he hurried toward it.

Carefully, he pulled out the fisherman's bobber. Holding it, backing away, he retrieved twenty feet of monofilament line—and at the end, a rusty hook and sinkers still in place, a complete terminal tackle, "hook, line and sinker."

"Aw-right! Hey, Lee!" he called toward the campfire. "Guess what?"

Mitch was out of breath when he reached the fire. "Hey, Lee, check it out!"

But Lee shook him off, engrossed in the stalk of yet another trout.

"Shh! Shut up, you'll scare him. Oh, yeh," he breathed, lifting the rock. "*Now* I got the little …"

Lee was soaked from head to toe, water-darkened hair plastered to his head. He looked miserable, teeth chattering in the chill of coming night. Now, with both hands, he raised the rock high above his head, swaying with the effort, and launched it.

Another geyser leaped in the air. Mitch danced nimbly away as buckets of river rained on Lee. The trout shot away, every scale in place.

Lee turned to his brother, dripping, shivering, cursing, and Mitch meekly held out his find. Lee regarded the tackle stupidly.

IN THE LAST LIGHT, THE BROTHERS SPLASHED through the shallows on the backside of the island, turning over rocks. Finally, under one algaed stone, Lee found a spring lizard and trapped it beneath his bare foot. Carefully, he pinned it behind the head and lifted it for Mitch to see.

Back on the beach, Lee hooked the lizard through the tail and cast it out. He had attached the line to the fire-drill bow, and holding the bow, curved and short as a dowser's witching stick, he hunched forward, teeth chattering. Mitch leaned against him for warmth, for shelter from the rising night wind—until Lee thrust him roughly away.

"Quit it! Get off me!"

The river whispered softly between its wide cattail banks. Upriver, the moon sat on the mountaintop, its face crisscrossed by trees. The air was losing the day's warmth, and a mist rose on river and marsh. In the stillness, fog hung in the willows like smoke from the fire.

All around them, the forest pulsed with the sounds of coming night. Rainfrogs, bullfrogs, crickets and cicadas laid down a counterpoint of peeps, croaks, grunts and chirps. In the cattails across the river, a bullfrog thrummed; another answered from the backside of the island; and the two adversaries dueled on in deepening register. Somewhere high on the mountain behind them, an owl hooted, and nearer, a whippoorwill warbled in the trees along the river. From the mountain beyond the marsh, a fox barked at the moon, its yipping high-pitched as a chihuahua.

Behind them, the fire threw ominous shadows in the willow rooms. Now the wind rose, the shadows quickened, and the rustling leaves gave them footfalls. Gulping, Mitch moved nearer the fire. He took in the colossal shadows he and Lee cast across the river. It was as though giants were standing behind them, and twice, Mitch turned to reassure himself.

"Hey, Lee, how come they to call this here Yeller Banks Island?" He had posed the question more to hear the sound of a human voice than to elicit information.

Without taking his eyes from the bobber, Lee pointed to the riverbank behind them. Mitch followed his water-pruned finger and saw the yellow-white, marly clay that formed it.

"Oh."

"'Duh, oh.' Mister Straight-A's." Still watching the float, Lee held up his middle finger. "'Duh, hey, Lee, how come they to call this here a finger?'"

Mitch laughed in spite of himself—but again, looking

61

toward the bank, he saw the high-water mark.

"Hey, Lee?"

"*What?* Jesus, Mitchell! Do I look like a encyclopedia?"

"What causes them?" Mitch said, pointing. "Them water-rings? Look up on that tree trunk yonder. They all up and down the river. Bank too."

Sighing, Lee gave the bank a cursory glance. With a shrug, he returned his attention to the float.

"Dunno. Floods, I reckon. Log drives in the springtime. Who cares."

"Oh. But how come they—"

Lee held up his hand and pointed at the float. Turning, Mitch saw the bobber trembling; the monofilament starting to move off. Now the bobber disappeared in a strong, slantwise dive. Standing, Lee set the hook, and the little willow bent over steeply.

Upstream and down, the taut line cut the water. Lee played the fish gently, fearful of the rotten line. Twice, he went waist-deep to stop a downstream run. Twice, the trout pulled the willow completely underwater, and Lee splashed after it, his arm submerged to the shoulder. Each time, with gentle pressure, he coaxed the fish back to the surface.

At length, he worked the trout—exhausted, lying on its side, its rainbow vivid in the firelight—into the shallows, skating it toward the beach. The fish was nearly aground when the line broke. Lee leaped and, with both hands, scooped fish and water onto the island.

There, the trout flopped around on the sand so that when Lee finally caught and lifted it, the firelit fish seemed sugar-coated. The big lake-run rainbow was every bit of eighteen inches.

"Aw-right!" Lee whooped. "Curb service!" He held out his hand. "Gimme five, baby bro! High five! On the side! *Skin it!*"

The brothers shouted and slapped hands. Puckering, Lee gave the squirming fish a farewell kiss.

15

THE LINE OF CARS FOLLOWED THE PICKUP off the river road and into a littered, riverbank clearing, the kind used by fishermen for parking. The cars came to a stop in a tight semi-circle, power-steering groaning, big engines idling. Through the trees, the white-water river was frozen like a glacier by the brilliant high beams.

As the men dismounted, the echo of slamming car doors, *chunk, chunk, chunk,* punctured the night. From the number of door-slams it was clear, even before the men stepped in front of the lights, that Tony had mustered a sizeable army.

Out in the headlights, the men -- black silhouettes against the blazing high beams -- got ready to start downriver. They were a group of maybe fifteen, all city-bred. Three had come in coats and ties and wore wingtip dress shoes. The others, in their deck shoes and golf shirts, seemed dressed for a day on the links or at the racquet club. Only Eggar, in his bib-overalls and workboots, seemed at home.

He stood at the edge of the clearing now and watched the others pass the insect repellent and a bottle of rum. At some point, Eggar had worked with Day-Glo paint, and the streaks and splats vaguely outlined him. Chewing, he watched the men with an expression that suggested he'd swallowed his tobacco.

They were treating it as a damn outing. There was the excitement, the enthusiasm in their voices of children poised on the lip of summer vacation. It reminded him of the spring and summer he'd taken to guiding city fellers for trout. Like painter-work, he'd give it up after one season. There wasn't enough money for that aggravation. Better he outright baby-sit like his oldest girl, May Ellen: Same money without the heavy lifting. His deal with Tony was as go-between with area farmers willing to grow the new cash crop—simple enough since Eggar was blood-kin to most of them. But here he was baby-sitting again.

Eggar spat at the thought of the long night before him. In summer, with the snakes crawling, the woods was no place to be after dark. He spat again at the sight of Tony topping off the silver flask.

Now there came the clicks of cartridges being fed into clips and magazines. The snap of shotgun breeches being closed on loads of double-ought buck. When they shut off the engines and killed the headlights, the clearing was plunged into perfect blackness. The seamless silence of the deep woods descended.

For the first time, some of them sensed what lay ahead. This was something unfamiliar to these men of the city, where always in the darkest corners, there was the alpenglow of neon. Somewhere always a leaking night-light or prowling car lights.

Unnerved, several snapped on their flashlights, and circles of illumination darted around the clearing. Blackened hearthrocks, scorched beer cans and the silver dollars of discarded condom foils were suddenly spotlit by the moving circles of light.

"This here looks like a fun kinda place," one of them observed with a bolstering chuckle.

"Yeh," said another. "Wish I'd brought my rod." He was looking at an accordioned bait carton.

"Hell, I brought my *rod*," the first man laughed, looking at a condom foil. "Wish I'd brung the *wife*."

The other men chuckled dutifully, but the laughter was forced and quickly died.

Tony stood a little apart from the others, oblivious to their chatter, nervously eyeing the night. In the jacket pocket, his sweaty hand palmed the checkered grip of the revolver.

A full moon had topped the mountain, an aspirin dissolving in the clouds of a moving front. Fog had climbed the riverbank and hung in the trees like cotton. Below, it lay on the river in a vaporous blanket. Their commotion had silenced the cicadas, and the only sounds filtered up from the river. Straining, Tony heard the faint roar of the rapids upstream. The splashing scutter of a startled raccoon. The purl and slap of feeding trout. An owl hooted on the mountainside across the river, and Tony turned toward it, shivering, watching the fireflies wink in the cavernous blackness beneath the trees.

It had been a long time since he was in the boonies, and just the feel of the velvet night around him, now that the civilized sounds of cars and voices were stilled, was enough to waken old fears, an old dread. He was suddenly warm, sticky, and sweat had popped out on his face. Angrily, he wiped it away with the palm of his hand.

"All right," he told them gruffly. "Let's move out. And stay together. No screw-ups, Roselli. I mean it. Eggar, lead off."

The men shouldered their packs, and in single-file, started down the river; down the dark and narrow riverbank path, already stumbling after Eggar's overalled back.

Tony brought up the rear. Through the trees, the river moved in the night, a riffle here, an eddy there; the widening rings of a rising trout, all catching the faceted flash of moonlight. Beneath the windy trees, there was the glint of gun-metal, of blued steel, gleaming evilly beneath a bad moon rising.

16

THE BUTTERFLIED TROUT POPPED AND SIZZLED, roasting on the fire-drill planking the boys had propped before the fire. Cattail tubers were turning brown atop the coals, and Lee rolled them over with a stick. Hunched over, the brothers sat as close to the fire as they could get. Their wet clothes steamed in the heat, as did their sneakers, inverted on sticks stuck in the sand.

As the fire burned down to cooking coals, all around them the forest night closed in. Firelight reached back beneath the willows in a *chiaroscuro* of dancing dark and light. Above the fire, the willow canopy stirred in the updraft, inflating like a green balloon, revealing further firelit rooms. The moon was over the mountain now, and on the riverbank, the wind roared through the great spruce. Whitening in the moonlight, they were suddenly visible.

Lee rolled onto his knees, pulled a small piece off the fish and put it in his mouth. He chewed critically, smacking his lips.

"I reckon she's done," he said at last. "Done enough anyways."

With the plank on his lap, he grasped the trout's backbone and pulled the fish's skeleton away intact. He lifted the steaming trout, juggling it, and tore it in two. Mitch got the smaller half.

"Eat it slow. That's all they are."

Mitch nodded, but ravenous, he dug in. He chewed gingerly, though, picking out the flybones.

"I wisht we had some salt," Lee said.

"I got some."

Mitch stood and dug in the pocket of his overalls. When he pulled the salt out, the packet came away in a wad.

"I reckon it got wet."

"Duh," Lee said. "Wonder how that happened?"

He pointed to Mitchell's pants.

"What?"

"Drop trou."

"Unh-unh!"

"Drop 'em, I said!"

Mitch unhooked his suspenders and his overalls fell at his feet. He stepped out of them with embarrassment and handed them over. Lee held the pants over his fish and slowly turned out the pocket. Salt—and sand—fell in sodden clumps on the blackened trout.

"Don't take it all."

"I ain't. Crybaby! Shut up!" Lee dropped the remaining clump of salt on Mitchell's trout. "Spread it around some."

"Gimme back my overhauls."

"Okay. Here."

He held them out to Mitch—but when Mitch reached for them, Lee threw them across the island.

"Fetch, Fido!" he told his brother, laughing.

Mitch hurried to retrieve his pants and quickly pulled them on. Sitting again, he dug back in, eating hungrily. He didn't worry about bones now.

After a time, he told Lee, his mouth full, "I wisht we had some ketchup."

"I wisht you'd shut up! 'Lee, I wisht we had some ketchup.' I wisht we had a helicopter."

Mitch took another bite. Chewing, he looked at Lee. "I surely do hope Mica and Suellen got home okay." Lee didn't answer. "They wouldn't hurt 'em … would they, Lee?"

Lee looked down. "I reckon they can take care of theirselves. More'n we can say."

Mitch nodded, but he didn't look so sure. He dug back in. After a time, he asked Lee—who was deep in thought, "What we gone do, Lee?"

"Ain't but one thing to do. Head downriver. Make for the high bridge. It's the only way out."

"Reckon how far it is?"

"I done told you. Five miles. At least. Maybe six. It ain't got no closer since this afternoon."

"Well, that ain't so bad, right? We oughta make the bridge by tomorrow evening. Right, Lee? Maybe sooner."

Lee snorted and gave his brother a disgusted look. "Moron, it's what's *'tween* here and the bridge that's bad. Ain't no

Interstate highway."

"You mean The Wall?"

"For starters. The Narrows starts up jist below The Wall."

"How we gone get through, Lee?"

"You don't get *through* The Narrows—'less'n you're crazy. We gotta climb out. They's 'posed to be an old game trail 'bove the falls. *'Posed* to be. I ain't never seen none."

"And then the bridge?"

"No, then Green River Gorge—if we make it that far." Lee took another bite. "We hit The Cables right below The Gorge. We can get acrost there—if that big rain we had last month ain't tore 'em out. She took out the foot-bridge on Camp Creek— daddy said—and it's a whole *bunch* higher."

"*Then* the bridge?"

"Yeh. *Then* the bridge."

Mitch sat back, smiling. "Good."

Lee rolled his eyes. "'Good.'"

Mitch settled back on his elbows and fell silent. There was a piercing twinge of guilt—that registered on his dirty face as a scowl—as he imagined the dimensions of his mother's alarm. She would be beside herself by now; beyond anger.

At length, he asked his brother, "Reckon what mama and them's doing 'bout now?"

"Mama's boy."

"I ain't done it!"

"Goody Two Shoes."

"I ain't!" Mitch said with heat.

Lee laughed. He knew all his brother's hot buttons. "Crybaby" at this point would have sent him into tears. For once, it didn't seem worth the effort. There were more pressing concerns.

"What time's it getting to be?"

Mitch consulted his wrist watch. The face was cracked and fogged, Michael Mouse a little watermarked, but it still worked. Mitch put it to his ear and heard the tiny vermin heartbeat.

"Nine. A little after."

"Eating supper, I reckon—'less they out looking for us— both of 'em with a big hickory." Lee sniffled. "Mama's boy's gone get a striping. I reckon he'll cry then."

Lee imitated Mitch crying, sniffling, lower lip run out in a pout—but Mitch wasn't listening.

"Wonder what they having?" He looked wistfully at the trout skeleton, blackening on the coals. "For supper, I mean. Probably pork chops … and corn on the cob … and strawberry shortcake … and ice tea … and cracklin bread … and peas 'n' hock …"

But Lee wasn't thinking about food. Shaking his head, grinning, he told Mitch, "God, I bet the old lady's fit to be tied." He chuckled. "Old man too."

Contemplating his parents' consternation, Lee's grin widened.

17

MR. AND MRS. RAINEY WERE WORRIED. Sitting at the kitchen table, they ate their supper in silence. Gladys Rainey, thirty-five and built along the racy lines of a VW bug, picked at her pork chop. At the other end of the table, her rail-thin husband ate mechanically, joylessly shoveling it in. His white coveralls and green John Deere cap boasted a psychedelic profusion of splats, streaks and drips. He had spent the day painting at Kentucky Fried Chicken, and the Colonel's corporate colors glistened under the bare light bulb.

His wife was of Pentecostal bent, and the kitchen, like every room in the Rainey house, looked like a set from a vampire movie: Every wall held a crucifix. On the wall over the sideboard, a tintype of a haloed Jesus, His arms spread wide, "suffered the little children to come unto Him." On another wall, a cross-stitch sampler proclaimed: "King of Kings and Lord of Love." The Rainey menage was just that kind of hard-rocking place.

In the heavy silence, the only sounds were the clicking of their cutlery and the ticking of the wall clock above the sink. For the tenth time in ten minutes, Mrs. Rainey looked up at it, saw that it was five after nine and her look of concern deepened.

"I swear! Reckon where them boys is got to this time?"

She put down her knife and fork, abandoning any pretense of eating. Noisily, she pushed back from the table with an indigestive wince.

Mr. Rainey sighed. "Lord only knows. They be okay, I reckon."

An hour earlier, he had checked Mitchell's closet for the deer rifle. Its presence there had been somehow comforting.

"I don't know, Cleve. It ain't like 'em to run off like this—not without telling nobody. Not even Lee—fer all his devilment …"

Mrs. Rainey had checked for the gun two hours before and said a silent prayer at the sight of it.

"First time fer ever'thing."

"I'm half a mind to call the sheriff."

"Now you jist cool your jets. No sense to go off half-cocked. Sheriff got a full plate ... without some tomfool, teenage ..."

But his expression told her he was far from sure.

"I bet I know one thing," his wife said.

"What's 'at?"

"Them two'll be eating off the mantel a solid month when I get done with 'em."

"I reckon you'll have to get in line."

Mr. Rainey paused, shaking his head, looking off into space.

"What, Cleve?"

"I can understand Lee pulling a damn-fool stunt like this ... but Mitchell ..."

Mrs. Rainey was near to tears as she nodded her agreement. "'Less'n Lee went and got him into something. Wouldn't be the first time neither."

Mr. Rainey sighed. "Well, they's no use supposing. Let's jist sit tight and see. They'll come adragging in here sooner or later, 'less I miss my guess."

But Mr. Rainey's troubled face belied his words.

0

18

ON YELLOW BANKS ISLAND, THE FIRE HAD BURNED LOW. Lee belched softly and lay back. Watching him, Mitch managed an imitative croak of his own. He settled into the identical position, back on both elbows, bare feet to the fire. Like Lee, he picked at his front teeth with a stem of marsh grass. Lee's sodden wallet was out, open on the footprinted sand beside him, and in the firelight, he studied a wrinkled, watermarked photo of Jennifer. Looking up, he sighed as he regarded his ruined letter jacket, cracked and steaming before the fire. The two remaining sports bars were tarnished, and the red W hung by a single serif. By morning, it would be too small for Mitchell.

"Thinking about Jennifer?"

"Yeh." Lee shook his head. "I reckon she's history now."

"Lee, Jenny don't care 'bout the money. She likes you. She told me so. Always has."

Lee snorted. "A lot you know. 'Fore I got that letter jacket, I was invisible." He sighed. "Four varsity letters and nothing to put 'em on. We a pair, Mitchell. Losers."

The boys fell silent and returned their attention to the fire. The coals reddened as it popped and cracked in the night wind.

Finally, with a sigh, with a final, lingering look, Lee put the photo back in his wallet. He rolled up on one hip and put the wallet away.

"Lee?"

"Hm?"

"I reckon the money was theirs."

"Right. Sherlock Holmes."

"Lee?"

"Huh?"

"What if we was to give it back? The money?"

"Wouldn't make no difference now. We seen 'em drown that old man." Mitch shivered at the recollection. "You heared what they said. We could send 'em to the gas chamber."

"Yeh ... but what if we promised not to tell?"

"They wouldn't believe us, Mitchell. They wouldn't take the

chance."

"Yeh, I guess not."

Mitch sighed and sat up. With an unburned end of driftwood, he began to absently stir the fire. After a time, he asked his brother—who was again deep in thought, "Lee?"

"What?"

"You guess they got a pot farm around here somewheres?"

"Nah, these here fellers ain't got no farm. They don't grow it, they sell it. The old man grew it. That's what the money was for. Like as not, they run a club somewheres over Asheville-way."

"Oh. You sure do know a lot, Lee."

"Reckon I don't know much—else I wouldn't be here now. I knowed it were drugs right from the start. Shoulda stayed clear away."

"Lee?"

"What, Mitchell? *Damn!*"

"I feel real bad 'bout that old man. *Real* bad! I reckon we was the cause of that. Sorta."

"Don't think about it. Guess he had it coming. Lie down wid dogs, get up wid fleas."

Lee sat up and threw the last sticks of driftwood on the fire.

"Don't do no good to worry," he said. He rolled onto his side and squirmed a hip-hole in the sand. "Let's get some sleep—while the getting's good. Gotta far piece of ground to cover tomorrow. Ain't gone be no cakewalk."

Mitch nodded and rolled onto his side, facing the fire. There was twenty degrees difference between his front side and backside. He was freezing and burning up. Mitch looked fearfully around. Firelit shadows danced on the willow canopy and trembled on the river. Beyond the willows, the moonlight showed the silver current as clearly as a hydrograph. Downstream, the bullet-riddled log had beached itself, the bullet holes white in the black bark.

The boys curled into fetal positions before the crackling fire, but Mitchell's heat-flushed face, as he stared across the leaden river, revealed his big-eyed wakefulness. Rolling over, his back to the fire so Lee couldn't see, Mitch folded his hands and began to pray. *Our Father, Who art in heaven, hallowed be thy name ...*

A RABBIT EMERGED FROM THE CATTAILS AND CAME DOWN to the river to drink. Suddenly, it looked up, nose twitching, and disappeared into the forest. Moments later, an emaciated gray fox came down the river, tongue out, trailing at a lope, and plunged into the marsh.

Their dorsal fins leaving wakes, trout fed in the cattail shallows with noisy, slashing strikes. Now a luna moth flew downstream, just above the surface, and a huge brown trout left the river to engulf it. All that remained when the ripples had subsided was a powdering of wing dust on the moon-struck water.

In the cattails across the river, a raccoon cornered a small trout and, with a bearlike flip of its forepaws, threw the fish onto the bank. Now it bit through the head, and the trout shuddered and was still. The raccoon sat back on its haunches and began to eat.

ACROSS THE RIVER, MITCH WAS DREAMING, tossing and turning beside the dying fire. Now he woke with a yell and sat up, his face covered with sweat and sand. Trembling, he moved nearer the fire. Shuddering, he took in the dark willows behind him. Wide-eyed, he checked out the river upstream and down. In the nightmare, the old man had crawled from the river, nose bleeding, eyes full of blame. "The hole was allus empty," he said over and over. "I swear on my mother's grave." He had tried to drag Mitch into the water.

Mitch looked across the river and saw a rabbit drinking from the shallows. Nose breaking the perfect pane of moonshine. Nibbling at the marsh grass along the shore. As Mitch watched, smiling, a second rabbit joined it, and the two cavorted along the riverbank. Chasing each other in tight circles. Butting heads. Touching noses.

Mitch watched them, wholly entranced, completely distracted—when in a rush of wings, a Great Horned Owl swooped down and took a rabbit away in its talons. The rabbit screamed pitifully.

Far in the night, high above, the rabbit's screams went on, growing fainter and fainter, until Mitchell could stand it no longer. He jumped his feet and threw a rock high into the night.

"Murderer! Murderer! I'll kill you! I'll kill you!"

Mitch threw rock after rock, but all splashed harmlessly into the heartless river. The ripples were soon lost in the current.

Finally, his screaming woke Lee.

"Mitchell! Mitchell, shut up! You want 'em to find us? Huh? You want 'em to find us? Now jist shut up! Go back to sleep!"

And Mitch slumped to the sand, sobbing, firelit tear tracks on his dirty face.

19

ELEVEN O'CLOCK: THE MOON LAY ON the current-wrinkled river with the abstract toolings of demented silverwork. The boys slept the bottomless sleep of total exhaustion, curled into fetal balls on either side of the smoldering fire. The blackened trout skeleton was visible on a hearthstone, burned feathery as the ash of a fern. On the stakes, their shoes had scorched, and the waffle pattern on the soles sagged out of shape. Still steaming, the letter jacket continued its progress toward the children's rack.

Beyond the fire, that crimsoned in a breath of night wind, crickets, cicadas and rainfrogs creaked like a contraption made of rotary parts, and the backwaters vibrated with the baritone of bullfrogs. On facing mountains, owl and fox maintained their two-part disharmony, while on the riverbank, the whippoorwill continued the tireless repetition of its name, a bird with an ego or identity problem.

Fireflies flashed in the green rooms of weeping willows and winked across the quicksilver river, where occasionally they were intercepted by airborne trout. In the backwater behind the island, a whitetail doe and two fawns fed like moose, withers-deep in the lilypad shallows. Just upstream, a raccoon splashed along the sandbar, turning over stones. Now it found a crayfish and sat up on its haunches to eat. In the stillness, the cornflake crunch of shellfish was loud.

And now a snake, a venomous, thick-bodied water moccasin, slithered ashore on Yellow Banks Island. It stopped on the warm sand at the river's edge, thready tongue working, looking toward the sleeping shapes of Mitch and Lee. Mitch turned over and mumbled in his sleep, sand sticking to one reddened cheek. Lee snored lightly, upper lip aflutter. The snore fit seamlessly into the rhythmic throb of the bullfrogs.

A MILE UPRIVER, THE MEN STUMBLED ALONG the footpath, metal objects clanking together in their knapsacks. Eggar held the lead, and Tony pushed them hard from the rear. It had rained the day before, and the trail was a soup of mud and standing water. The snaky undergrowth grew thickly along both sides of the path, and in the silence—the night-sounds stilled by their clumsy passage—there was only the swish and trill of pants legs. The city men were not in the best of shape, and they panted and puffed, pissing and moaning, stumbling and cursing the darkness; cursing the sputtering surprise of a spider's web. Their flashlights were off, and the barrels of their rifles and shotguns gleamed in the moonlight. Below, reflected in the river, the moon followed along as though current-borne.

Slowing, dropping back, Tony stared at the sky. Though the moon was well up, it was dark beneath the trees. Now the wind picked up, gusting, and stirred the limbs overhead. Through it, Tony saw a cloud moving swiftly across the moon. At its edges, the cloud gleamed like silver, in bars like silver sunbeams, its wispy margin bright as light-struck angel hair. Now the cloud passed and forking shadows reappeared on the rutted trail. The fog was thickening over the river, climbing the riverbank through the dark trees in wisps and feelers. It was chest-deep on the footpath and swirled into ghosts at their passage. The moisture-laden air clogged the lungs of the smokers, and all up and down the column came the sound of phlegmy, fist-muffled coughing.

Tony looked down at the moon-silvered river. He saw the reeds growing in the black shallows and then a clump of bamboo. Suddenly, the moon, the river, the bamboo, the shuffling, coughing defile of men, his shoulders chafed tender by the straps of the heavy pack, brought it all back—the night patrols in the Delta. For the first time in years, he felt the heavy night sweat coursing down the indent of his spine; tickling in his scalp; in his eyes blurring his vision; tasting of seawater in his mouth. Trembling, Tony reached back and found the flask. He uncapped it one-handed and took a long drink.

Now, near the middle of the column, the short gangster named Messina stumbled headlong and fell with a splash. He got to his feet furiously.

"Damn roots! Dark as a damn pit! And slow down, Eggar! I

ain't no frigging mountain goat!"

"Dammit, Messina!" Tony hissed. "*Stow it!*"

Near the front of the line, the tall mafiosi named Roselli whispered to Eggar, "I can't see nothing, Eggar. Come on, man—gimme some light."

"No lights," Tony told him, capping the flask, wiping his mouth with a trembling hand. "No cigarettes neither. We getting close. Might be an ambush."

"Huh?" said another man. "I thought you said they was unarmed?"

"They got their ways, Nicky New. You better believe it. They got they ways. Once they locate you, they pick you off like flies."

Messina and Roselli exchanged a look.

"My name's Frank, Tony, Frank Piscopo. *You* know."

"Your name's dumbass, dumbass. Now shut up. Get back in line."

"Right, Tony, sure. Whatever you say."

"Said shut up. Ain't gone tell you again."

As they continued down the path, Tony's eyes flicked ahead, looking for trip-wires and booby-traps; searching the high ground for an ambush; scanning the dark treetops for the head-and-shoulders outline of a sniper. He was glad Bodarsky was walking point. Below him, in the moonlight, the river moved ponderously … between thickening cattail banks.

ON YELLOW BANKS ISLAND, MITCH WAS TAKING his history final—but in the dream, there were hundreds and hundreds of questions, so many he could never answer them all before the bell. Furiously, he checked the multiple-choice questions, guessing now, as Mrs. Frankhausen piled his desk with the mimeo-blue test pages.

Again, the wind rose—in the dream, the draft generated by the cascading pages—and the fire's dying embers reddened. An owl hooted on the mountainside, and at the sound, Mitch stirred in his sleep, mumbling.

The water moccasin had crossed half the distance between

78

river and fire, the wet sand embroidered with its sidewinder track, and at Mitchell's sudden movement, the big snake stopped and coiled, forked tongue flicking, tasting the night air for danger and for prey.

20

IT TOOK A LONG CAST TO REACH THE FLOODLIT DAM from where Codge Loflin sat in the bow of the borrowed johnboat. The boat had swung around against the taut anchor line, the square bow into the outfall, and rode the upwelling like a surfboard. The aluminum bottom slapped the water with the gong of an empty oil drum. Codge felt the steam rising off the water, still warm from its passage through the turbines. For the tenth time in as many minutes, he took off his glasses and wiped them on the tail of his chamois shirt.

Codge's teenage nephew, Ronnie, sat in the stern, listening to his Walkman, fretting his fishing rod like a guitar. He had the rock music cranked to such a volume, Codge could hear it faintly over the roar of the tailrace. Thus deafened, Ronnie complained loudly of the cold and wet, and Codge silently resolved—for the tenth time since their arrival—not to bring him again. It was a resolution that would be forgotten within the hour.

Now, feet braced against the bow, Codge drew back his bait and let go. The chicken liver hit the face of the dam with a bloody splatter—it looked chocolate in the sodium-vapor light—and tumbled down into the roaring white outfall. The rodtip jerked sharply down. It was like surf-fishing, Codge thought, taking up slack as the current tumbled the bait back to him. You never knew when you had a damn bite.

In the blackness left and right of the dam, lanterns marked the locations of bank-bound anglers. Caught in the glow of the white-gas lanterns, they seemed to hang in the blackness like men on magic carpets. Codge could see them as clearly as though they stood under streetlights. Squinting, he recognized two. There was a milky nimbus where the lanterns struck the driven mist, and rainbows glimmered at the edges.

There were floodlights on the face of the dam, trained down on the boiling tailrace. The lights spotlit other boats on either side of Codge. Squinting into the lights, Codge looked up the face of the great dam. It towered over him, a skyscraper of concrete lodged in the gorge, glimmering in the moonlight.

Looking up, hands in his armpits to warm them, his rod resting on the bow, Codge watched a pair of blue-coveralled workmen cross a guardrailed scaffold a hundred feet above. A pistol-packing nightwatchman with a time-clock hanging from his shoulder negotiated a catwalk even higher up. Watching him, Codge, who was himself a security guard, mouthed a silent prayer of thanksgiving that at least he was off graveyard.

There was a glassed-in control room low on the dam-face. The room was darkened and the glass red-tinted from the panel lights inside. Codge could see white-coated engineers moving around a control panel, monitoring the rows and rows of voltmeters and switches with positions marked by red and green lights. Most of the lights were red. Behind them, another panel was lit up in red and green like Christmas. Some of the men carried clipboards and cups of coffee. Their downcast faces looked sunburned.

As Codge watched, more men entered the little room. He looked nervously at his watch, the Roman numerals ghostly green, and saw that it was nearly midnight. He began to reel in his line.

Suddenly, from the face of the dam, a powerful horn began to sound, echoing down the gorge. On both banks, fishermen grabbed their rods and lanterns and bait buckets and began to scramble toward the parking lots. As one, the boaters fired their outboards or put their backs into their oars.

The horn startled Codge's nephew. So he wasn't totally brain-dead. He wiped the headphones off in a single motion and quickly reeled in.

In the bow, his uncle strained at the anchor, but it was stuck fast, a hundred-dollar Danforth.

"Slack off on her, Ronnie," Codge told him, puffing. He had had the flu and still didn't have his strength back. "She's hung up on us."

The boy came ahead on the electric motor, and when the boat was nearly vertical above it, Codge felt the fouled anchor let go. With a sigh of relief, he hauled it in—the braided, yellow line slick with algae and stinking of the river bottom—and dropped it, gonging, into the boat. Ronnie—who'd kept the motor wide-open during the operation—had nearly reached shore.

At the launch, they dragged the boat up the concrete ramp, huffing and puffing, the bottom grating, the bait-bucket turning over.

Now, as Codge stood at the edge of the parking lot, watching the river, a shiver of anticipation ran over him. He had helped build the dam and remembered the first pour of concrete. He had been a young man then, not much older than Ronnie.

"It's something else, ain't it?" he said, turning to his nephew, smiling. The excitement in his rheumy eyes made him look ten years younger.

But the boy was back in his headphones and stood across the access lane, admiring a candy-apple Corvette. The car looked purple beneath the sodium-vapor streetlamps.

"Far out!" Ronnie said loudly.

You got that right, Code thought. You and the deaf leopard.

Ronnie danced up to the driver's window and leaned down to see past his reflection in the tinted glass, hands up on either side to form a visor. He patted his sneaker in time to the music. The song's lead guitar lick inspired a moment of frenzied air guitar. From behind, to his uncle, it appeared as though he were trying to pass a peach seed.

Codge shook his head and began to gather the spilled minnows. Most of them were still alive, fluttering, trapped beneath the boat's molded ribbing. More'n I can say for the boy. Now, gathering the minnows, he found a $20 bill.

INSIDE THE CONTROL BOOTH, THE ENGINEER STEPPED to the master panel. He looked at the wall clock, saw that it was midnight and made a note on his clipboard. With a final glance down at the tailrace pool—and everyone appeared to be clear—he threw a switch on the panel and the remaining lights went from red to green. Quickly now, he pushed a series of buttons.

Outside, there was a high-pitched, hydraulic whine as the

flume-gates rose. Fully open, they ratcheted into place with a *clang,* and a wall of white water twenty feet high roared into the gorge. Vertical as a tidal wave, it boomed through the tailrace, echoing off the dam, deafening in the canyon of granite and concrete.

Where the gorge narrowed, it deepened accordingly, rising on the vertical walls like a flooding canal lock. As Codge watched, smiling, the flumewater thundered into the gorge, gathering its freight of sawlogs, floating them as easily as the Styrofoam cups and beer cans it gathered from the shore.

Over all, the electric honking of the foghorn ripped the night.

21

MITCH MUMBLED IN HIS SLEEP. THE WATER MOCCASIN was only an arm's length from him. Now the wind stirred the sand, and it pricked his face. When he moved, rubbing his cheek, the snake oozed into a coil, scales sparking in the moonlight, the liquid tongue flicking out. Mitch rolled away, mumbling, and when he rolled back, the snake had stopped a foot from his face.

Suddenly, the crickets, cicadas and rainfrogs ceased on a single high note. The silence that followed was profound. Even the night wind grew still. Across the backwater, the deer looked up, looked upriver and disappeared into the woods with whitetailed leaps. The raccoon scuttled, splashing, into the streamside forest, still holding the crayfish.

Mitch stirred in his sleep, turning, and again the snake coiled, its head cocked back to strike. But Mitch settled on his back and began to snore, and the snake oozed out of its coil.

Across the fire, Lee was dreaming, already wrestling with summer school. He mumbled some terms of geometry – "Don't tell me, Jen. Hypotenuse. No, scalene." -- then rolled over and his mumbling stopped. The fire had burned lower still, and beneath the overlay of ash, the coals glowed in a sudden breath of wind.

IN THE LIGHTLESS CAVERN OF THE UNDERSTORY, the footpath rose, scaling the riverbank to pass an ivied boulder, the vines black-looking in the darkness. From the top of the incline, Tony saw the river moving slowly between reedy banks, gleaming battleship-gray in the moonlight.

Now the path dropped down, leveled out, and from the rear, Tony watched the men stumbling ahead. In depthless silhouette, their heads shuttled up and down like some kind of pop-up arcade game. The wind rose, the moon peaked through the canopy, and he saw the gleam of moonlit gun-metal. Heard the shuffling footfalls of fatigued feet. Felt the twinge of his abraded shoulders.

In a rush, the sights and sounds of a firefight assailed him. The hollow popping of an AK. The red laser-streaks of tracers. The firefly winking of muzzle flashes. The screams and groans of the wounded. "Medic! Medic! I'm hit! I'm hit!"

"Ouch!" said Messina. He slapped viciously at a mosquito on his neck. "Frigging bugs!" He slapped his arm. "*Damn!*"

At the sound of Messina's voice, the hallucination broke like a fever. Tony stopped in the path, shivering as from a malarial chill. With the edge of his hand, he squeegeed the sweat from his brow and flung it toward the river.

"Shh! Shut up, I said! We getting close. Sound carries over water. No more talking from here on. You hear me, Messina? *Stow it!*"

"Yeh, okay, Tony. Nothing that a transfusion wouldn't fix."

"Roselli, quit your damn crying."

Roselli seemed genuinely hurt. "*What,* Tony? I ain't said *nothing.*"

"I guess it's my imagination."

Roselli and Messina exchanged another look.

"Yeh," said Roselli. "I guess so."

UPRIVER, THE FLUMEWATER WAS GAINING STEAM as it dropped off the mountain. The leading edge, the tidal wave, bulldozed a tumbling, rumbling wall of logs before it. Now it churned up a crushed canoe from a summer camp. (In the moonlight, the Indian name on the bow was visible for an instant.) Now it disgorged what appeared to be a dead deer. Great sawlogs continued to accumulate on the crest, buoyed as easily as balsa. Already, the ends were white-splintered, the bark scarred white. They rode the frothing crest, bank to bank, tumbling in the moon-white water, creaking and cracking with each collision. In the moonlight, the snow-white crest gave it the look of a glacier moving in time-lapse photography.

Now the tidal wave reached The Money Tree and roared past. Tearing driftwood from the banks. Floating uprooted trees as easily as twigs. Undercutting the bank and causing a mudslide. Now it reached Mine Falls and went over with a thundering roar, launching sawlogs the size of phone poles, javelining them far downriver. On both banks far back of the river, the ground shuddered from the weight of falling logs and water. The creaking and cracking of the great logs as they slammed together, splintering, echoing, had the deep bass booming of an ice-floe breaking up.

ON YELLOW BANKS ISLAND, THE WATER was finally audible as a faint and faraway roar; like the wind in the tops of the great spruce, or like distant summer thunder. As the roar increased, Mitch stirred in his sleep and rolled over.

Instantly, the startled snake went into a coil and drew back to strike him in the face—when the Great Horned Owl swooped down and plucked the moccasin soundlessly into the night, without disturbing so much as a grain of sand.

Mitch rolled over and slept on, mumbling, rubbing his sunburned face. But as the roar continued to grow, his eyes opened. He lay still, groggy with sleep. With a frown of puzzlement, he sat up and looked upriver.

"Lee!" he whispered across the fire. "*Lee!*"

Lee woke with a start; then rose groggily on one elbow.

"What's that?"

Lee looked blankly at his brother and lay back down. "What's what?"

"That noise. Hear it?"

"I don't hear nothing. Is that how come you woke me up? Butthead! I was asleep!"

"Listen close!"

Again, Lee rose on one trembling arm and followed Mitchell's gaze up the moon-bright river. His face darkened with perplexity and growing unease.

"It's the wind," he said, frowning. "I reckon."

THE WOODS BEGAN TO OPEN AS THE FOOTPATH DESCENDED to the river. Tony had joined Eggar on point, and now, fifty yards downstream, he could see the hayrick outlines of willows and, beyond them, what looked like a lake. Now the wind picked up, inflating the willows, and from the height of the riverbank, Tony saw a spark of firelight. As the wind died, the spark winked out.

Tony stopped and held up his hand, and the other men stumbled to a stop behind him. Eyes on the fire, which flickered wildly through the willows now, he drew his pistol. Watching him, the others followed suit.

Tony smiled. "Oh, yeh," he said, more to himself than his men. "*Now* we got the little punks."

With a wave of the snubnose, he motioned the men forward.

AT THE CAMPFIRE, THE BOYS WERE SITTING UP. They stared up the river with frowns of puzzlement. Mitch glanced at his brother across the fire.

"Maybe it's rain," he said. "You reckon?"

Lee looked through the willows at the sky. Even with the moon out, the brightest stars were still visible. He shook his head. Standing, he put on his shoes and walked the few steps down to the river. Mitch slipped on his shoes and followed.

Both boys stood on the sand beach, staring upriver, where the peculiar thunder continued to grow. It sounded like wind, but somehow with a shuddering, underneath bass. They stared into the black cavern beyond the cattails where the river came out of the trees. In the moonlight, the fog was thick as woodsmoke, cottony on both shores and streaked above the river where the current pulled it along.

GUNS DRAWN, THE MEN HAD REACHED the backside of the island. Now, as the path dipped down and left the woods, Tony saw the boys standing at the river's edge and sighed with relief. Out of the trees, his demons seemed to desert him. Smiling, he wiped his face and with hand signals directed half the column past him, down the path to cut off the boys' escape. But before they could move, they too stopped and listened to the growing thunder behind them. Frowning, they turned and looked upriver.

"What the hell...?" Tony said. It sounded a little like an airstrike, the Phantoms carrier-based, still out over the Gulf.

Eggar grabbed Tony's sleeve. "Hey, what time is it?"

"Whatsa matter, Egg?" Tony snickered. "Gotta hot date? Hey, fellas, Eggar's in love."

"What time is it, dammit!"

Tony was impressed with Eggar's fear. He turned his back to the campfire and checked his watch with the flashlight.

"Twelve," he whispered. "Ten after. How come? What the hell's eating you?"

Slowly, Eggar turned and looked upriver. When Tony put the light on him, he saw the fear in Eggar's eyes.

22

THE BOYS WERE ON THEIR FEET, LOOKING UPRIVER, when the wall of water avalanched out of the trees, the frothing crest glittering in the moonlight. The flumewater thundered into the oxbows, flattening willows in its path. The cattails shivered and were inundated, bulldozed by the leading edge of timber. Out of the gorge, it had lost half its depth, but still towered over them like a collapsing dam, tumbling its tonnage of sawlogs and riverbank debris.

"Oh God!" Lee screamed. "They opened the flume-line!" Lee ran to a willow and began to climb. "Climb, Mitchell! Hurry! Don't look at it! *Climb!*"

Mitch ran to the adjacent tree and began to climb.

UPRIVER, THE FLUMEWATER ENGULFED THE MEN. Several were swept off the narrow path into the churning river. Somersaulting, they went under, screaming, into the grinding, cracking, tumbling logs, some still clutching their rifles and shotguns.

THE BROTHERS CLIMBED LIKE HERETICS at the burning stake. As the water hit the willows, they bent over steeply, and the water level began to rise faster than the boys could climb. Now it was below their tennis shoes; now it submerged their feet; now it was up to their knees; now their waists, as overall, there was the jetport roar of white water. The boys had to scream to be heard.

"Lee! Lee, I'm going under! I'm going under!"

"No, you ain't! Keep climbing, Mitchell! Don't look at it! Don't look! Jist climb! *Climb!*"

Finally, arm-weary, the boys could go no higher. They hung to the bowing trees, exhausted. Yet still the water rose.

UPSTREAM, THE MEN HAD ALSO TAKEN REFUGE in the trees, but they lacked the agility of the boys. Now Martino, big and paunchy, got caught by the water halfway up a steeply bending sapling. With a scream, he was torn from the branches and sucked into the white water. He went under, screaming, terror on his big-eyed face. Thus inspired, the other men climbed higher, faster.

THE BROTHERS HUNG TO THEIR SWAYING TREES, exhausted, but as the water neared their heads, they began to climb again. They were near the tops of the trees, as high as they could go without riding them down, and already the water had reached their feet.

"Lee, it's still coming up!"

"Don't look at it!"

"I cain't hold on much longer!"

"Yeh, you can! Yeh, you *can,* Mitchell!"

It was then that Lee looked toward the riverbank and saw the oak tree. Flooding had undercut its root-system so that it projected out across the river at a nearly horizontal angle, forming a bridge between the island and shore.

Carefully, Lee inched his way higher until he was at the very top of the willow. Leaning back and forth, he set the tree rocking, bending on a line with Mitchell's tree. (Mitch watched him with wide eyes and an open mouth.)

Now, as the tree straightened, Lee jumped, and the willow catapulted him across the water into the top of Mitch's tree. There, the combined weight of the boys was too much for the willow, and they began to ride it down, sinking toward the roaring white water.

Mitch screamed, eyes huge in his ashen face. "We sinking, Lee! We going under!"

"No, we ain't! Hang on, Mitch! Hang on!"

And they rode the tree down until they could reach the top of the adjacent tree. Lee grabbed the topmost limb, pulled the tree over and they clambered into it—but that tree too began to sink toward the river—and toward the adjacent tree—which they gripped, scrambling into the top—and it too began to sink toward the next tree—and the next—and the next. And in this fashion, the brothers walked through the treetops like a pair of spider monkeys, getting closer and closer to the riverbank and the uprooted tree.

Finally, they reached the willow overlooking the undercut oak, and rocking the willow, they catapulted themselves down onto its branches—but the tree wouldn't support their combined weight! Undermined by flooding, it began to sink, settling to the surface of the icy white water, bending steeply downstream. The boys were swept into the rapids, the bibs of their overalls ballooning with water, impossibly heavy. At the last second, they caught onto limbs by their very fingertips. Slowly, hand over hand, they managed to pull themselves back to the trunk—where, limb by limb, they inched their way along the tree toward the riverbank.

They were nearly to the bank when Mitchell lost his grip and was swept into the current. Lee lunged and caught him by a suspender just before the river could sweep him out of reach. Straining, he pulled Mitch back to the inundated tree, where again, they began their hand over hand crawl up the trunk toward the bank.

Finally, sobbing for breath, Lee pulled himself out of the water and onto the bank—and reaching back, he hauled his brother onto the high ground beside him. There, they collapsed side by side, exhausted, chests heaving. Mitchell's whole body shook with weary sobs.

The boys lay on the riverbank, gasping for breath, and looked back at the island. What had been a stagnant backwater was now a roaring white water. What had been their campsite was now under ten feet of boiling rapids. The island's trees were submerged nearly to their tops, and under the moon, the current frothed whitely as it surged around them. The brothers shivered as they watched. Lee gulped and started to speak—when the rapids swept a man by, close enough almost to reach out and touch. He screamed to them for help, eyes wild with fear, arms pinwheeling madly.

He was almost past when he grabbed an exposed root and began to pull himself toward the bank. As the boys watched, wide-eyed, transfixed, inch by inch, he pulled his way toward them, tendons standing out in his neck. He had nearly made the bank when the current tore the root loose, and he was swept violently past, screaming, spinning. Downriver, they saw his waving arms disappear under the boiling white water, silencing his screams.

The brothers recoiled. They crouched behind a spruce on the riverbank, shivering with cold and fright. Staring up the riverbank footpath. Into the dark woods behind them.

"Lee, you reckon they all drownded?" Mitch screamed to be heard.

"Nah."

"Me neither."

Lee stood then and looked up the dark footpath. "They right around here somewheres. We gotta keep moving."

Mitch nodded dumbly, crying, and with Lee in the lead, they started off down the dark, riverbank trail.

23

DAWN FOUND THE BOYS ASLEEP ON AN OXBOW, embracing like newlyweds. They slept spoonstyle, and Mitch had his brother's back in a fierce embrace. Birds were singing in the streamside trees; an orange sun crested the mountaintop and turned the river to gold. With the surface unbroken, it looked like a narrow lake. Across the river, the marsh stretched to the very foot of the mountain, and fog lay on the cattails in a vaporous blanket. Now, sunstruck, the mist began to rise in wisps like genies unbottling, revealing the sheer, granite monolith of The Wall, rising out of the fog beyond. Of a color, the cliff-face was nearly invisible.

With a yell, Lee sat up and looked fearfully around. The boys had fallen asleep on the last of the oxbow islands, and downstream, the view was unobstructed. A quarter-mile away, Lee saw the river whiten as it turned the curve at the end of the marsh, turning back toward the white water at the base of The Wall. Upstream, his view was blocked by the willows that overhung the river in a cumulous hedge.

Suddenly, Lee stiffened. Something was moving in the willows on a line with the boys' position. Crouching, he watched intently, a rock in each hand, as the canopy jerked and trembled. When the movement reached the last willow, Lee's right hand drew back. Now the tapestry parted, revealing the white-spotted, cud-chewing head of a fawn. Lee released an audible sigh, as the little deer bounded away upstream, flag waving.

"Mitchell!" Lee roused his brother roughly by the shoulder. "Wake up! Wake up!"

Mitch sat up groggily. He hunched over, hugging his knees, teeth chattering. His breath was visible in the chill air.

Both boys shivered miserably. They looked drawn and tired from the night's events. Looking at the river, they saw the water level was back to normal. Mitch shuddered as he regarded it.

"I'm so cold, Lee! I'm *freezing!*"

Mitch started to cry, and silent tears quickly gave way to sobbing.

Cursing, Lee gave him a hard shot to the shoulder. When the crying continued, he took Mitch by the suspenders and shook him violently.

"Shut up! Shut up!"

Mitch sobbed on and on. "I'm so hungry! I'm *starving* to death!"

Lee slapped him again and again. He gripped the suspenders and gave Mitch another good shake.

"Shut up, I said! Crying ain't gone help you none this time, Mitchell, so jist shut up about it. *Shut up!*"

Slowly, Mitchell's sobbing subsided. He inhaled deeply, sniffling, and wiped his eyes with the grubby back of his hand. Tears streaked his dirty face, and his cheeks were red from the force of Lee's blows.

Looking at his brother, Lee relented, releasing him.

"I'll build a fire," he said. "Maybe we can catch us another trout." He pointed downriver to a bank of driftwood. "Go and check out that driftwood yonder. See if you can find us another hook 'n' line."

Mitch stood up. "Okay."

"And hold it down."

"You reckon they still after us?"

"Yeh."

Mitch sniffled. "Me too."

"Then—get going!"

Lee knelt and began to unlace his remaining shoe.

AS HE LIMPED ALONG THE RIVERBANK FOOTPATH, Tony uncapped the silver flask and drank deeply from it. He wiped his mouth with the palm of his hand.

"Some frigging guide you turned out to be," he told Eggar's overalled back. He capped the flask one-handed and put it away. "I coulda got us all drownded."

"I told you this here river wunt no place to be attar dark." Eggar spat. House-painting was looking better all the time. "You wunt listen."

"Hell, my mama coulda told me that—and she ain't on the

94

payroll."

"Yeh, well, she needs to be. Maybe you'd listen to her."

"Never happen."

Upriver, the surviving men, possibly a dozen of the original fifteen, followed Tony and Eggar along the trail. Their faces and clothes were dirt-streaked, and a couple had lost one or both shoes and walked sock-footed. The men in suits had discarded their coats and ties, but most still had their guns. As they trooped down the trail, their stubbled faces were grim, ugly.

"Come on, Tony, man," Roselli said. "Let's go back."

One shoe was missing, and a sleeve had been torn from his blue windbreaker. The alligator logo hung by its tail. His hat lost, he wore a red bandana around his head now, and with two days' growth of beard, he looked like an Italian wino limping toward the Salvation Army. With his pistol, he hacked dispiritedly at the foliage along the trail.

"There ain't no frigging way them kids survived all that water."

"We did, didn't we?"

"Sort of."

"We ain't going nowheres till we get a body-count. I want them kills confirmed."

Messina groaned. The joy at simply being alive had passed in the night; during the eight hours he'd spent in carnal embrace with the oak tree. His chest, arms and thighs were rubbed raw from the rough bark. Now he remembered Atlanta was playing the Dodgers at two, and he was going to miss it. Plus his wife would be raising holy hell. He had promised her no more nights out with the boys. Divorce court loomed large once again.

"Tony, man, them kids could be ten miles downriver by now. In little pieces."

"Yeh, and they could be headed for a telephone."

"E.T. phone home," Messina said and kicked viciously at a root. He tripped and went giant-striding down the trail.

He was wishing now he'd stayed in Atlanta. His idea of country was like in country club. Like the other men, Messina's heart wasn't in it. Unlike Tony and Eggar, they weren't wanted for murder—at least not until they found the boys. Most of them had kids of their own. Messina had two boys, though the oldest was younger than Mitch. When the time came, he wasn't sure how he would react. Failure, though, would bring heat from Atlanta. When the order came down, you responded—or else.

"Hey, Tony, what say we—"

"Shut up and move it! Bunch of damn girls!"

SNIFFLING, MITCH WANDERED AWAY DOWN THE ISLAND. Near the middle, he came upon a shallow flood pool, full of trapped minnows, and gave futile chase, stumbling and going down face-first. Wet again and shivering, fighting back his tears, he headed for the driftwood.

He was digging in the silt-chinked wall—pulling out the paper woven seamlessly as a bird's nest; now unearthing an outboard motor oil bottle—when, looking beyond it, he saw a quarter-acre of blackberries growing in the sandy soil of the rocky high ground. His face lit up.

"Aw-right!"

With a whoop of delight, Mitch ran to the berry patch. There, he picked with abandon, with both hands. He stuffed them into his mouth until it was purple, until purple juice dripped off his chin. He ignored the thorns that scratched his arms and face.

When he had eaten his fill, he heaped both blue-stained hands and ran back up the island toward Lee.

As he came into sight, he saw Lee kneeling over the fire-drill, the first wisps of blue smoke curling up into the still air. Smiling, Mitch held up his heaped hands and prepared to call out -- when a movement on the riverbank above and beyond Lee caught his eye—the glint of metal in the morning sun—and watching with wide eyes and open mouth, Mitch saw the entire column of men materialize on the footpath.

He dropped the berries and screamed to his brother, pointing. Lee turned, saw Mitch and stood, unsmiling. He waved him impatiently to the fire.

At that moment, gunshots exploded off the rocks at his feet.

The boys hit the ground. Lee raised his head and saw the

men running down the footpath. Eggar was in the lead, his rifle halfway to his shoulder. In his red cap, eyes shining, he looked like a deer hunter approaching a wounded kill.

The brothers broke for the river then, zigging, zagging, using the one or two small willows for cover. Bullets raised sand in spurts at their feet. River rocks exploded in bursts of stinging shrapnel. Sand and rock shards sprinkled the river beyond.

Without breaking stride, they hurdled the fringe of cattails, dove headfirst and swam hard for the far shore. Though the current was minimal, it still managed to sweep them downstream.

The men quickly crossed the island and stood on the beach, firing. Tony dropped into the Weaver stance, his snubnose chest-braced, and fired with both hands. The revolver was a .357, and the big magnum leaped with each report. Water geysered around the boys, and the jacketed bullets glanced off, whining. They ripped through the cattails beyond, and tassels fell heavily as corn.

Redwing blackbirds rose with a squawk, and now an errant bullet brought one down in a cloud of red and black feathers. The gunfire echoed off The Wall beyond, and rolled back like thunder, booming, starting flocks of strident blackbirds all across the marsh.

The boys dove then, and swimming hard underwater, they let the current take them downstream.

24

THE BROTHERS SURFACED ACROSS THE RIVER and scrambled into the cattails. They crouched inside the fringe, submerged in the brown water to their chins, and watched as the men milled about on the far shore. The cattail heads were full and waved deeply at the slightest breath of wind. Pollen filmed the stagnant water, and each motion of the cattails filled the air with a fine yellow dust that hung above them in sunbeams. Mitch sneezed again and again.

Shivering, they watched the men through the screen of sausage-shaped tassels. Mitch rose to better see, and Lee forced him down. They recognized Eggar and the one called Tony, but the other men were strangers. Lee counted twelve of them, all armed, and tasted again the ammonia wash of fear. He looked at his little brother. Mitch was watching him expectantly, shivering so hard he sent out ripples. Lee looked away.

When they saw Tony direct the others to enter the river, the boys started off, breaststroking through the cattails, heads down, slowly parting the thick reeds with water-pruned hands. Fifty feet from the river, Lee stopped and looked back. He groaned at the sight of the mud-trail they were leaving.

THE MEN MADE THE FAR SHORE AND STOOD, dripping, in the fringe of cattails, squinting across the marsh. The thousand acres of cattails waved like October wheat in a Nebraska field, green and gold. The sun was well up now, luminous in the dissipating mist, and rainbows trembled all across the marsh. At the end of the floodplain, vertical as its name, stood the gray, granite fortress of The Wall.

Hands visored to shield his eyes—he had lost sunglasses and cap in the flood—Tony saw the vast dimensions of the marsh and the task ahead of them. Cursing, he removed the flask.

"All right, dammit, spread out. Don't ever'body bunch up here. And hold it down. Piscopo, Buttafuco, over there. Messina,

Milano, take the right. Roselli, don't screw up."

"What, Tony? I ain't done nothing."

"You can say that again."

"Okay, I ain't done—"

"Shut up, I said! This ain't no game!"

The men fanned out and started off. Spread out in a line, rifles and shotguns at port-arms, they looked like pheasant hunters jump-hunting a cornfield.

Now a flock of blackbirds did get up, and Roselli doubled with his pumpgun. As he watched the feathers twirl down, he cackled in insane imitation of the birds.

"Oh, wow, Tony! You see that? A frigging double, man! American frigging Sportsman, man! Far out!"

Tony let go with both barrels. "Roselli, you idiot-moron, what did I just say? *What?* Are you three years old?"

"What, Tony?"

"These little punks get by us, I am personally gonna whack you. *Capisce?*"

"Sure, Tony, sure."

THE BROTHERS KEPT MOVING, KEPT BREASTSTROKING through the reeds. Pollen hung in clouds in the still air, and both boys were sneezing now, bending close to the water with hands over their faces to muffle the noise. Yellowjackets and hornets rose loudly at their passage. Paralleling the river, they angled downstream toward The Wall. With the fog lifted, the gray cliffs stood up beyond the marsh like a fortress beyond a moat.

The boys were halfway down the floodplain when they flushed the blackbirds. At arm's length, the flock thundered up, water streaming, in a confusion of exploding seedpods and driven spray. Mitch shrieked and climbed on his brother's back. Cottony seeds and pollen swirled above them in a sunstruck cloud.

From the middle of the marsh, Tony heard the birds and, whirling, saw them rise across the flat, back in the direction of the river. He watched as the birds strung off up the marsh, settling on banked wings near the river. Quickly, with hand signals, he deployed the men left and right and sent them in the direction of the boys.

Their position given away, Mitch and Lee started off again. Half-swimming, half-walking, they pushed through the heavy reeds. With their heads down, they could see barely a yard in front of them. From time to time, Mitch lost sight of his brother, and rising on tiptoe in the squishy mud, he watched the trembling cattails for direction.

Now Lee stopped and slowly raised his head. The men were coming, fanned out ten feet apart. They were only a hundred feet away now and coming on a line to their left. Quickly, he ducked down and pulled Mitch down beside him. Lee put a finger to his lips. One look at his pinched expression told Mitchell all he needed to know. The boys froze, trembling, and submerged to their noses in the pollen-filmed water, their sneezes blew bubbles.

IT WAS HEAVY GOING FOR THE MEN IN THE REEDS AND MUD. The water was waist-deep, the mud knee-deep, and they splashed clumsily, arms waving, as they tried to keep their balance. In places, the water dropped off into chin-deep gator-holes, the work of beavers and river otters. Several of the men had now experienced these sudden changes of depth, and they inched ahead fearfully, using their shotguns and rifles to sound the depth.

"Hey, yous guys, wait up!"

Fatty Buttafuco, a hundred pounds overweight, was fifty yards across the marsh. Like a vaudeville pratfall artist, he was all windmilling arms and body English as he struggled toward them.

Eggar was at the forefront of the straggling V, and now he stopped and turned, waiting for the others to catch up. He watched their exertions fearfully.

In the night, Eggar had cut a deal with himself; reached a compromise he could live with. While he wouldn't take an active part in the killing of the Rainey boys, neither would he help nor hinder the other men. Now, as he saw what stood between him and the apple-green room in Raleigh, his heart turned over and stuck in his throat. For the first time, he knew what the expression meant. They said the gas smelled like cherry pits. They said you turned blue and messed yourself. His name would be in all the papers. He thought then of his mother. Her heart was already bad. It would kill her as surely as it killed him.

With a groan, Eggar closed his eyes, the sun glistening on his sweaty face.

Now Roselli stuck in the mud, lunged forward, and with a sucking sound both shoes came off. Cursing, he went down on his knees, feeling up to his sunburned neck in the paddy-water. Finally, he found them.

"Frigging mud!" He eyed his ruined wingtip miserably. "Suck the chrome offa frigging trailer hitch! Hey, Tony, man, wait up!"

Now Buttafuco, waded up, pushing a muddy wake ahead of him.

"Hey, Tony. Ain't this mud a bitch."

Tony gave him a withering look and turned away.

Buttafuco took a step, lost his footing and, arms pinwheeling, eyes wide, went down backwards. His pratfall raised a titanic splash that started another shrill flight of blackbirds.

The other men rocked with laughter—until Tony silenced them with a look.

Buttafuco wallowed to his feet and captured his Braves cap. His wet clothes clung to him like polyester skin, revealing tubes of buttery blubber that quaked from his chill.

Tony watched him with disgust. Now, from the corner of his eye, he saw that Eggar was hanging back.

THE BOYS PUSHED AHEAD. THE CATTAILS GREW so thickly that from time to time, Lee lost sight of Mitch and had to wait for him to catch up. Moving ahead again, parting the cattails, they came face to face with a huge water moccasin. As the snake drew back to strike, the cottony mouth wide, the brothers screamed and leaped completely out of the water. The big snake struck and missed.

Seconds later, gunshots rang out, and bullets geysered in the muddy water around them. Glancing off the water with a whine, the rounds tore through the reeds. Cattail heads exploded, and cottony seed pods and pollen filled the air in swirling sunbeams. Mitch sneezed until his nose bled.

The men floundered wildly toward the boys. Now Pompetti lost his footing and fell sidelong like a breaching whale. The cattails rocked in the wave he sent out—but this time, the others hardly gave him a backward glance.

At the sound, Lee raised his head and saw the men coming. This time, they were no more than fifty away. With his pocketknife, he cut two reeds and gave one to Mitch. With the men quickly closing, the boys submerged in the water and breathed through the hollow stalks.

Moments later, the men passed so closely, the boys could have reached out and touched them. Underwater, they saw their legs go by, pants clinging from the suction.

Topside, Eggar saw the trembling reeds with the fresh knife cuts. As he regarded the reeds, his sunburned face held a measure of fear; a measure of admiration. Now he spat, his quid making rainbows in the roiled water, and waded on by.

AFTER WHAT SEEMED HOURS, LEE SURFACED. He turned slowly, periscoping, just his eyes above swaying cattails. The men had passed them by fifty yards and were still moving away. Lee pulled Mitch to the surface, and he came up coughing. Lee covered his mouth with a water-pruned hand.

Mitch looked fearfully around. "Where…?"

With his chin, Lee indicated the line of caps above the cattail heads. On tiptoes, Mitchell saw them and smiled.

Across the floodplain, Tony came to a stop and raised his hand. The other men splashed to a halt behind him. Slowly, he scanned the flat. Somehow, the boys had given them the slip.

"Dammit! The little punks!"

CIRCLING WIDE, PUSHING QUICKLY THROUGH THE REEDS, the boys approached the end of the marsh. When Lee stopped again, shivering, teeth chattering, they could hear the roar of white water. "Listen!"

"What, Lee?"

"It's The Wall! Come on!"

The boys made for it, steering by and toward the sound of white water. They ran now, and Lee's skin crawled at the prospect of another water moccasin.

They were nearly to the river when the men saw them far across the waving cattails. Roselli threw up his shotgun—but Tony pushed the barrel down.

"Save it. They outta range. Come on."

Running in the cattails with a high leg-kick, sunstruck pollen and swarming bees rising in a cloud behind them, the brothers made the edge of the marsh. They stood, chests heaving, and looked up at The Wall. The fog hung at the level of low clouds now, and the gray cliff-face disappeared smokily into it. To Mitch, it looked like an evil castle in a fairy tale.

With Lee in the lead, the boys splashed down the narrow beach. Broken lose from the cliff, scree lay strewn along the shoreline. Lee had lost both shoes—without laces, the mud had quickly sucked them off—and he ran gingerly on the sharp rock. Mitchell still wore one high-top, clubfoot-looking with its boll of mud, and he humped along like Grandpappy Amos.

Now the beach became a boulder field as it neared the flank of the cliff. When boulders blocked their downstream passage, the boys waded into the river, shallow and glass-green where it ran over a sluiceway of algaed bedrock. Mud swirled from their overalls, discoloring the water. Already, the current had quickened. Here and there, the water broke white as it surged around boulders.

Mitch tensed as he felt his traction begin to leak; the current begin to skate him along the orange riverbed. Downstream, he saw the glassy headrace bend into a small waterfall. Beyond was the leaping white water of the gorge, wall to wall, white as a glacier in the morning sun. Mitch gulped as he regarded it.

"You ready?"

"I guess so, Lee."

"Stay close to shore, Mitchell."

And pushing off, the brothers body-surfed the current toward the base of The Wall.

MOMENTS LATER, THE MEN PUSHED THROUGH THE CATTAILS and hustled down the beach, knapsacks banging. They were strung out now. It was fifty yards between pace-setting Eggar and Buttafuco, the gasping fatso at the end of the stumbling defile. A heavy smoker, Buttafuco's carbonized air passages whistled flutelike, and his face, visible in patches through the mud, was scarlet. His love-handles shivered as he pounded down the rocky shoreline.

"Hey, yous guys, wait up!"

A hundred yards downriver, the boys beached themselves above the waterfall and splashed ashore. Here, the rocky beach ended in monolithic granite, the boulder field a hem of tumbled rubble. Lee looked at the river roaring into the gorge, sheer-walled as a canal lock. Then, gulping, he looked up and saw the narrow handholds and footholds that climbed the vertical cliff-face into the clouds.

25

BELOW THE OXBOW ISLANDS, GREEN RIVER didn't rest for long; just a few hundred yards to catch its breath. Just beyond the last oxbow, the mountain steepened, and the river ran to catch up. Bending green into riffles. Breaking white on scree fallen from above. Teetering over a first small cataract as it accelerated into the wild white water of The Wall. From here, facing cliffs stretched two miles downriver, hewn foursquare as the walls of a corridor, as though a giant stonemason had hacked them from the flanking, rock-ribbed mountainsides.

Nowhere now was the river green. It frothed white as winter surf with a roar that loosened boulders, fallen from above, new-cracked and white, strewn along the shoreline shallows like blocks of ice. Saplings grew horizontal from the rockface, tenuously gripping the thin soil of the mossy crevices. Below them, the guano of roosting hawks and eagles streaked the granite.

Once in, the boys would be committed. The only way out lay two miles downriver where the gorge ended in a fearsome chute of wild white water known as The Narrows. It was, to all intents, a box canyon. The game trail in which Lee had placed his faith did not exist.

THE BOYS CLIMBED FOR THEIR LIVES, but as they climbed the sheer rockface, they came back into view of their pursuers. Bullets ricocheted off the granite in long leaden streaks. Spent buckshot showed in silver splatters. All around them, summer-sere lichen exploded in puffs of green dust.

Below, Tony fired his snubnose with both hands, chest-braced. Raising his rifle, Eggar took careful aim, and the V of his sights aligned the little gold dot squarely on Lee's back, on the crisscross of his brass-buckled suspenders. But as he prepared to squeeze off, he adjusted his aim, and the bullet went wide, *cracking* off the cliff, throwing splinters of rock beside Lee's head.

The near miss stung Lee's face. Quickly, he scrambled up and rolled onto a narrow ledge. He reached down and with one hand heaved Mitchell up beside him.

Out of sight now, they lay against the cliff-face, breathing hard. Lee touched his cheek and saw the blood. Furtively, he wiped it away and looked at Mitchell. His little brother had pressed himself to the cliff, his face to the wall. His little back heaved as he sobbed for breath. For a moment, Lee thought he was crying.

DOWN BELOW, THE MEN REACHED THE BOULDER FIELD, and wading in, they tried to follow Eggar down the river. But their leather soles were no good on the algaed riverbed, and loaded down, they foundered in the current, arms windmilling.

Again, it was Pompetti who lost his footing and fell. His compatriots lunged for him, but weren't fast enough. He struggled wildly as the current grabbed him and swept him away, sitting up, bobsledding down the sluiceway.

Now he went over the waterfall, and his waving arms disappeared in the white water, his screams abruptly ceased. Throughout it all, he had kept on his Braves cap, and it rushed downstream, a vivid dot of red and blue, spinning, leaping, reappearing.

The other men stood, teetering in the current, and watched the cap race into the gorge. They were sobered, subdued by the what had happened; by the power of the river.

"Jesus Louise! You see that?"

"Are we having fun yet?"

"Excuse me—but this sucks!"

Tony saw that he was losing them. He waded among them, pushing and shoving, waving his pistol.

"Okay, dammit, move it! Move your candyasses! *Now!*"

HIGH ABOVE, THE BROTHERS WERE MOVING AGAIN. Breathlessly, they climbed, feeling out each handhold, each foothold. They had climbed through the clouds, and now, out on the dazzling ledges, sunning lizards skittered away at their approach.

Finally, they rolled onto a ledge three-hundred feet above the river. Lee sat up, gasping, and checked out the way ahead. The ledge stretched on, barely a yard wide, the fault-line flat as a sidewalk, the cliff-face sheer above and below. Fifty yards ahead, it curved out of sight around the belly of the cliff. The sun was high in the sky now and reflected brilliantly off the granite. The patches of lichen looked black. Already, the boys were sunburned.

Amplified by the facing cliffs, the river's roar came up from below, softened by distance, hardened by echo. Far below, they could see the action-figure men making shore, an eddy of blue-capped motion.. As they watched, the eddy strung out as the men began to climb. Red-capped Eggar was still in the lead, showing the way. Already, he was outdistancing the others. He climbed one-handed, gripping his squirrel gun, and the octagon barrel flashed like a steel splinter.

Lee sat back against the rockface and looked across the hundred yards at the mirroring cliff. There was an eagles' nest on a crevice there, and the female hovered over it, a squirming trout in her talons. Now she dropped the fish among the eaglets and banked away, screeching, wings flaring, into a glide toward the river. Her primaries and head were snow-white in the brilliant sun.

Lee's eyes followed her flight downriver where, looking up, he sighed. Mitchell's eyes shortly followed, and they gazed together at the Interstate bridge. From this height, the entire bridge was visible; from the concrete foundations in the granite riverbed to the five great horseshoes of the archwork. Four lines of gnat-cars sped across in both directions. Chrome and windshield sparked minutely. A tractor-trailer crept along one shoulder, and the southbound traffic thickened into a single, multicolored strand to pass. The morning had brought them perceptibly nearer. Even so, they stared at the bridge hopelessly.

"You ready?" Lee asked his brother.

Mitch sat up. "I reckon. As I'll ever be."

He rubbed his eyes, and the sweat in them stung like

107

seawater. He sobbed for breath.

"Let's go then. And stay close to the wall."

"We ain't gone make it, Lee."

"Not sitting here, we ain't. Let's go. And try and keep up, Mitchell."

"I'll try, Lee. My legs ain't long as yours."

The brothers stood and started along the ledge, giddy with the height, a hand on the scorching rockface for balance. Mitchell's eyes were glued to the brass buckle on Lee's suspenders. It took a supreme act of will to keep them off the river below.

WITH A CLANG OF KNAPSACKS, THE FIRST of Tony's men rolled onto the ledge and collapsed. They lay along the granite, chests heaving, their shirts soaked through. Roselli sprawled face-down. His crucifix hung through his open shirt, and he squeezed it in a sweaty fist.

"*Basta cosi!*" he moaned. "*Basta cosi!* That's enough!"

With a groan, Messina and Piscopo roused themselves. Sitting up, they lit cigarettes, which only served to intensify their wheezing and coughing.

"Mother of the bleeding ..."

"You got that right!"

Now, knapsacks clanging, two more red-faced men rolled onto the ledge. They were covered with the green dust of the desiccated lichen, and in places, sweat had turned it to rivulets of green dye. Their knees and elbows were green-stained.

"Jesus Christ Almighty!" Giordano wheezed. "Whose good idea was this? Oh—hey, Tony."

"I ain't believing this!" Guiliani said. He was examining his bleeding fingernails. He'd had them done day before yesterday, and the cuticles were ruined.

"Anybody bring any water?"

"Yeh, but I poured mine out. Too heavy."

"That was smart. That was frigging *brilliant.*"

"Where's *yours*—you're so damn smart?"

Tony had his flask out and drank deeply from it. Sweat

streaked his face in dirty rivulets. His air passages were raw from breathing Eggar's dust, and his thighs trembled so badly from the exertion, he could barely stand. Now he leaned against the cliff-face and slid down into sitting position. Capping the flask, he looked down the dazzling ledge and thought of his sunglasses, lost in the flood.

Eggar stood a little apart, watching the group with detachment. Rifle folded into his arms, he bit from his plug and began a ruminative chew. With the thirty-minute rest, he seemed hardly winded by the murderous climb.

"Hey, yous guys, wait up!"

Eggar looked down and smiled as he spotted Buttafuco. Last in line, the fatso was only halfway up and clung to the incandescent cliff-face like a polyester blister. Unbuttoned, his yellow shirt billowed in the breeze. He looked up, his red face bright as the colors of his clothes, and Eggar waved him on. Grinning, he spat and watched his quid streak past Buttafuco, unawares.

Now two more men rolled onto the ledge, gasping. Salt streaked the backs of their blue dress shirts where perspiration had dried in the sun. Their ears and necks were crimson with exertion and sunburn.

"Christ on a crutch!" Milano said. He had lost his hat, and his bald head was already blistered.

Licavoli sobbed for breath. "Jesus - Joseph - and - Mary!"

"Shut up your bitching," Tony told them. "Eggar, lead off."

"Hold it, Tony! Jesus! We just got here."

"Sounds like a personal problem to me. Eggar, move out."

Following Eggar, the men started across the ledge. Now they looked over. Far below, the rivulet-river raced through the gorge, straight and white as a length of gauze, too brilliant to contemplate. To a man, they drew back and flattened themselves against the rockface. Roselli crossed himself so rapidly his hand was a blur.

"No frigging way, man! This is *crazy!*"

"Roselli, what's the problem? Hold it, Eggar. Roselli wants you to carry him."

"I'm going, Tony. Godalmighty! Just lemme catch my

breath!"

"Man, it's a long ways down!"

"You ain't said jack!"

"Move it, dammit!"

Slowly, the men began to inch along the ledge, looking fearfully below. Pressed back against the cliff, they looked like suicides on a midtown window ledge who'd had a change of heart.

Eggar waited up ahead, arms folded, chewing, smiling his orange smile. Now he leaned his rifle against the cliff-face and sat down. He crossed his legs.

Tony looked at Eggar and his rage boiled over.

"Get your candyasses *moving!*" he screamed from the end of the column. "Roselli, ain't gone tell you again! Milano, you oughta be in orthopedic shoes! Move it! Messina, *move!*"

26

THE BOYS HURRIED ALONG THE LEDGE. Shoeless on the sharp rock, Lee was limping deeply, and where the ledge began to climb, he stopped and leaned against the burning cliff-face to examine his feet. They were badly cut and bleeding. The prospect of infection produced a momentary frown, a compression of the lips. He was chilled by the thought that he would have to survive to infect. He had seen the men: The odds were against it.

As he waited for Mitch, he looked down the dwindling ledge. The sun was blinding on the granite; the ledge afloat on waves of heat. For the first time, he noticed his thirst.

Now Mitch hobbled up, red-faced and gasping, and they started off again.

They had gone barely fifty yards when the ledge suddenly widened into a bowl between outcrops. There was a boulder field in the little basin, an area of broken rock fallen from above.

Winded, Lee came to a stop so abruptly Mitch bumped him from behind.

"How come we stopping here for, Lee?" Mitch said. He leaned back against the cliff, breathing hard, and felt the heat of the granite through his teeshirt. Quickly, he stood.

"I gotta idea," Lee told him. "Go on ahead."

HUFFING AND PUFFING, THE MEN STUMBLED along the ledge. It was wider now, and under Tony's lash, they seemed to be coping with their fear of heights. Fifty yards ahead, the way widened and rose toward the summit in a creviced stair-step. There, an outcrop overhung the ledge. The shade beneath it was deep, black, and as he regarded it, Tony contemplated another breather.

"Hey, yous guys!" Buttafuco wailed from far down the ledge. "Wait up!"

On the outcrop, Lee lay in ambush, two angular chunks of

granite at his side. Nervously waiting, he looked at the river far below. The rapids were white as ice in the midday sun. Upstream, the flatwater where they had spent the night was green as the cattails and willows that flanked it.

As Lee looked longingly at the river bottom, his mind hatched plan after plan for descent. Maybe they could double back, once the men were past, and descend the way they'd come up. He quickly discarded that idea. The window for detection was too great. The descent would take an hour, and they would be sitting ducks with the men firing from above. Of course, it would be crazy to try after dark.

He was still watching the river when the men lumbered into view below him. When they were in sight of the boulder field, Mitch stood up.

"There they are!" Lee heard.

Down the ledge, Mitch ducked as gunfire smoked off the rockface. In the crevice where he hid, the ricochets made his ears ring, and he plugged them with his dirty fingers. His lips moved in furious prayer.

"Finally," Lee heard one of the men say.

"All right," the one called Tony said. "Let's get 'em and get the hell outta here. Don't wanna get caught up here after dark. And hey -- no bullet holes. They gone make like hillbilly birds." Tony laughed. "This here trout fishing is dangerous recreation."

With Eggar in the lead, the men took off down the ledge.

Lee flattened as they approached the overhang. When the caps reappeared beyond it, he raised the biggest rock with both hands and heaved it onto the line. A tall man in a green cap two behind Eggar took the rock in the back of the head. His legs buckled and he went to his knees; then flopped heavy-bodied, headlong from the ledge.

From his vantage, Lee could see him all the way to the river, rapidly shrinking, as he plummeted backward, screaming, arms and legs windmilling. His shotgun followed, flashing end over end. Near the bottom, it clattered down the cliff-face and discharged, sprinkling the water with buckshot. There was a narrow band of green water at the base of the cliff, and there the man hit with a tiny splash and went under. The shotgun whitened

112

the water in a line beside him.

Eggar fired just as Lee withdrew his head, and the bullet *cracked* off the granite with an explosion of rock. Lying on his back, Lee heaved a second rock blind, and it too found its mark, taking another man full in his upturned face. Nose broken, mouth bleeding, he pitched off the ledge, backstroking with his arms. His scream died like a wind, and shortly, there came a second minute splash. His Panama hat sailed out over the gorge, side-slipping like a Frisbee, and now, caught in an updraft, it pinwheeled downstream, rolling along the cliff-face.

The red-faced men withdrew to a point below the outcrop, breathing hard, perspiring heavily. Tony was white with fury.

"The little punks!"

"Christ Almighty! This ain't happening."

"That's what you think."

"This here be de real worl', Jim."

"Hillbilly birds, eh? Looked more like guinea birds to me."

"Frigging teenagers! Oughta be put in cryo-sleep for seven years."

"Shut up, dammit! Lemme think!"

As he sat beside Tony, Eggar chewed hard to suppress his grin. Cleve Rainey had raised a pair of hellcats. He was as proud of them as if they were his own.

27

Up ahead, Lee rejoined Mitch on the ledge. They too were winded by the climb, but Mitch was ecstatic.

"We done it, Lee!" he gasped. "Oh, wow! Did you see it? *Bull's-eye!*"

Lee smiled, his face flushed and perspiring. "Yeh, God! I jist wisht we had the thirty-thirty." He blinked away the sweat. "Wouldn't need no Interstate bridge then. I coulda got 'em all while they clumb up here."

As Lee looked back in the direction of the men, Mitch saw that a rock fragment had cut his head. The gash above his temple was bleeding in a steady stream.

"Lee, you're bleeding!"

Lee wiped his temple and examined the blood on his trembling hand.

"Ain't nothing but a scratch is all. Eggar's getting old. That's twice he throwed wide."

Down below, the men were moving again. Sandwiched between Tony and Eggar, the stick and the carrot, they were making good time on the widened ledge. Still, they panted and puffed, pissing and moaning, as they followed Eggar's overalled back. Their eyes scanned the cliffside now anytime the ledge approached an overhang, and they kept well back of Eggar, letting him draw the fire. In their fatigue, they stumbled over rocks that clattered down the cliff-face and slipped into silence. Seconds later, the rocks landed with a faint splash far below.

After the third one, Tony looked back and treated them to a malevolent gaze.

"Dammit!" he hissed. "Hold it down! Roselli, why don't you just send up a flare?"

"I can't help it, Tony."

"You better *start* helping it. You hear me?"

"Sure, Tony, sure."

THE BOYS HEARD THE ROCKS TOO AND PICKED UP THEIR PACE. They were nearer the top now, in an area of some vegetation. Here, the runoff had carried soil and seeds down from above, and the crevices supported oaks and maples and sourwoods, stunted by the thin soil to bonsai-size shrubbery. In places, ropey vines, some as thick as grape vines, followed gravity down the cliffside.

Lee's limping had worsened, and he had bound up his temple with a strip of undershirt. Already, it was sodden with blood. Even so, they were making good time, extending their lead when—

"*No!*"

—the ledge came to an dead end; dropped off in space as abruptly as the door of an airborne jet. The brothers stopped at the last minute, right on the edge, three-hundred feet above the river.

Quickly, Lee pulled Mitchell back against the cliff, breathless at their close call. They looked fearfully up the vertical rockface above them.

"Lee? Lee, what we gone do?"

Lee's terrified expression told Mitchell he hadn't a clue.

Now a rock clattered down the cliffside behind them. Lee trembled as he picked up a chuck of granite and put his back against the wall. Eyes on his brother, Mitch did the same.

Again, they heard a dislodged rock and closer now, labored breathing. Lee licked his lips and wiped the sweat from his eyes. Mitch was crying silently.

Suddenly, Lee looked back across the cliff and smiled.

"What, Lee?"

"Look!"

Mitch turned and saw the vine that grew down the cliffside there, just at the edge of the drop-off.

Quickly, Lee dropped the rock and took out his Swiss Army knife. With the sawblade, he worked furiously at the vine. It took him only a minute to cut through, but it was the longest minute of his life.

Now Lee gripped the vine with both hands and leaned back against it, testing it for strength, and as he did, the tendrils *ripped* loose from the rockface, twigs raining. Lee climbed a few steps up the cliff, putting all his weight on it, bouncing. He smiled when he felt no give. The vine was solid as a tire swing.

Lee limped as he backed down the ledge to get a running-go. He smiled at Mitch, took a deep breath, and legs churning, rappelled across the cliff to the ledge beyond. Safely on the other side, he whooped with relief. Quickly, he swung the vine back to his brother.

"Ain't nothing to her, Mitch! Jist like a grapevine swing! Like at the Swimming Tree! You can do it! "

Mitchell didn't look so sure. Holding the vine, he looked down, and saw beyond his bare foot and holey sneaker, the crawling white-water river. Of a color with the cliffside, it was like looking into a great crevasse. Mitchell's head swam, his legs swayed, and he closed his eyes.

"Don't look down, Mitchell! Come on, you can do it! Get a running-go!"

Again, they heard the men coming; heard them stumbling, cursing, gasping for breath. They were much closer now. Again, Mitch looked at the rivulet far below. In the sun, the river seemed frozen between ice-cliffs. He looked up at Lee with tears in his eyes, as again, they heard the men. They seemed to be just around the curve.

Now Mitchell backed down the ledge to give himself some running room. Eyes shut tight, he ran down the ledge and sailed out over the void—but his momentum wasn't enough to carry him across! Lee lunged for him but missed, and Mitch swung back into the middle of the wall, feet scrabbling for a purchase.

Finally, he found a toe-hold in a crevice, and as he jammed his toes deeper, wasps boiled out of the rockface. Hanging helplessly, Mitch cried out as the wasps stung him again and again.

"Dammit, Mitchell, swing over! Use your legs!"

Mitch began to swing, running back and forth across the vertical rockface. He gripped the vine with his right hand as he swatted away the wasps with his left.

116

Slowly, the arc of his swing widened … until the last swing brought the vine within reach. Lee hauled him up by the suspenders and pulled him onto the ledge out of sight.

Seconds later, Eggar appeared around an outcrop, whistling.

Sitting beside his brother, back against the rockface, Mitch sobbed as he pulled wasps from his face and arms. His breath came in broken gasps.

Now Lee looked down at the vine still in his hand and saw the little, three-leafed shoots. "Oh, no!"

"What, Lee?"

"Poison ivy."

MOMENTS LATER—AS THE BROTHERS FLATTENED against the cliff, hands over their mouths to muffle their breathing—the men stumbled up to the dead end and looked over. Whirling, they looked above and below, open-mouthed. The boys' Houdini-like disappearing acts were beginning to unnerve them, and it was apparent on a couple of sweaty faces.

"I ain't believing this!"

"Ain't no way!"

"The little punks got wings!"

"Shut up, dammit! They around here somewheres. Gotta be."

But Eggar, his face perspiring and his blue work shirt soaked through, saw the severed vine and smiled.

"They's a higher trail," he said, looking up the sheer cliff-face. "We gotta backtrack a ways."

As his eyes followed Eggar's gaze up the vertical granite, Tony's face for the first time registered some fear, some doubt about the whole enterprise.

28

THE LEDGE CONTINUED BEYOND THE DEAD END, and the brothers hurried along it, leaping boulders, a steadying hand on the cliff-face. Already, Mitchell's face was hugely swollen. He looked like a tiny boxer who had taken a terrific beating. Lee's limp was so deep, he seemed to be stumbling. Blood had seeped under his bandage, and crusted blood streaked his face, showed in the creases of his neck and plugged his right earhole. Teeshirt and bandage were starchy-stiff with dried blood. As they ran, all around them was the constant, scuttling movement of the green-striped lizards.

Up ahead, where two boulders flanked the widened ledge, Lee paused, breathing hard, and waited for Mitchell to catch up. Even hung out on the cliffside, there wasn't a breath of wind. The ledge was like an oven; the granite incandescent beneath a dome of cloudless blue.

Lee stared down the cliff foursquare as a concrete wall. With the fissures and shrubs and patches of lichen, it might have been the facade of some great ruin. Under the palpable weight of the sun, the whole wall seemed to shimmer, and for a moment, he felt faint, giddy; the granite underfoot seemed to lose its very solidity. He ran his tongue over his dust-coated lips. Never before had he been so thirsty, and the tantalizing view of the river below—with the constant sound of white water—was torture. He tried to summon some saliva to wet his lips, but his swollen tongue produced only gritty cotton.

Now Mitch staggered up and sank to his knees—a hopeless, dead look in his eyes; his lower lip Ubangi-big in his dust-gray face—and together again, the brothers started off. Scared though he was, Lee forced himself to slow. It was clear that Mitchell was on his last legs.

Ahead, Lee saw that the way was blocked by a rock formation, a monolith that rose by steps to a higher ledge. Reaching it at a run, Lee pulled himself up—and came face to face with the wedge-shaped head of a huge timber rattlesnake!

Startled, the snake's rattles buzzed furiously, and fangs bared, its lozenge head drew back to strike. Lee screamed and fell backward, as the snake struck and missed. It recoiled, white belly flashing, and struck again. Now, sidewinding, it angled away, and back against the rockface, it oozed into a half-coil. Its rattles continued to chirp as it settled itself irritably.

Below, Lee sat against the ledge, head back, mouth open, beads of sweat standing out on his forehead. The fall had re-opened the wound, and blood trickled down his face and neck, crimsoning the dried blood. He held a hand to his pounding heart.

Mitch regarded his brother with wide eyes. "What, Lee?"

"Snake," Lee managed.

Now, from down the ledge, a rock clattered away with echo clarity. Like the curse that followed, it sounded only feet away, though it was hard to tell in the echoing acoustics of the cliff.

Quickly, Lee stood and started off. Behind him, Mitch hesitated.

"Lee," he said, his eyes for the first time showing some animation, "I'm scared of snakes."

"Who ain't. Come on. Ain't no other way."

"I cain't, Lee! Don't make me!"

Lee jerked his brother to his feet. A swift soccer kick to his dusty seat sent him toward the stairs.

Climbing up, the boys started along the ledge only to find it covered with snakes. There were dozens of them—massive, black-banded timber rattlers and russet-and-gold copperheads— sunning on the hot rocks. The snakes coiled about each other tightly, white underbellies flashing. The whole cliff seemed alive with them; the very granite seemed to move, to ooze.

The boys were completely surrounded—and at the first footfall, the rattlers went into coils, rattles buzzing, forked tongues flicking out, wedge-shaped heads drawing back to strike. One by one, the snakes took up the alarm until the sound of rattles was all around them. Now a rattlesnake crawled onto the ledge behind them, and their exit was blocked. They could only go forward.

At the sight of the snakes, Mitch froze and began to sob. Lee grabbed him by the suspenders and slapped him again and again.

"Shut up! Shut up, I said! *Shut up!*"

Mitch covered his head with his arms. "Okay, okay, don't hit me, Lee! Please don't hit me no more!"

Lee released him. "Now watch! Step where I step. And move slow. Ain't gone hurt you none, Mitchell. Scairder of you than you are of them."

Slowly, the boys tiptoed through the snakes, sweating bullets, their sunburned faces pinched with fear. Mitch sobbed brokenly, the tears joining the rivulets of sweat in his dirt-streaked face. He held his brother by the shirttail and followed closely, eyes shut tight.

Finally, the boys made it across the ledge and into the shade of the overhang. There were no snakes on the cold stone. There, they collapsed with sighs of relief. Behind them, the snakes settled like the surface of a lake; the sound of rattles died like a wind in dry grass.

Looking back at the snakes, Lee smiled.

"What, Lee?"

"I gotta idea."

"Oh, no!"

WITH A LENGTH OF WEATHERED WOOD, LEE PINNED a rattlesnake and lifted it by the neck. Though he held the snake head-high, the rattles touched the ground. Now he tried to give it to Mitch—who started back with a shriek.

"No, Lee, don't make me! Please, Lee!"

"Take it, I said! Crybaby! Mama's boy!"

Mitch tentatively extended his hands, and Lee turned the snake and showed him, "See? Grab it behind the head. Cain't bite you then. How's it gone bite you, Mitchell? *Chicken!*"

"Okay, Lee, I will."

But at the first touch of the scaly skin, Mitchell's nerve failed him, and he jerked his hands back with an hysterical shriek.

"I cain't, Lee! Please don't make me!"

"You got to, dammit! Now take it!"

"No, Lee, I cain't!"

A rock clattered down the cliff-face, silenced as it slipped into space.

"They coming, Mitchell, and they a whole lot worser'n snakes. *Take it!*"

Again, Lee thrust the snake at Mitch—and this time, he took it, eyes shut tight, gripping the snake so tightly, its beady, vertical-pupilled eyes bugged out. Mitch held it at arm's length and averted his sweating face. When the big rattler coiled around his arm, rattles buzzing against his chest, he lost control of his bladder.

With the stick, Lee pinned another rattler, and holding it tightly, he and Mitch ducked under the overhang and climbed the cliffside. The rattles on both snakes moved in a blur.

EGGAR HAD LED THE MEN AROUND THE DEAD END, and back on the ledge now, they hustled along it, making up for lost time. At the end of the line, gun out, Tony herded the men before him. Eggar was a cruel pacemaker, strolling along the narrow ledge as though it were a city sidewalk. By now, even Tony eyed his overalled back with hatred. More than once, he had the fantasy of emptying his magnum into the sweat-darkened patch on the blue shirt. Lost in his murderous thoughts, Tony stumbled ahead, and the others hurried to stay out of his way.

Again, the brothers had doubled back and taken up positions overlooking the ledge. Mitch had a good grip on his snake and was much more composed. There was even a hint of excitement on his swollen face; the suggestion of a smile. Again, as they lay in wait, they looked downriver at the tantalizing prospect of the Interstate bridge. The concrete spires glittered in the sun. The four lines of ant-cars had grown and acquired individual color. Lee's look of intense longing was almost sexual. Mitch might have been contemplating a cheeseburger all the way.

Now they heard a rock clatter off the cliff and slip into silence. Now someone fell, cursing, and they heard the one called Tony hissing for him to be quiet.

Lee leaned close. "Get ready, Mitch. Won't get no second

chance."

Seconds later, the men stumbled through. When they were directly under the boys, Lee looked at Mitchell and whispered—

"*Now!*"

—and leaning out, the boys dropped the writhing snakes, white bellies flashing, squarely on the shoulders of two of the men.

Screaming, they slapped crazily at the rattlers, and both were bitten in the face and neck. In their terror, they knocked another man off the ledge, and he slipped into space, screaming. Still slapping at the snakes, men and snakes pitched into the gorge.

Panicked, the others scrambled up the stairway on hands and knees and ran into the field of sunning snakes. On all sides, the rattlers went into coils, rattles buzzing.

The boys stood and began to pelt the snakes with rocks, and they began to strike in every direction. Three more men were bitten, and shrieking, kicking, they backed to the brink, snakes hanging from their pants legs, and pitched into the gorge.

The brothers ran for it then, scrambling through the boulders, climbing ever higher up the cliff. Now Tony got free, and gunfire ricocheted, smoking, off the granite on either side of the whooping boys.

29

DOWN BELOW, THE MEN SAT AGAINST THE WALL, licking their wounds, whimpering like punished children. Several had been bitten, including Eggar who was sterilizing his pocketknife with a butane lighter. Leaning against the cliff-face, gritting his tobacco-stained teeth, he cut his swollen forearm with two quick slashes and yelled in pain. Only with effort did he manage to remain conscious. His face was ashen from pain and the powerful venom.

Now he fashioned a tourniquet from his red bandana and used the pocketknife to cinch it down. With the tourniquet in place, he began to suck venom from his arm and spit it on the rock.

The other snakebites watched him listlessly. They were beyond caring.

The snakes had taken the wind out of even Tony. Pale and shaken, he sat against the rockface, breathing deeply, trying to compose himself. Though unbitten, he was soaked with sweat.

There had been a snake in Vietnam called the Bamboo Two-Step—a reference to its habitat and fast-acting venom. Tony had once seen a point-man—a cherry named MacDonald—bitten on the hand when he'd opened a booby-trapped rice cache. The soldier had made it five steps, but was blind beyond two. He died, screaming, before the medic could even key the handset to call in a dust-off.

Then, one night, as Tony lay pinned to the ground in an ambush, one had crawled across his neck, down his shirt and out his pants leg. Only by chance that night had he left his fatigues unbloused. He had dreamed about it for years afterward, waking with the terrible night-sweats. He had thought snakes—like the sound of incoming mortar rounds—were behind him forever.

With a yell, he came to his feet. "All right, dammit, get up! *Up!*"

"I don't know if I can walk, Tony," Roselli said.

A copperhead had bitten him on the ankle, and now he raised

his pants leg and showed Tony his swollen foot. The area around the fang marks was livid and oozed a yellow-tinged blood. Roselli stared at it with objective distaste, as though the foot were attached to someone else.

"You can walk. Get up!"

"Come on, Tony, man. Lighten up. I was just snakebit."

Tony walked up to him and pressed the revolver to his neck.

"On your frigging feet, I said." He *cocked* the hammer. "*Now!*"

Roselli stood, swaying, a hand on the cliff-face for support. He had his wingtip in one hand, his pistol in the other.

"Okay, Tony, okay." Sweat poured down his stubbly, sunburned face. The red bandana was soaked through. "Take it easy, take it easy."

LEE WAS IN THE LEAD AS THE BROTHERS LIMPED along the ledge. The snake trick had lifted their spirits and picked up their pace. Mitch was smiling, though, with his parched and swollen lips, it was hard to tell. In the distance, they saw the Interstate bridge and took heart. The day's progress had brought it perceptibly nearer; enlarged its erector-set trusswork; enlarged the bumper-to-bumper cars whose windshields glinted in the declining sun.

After the heat of day, a thunderstorm was building, billowing over the river; stacking thunderheads as columnar as a tornado. As Mitch looked down the gorge toward the bridge, he noticed for the first time the mushrooming clouds. Faintly, there came the roofing-tin rumble of thunder.

WITH EGGAR BITTEN, TONY HAD TAKEN POINT. The men were strung out now with the bitten members and wheezing fatsoes straggling far behind. For the first time, Eggar faltered, stumbling, gasping for breath. Soaked through with sweat, his faded workshirt looked freshly dyed.

"Hey, yous guys," Buttafuco wailed. "Wait up!"

Now Tony glimpsed the boys above them and snapped off a

wild shot, just as they disappeared behind the cliff. It went wide, throwing rock-dust. The gunshot and ricochet echoed down the gorge, mingling with the growing thunder.

Ahead, the ledge had narrowed to barely a crevice in the cliff-face, and the boys moved along it with a slow sidewise step-and-slide. Above and below, the lizards rustled away at their approach. Lee pushed Mitch ahead to shield him with his body. Mitchell's face was so swollen, his eyes were closed, and Lee hobbled, dragging his cut feet. The bleeding in his temple had stopped, but his face, neck and shirt were covered with crusted blood. With no real food for two days, they were moving on adrenaline, and it showed.

Tony ran, holding the point, fifty yards back of the boys. Only a bellying in the cliff-face kept them out of sight. Ashen-faced, Eggar stumbled along near the end of the column, holding his tourniquet in place. Below the blood-soaked bandana, his forearm had swollen to twice its size, and the fingers of his hand were like sausages. Already, the area around the snakebite was blackening. Now Eggar took his quid of tobacco and plastered it on the bite, a country poultice to draw out the poison.

Tony was nearly in range when one of the snakebites, Constanza, collapsed on the ledge, his body in convulsions, foaming at the mouth. With his foot, Tony pushed him over the edge and watched coldly as he floated spread-eagle like a skydiver. He hit the river with a belly-flop, and the *crack* of his impact came up the cliff-face clear as a rifle shot.

The other men stared at Tony in disbelief. Furtively, Roselli crossed himself and mumbled in Italian.

THE LEDGE HAD WIDENED, AND OUT ON THE OPEN ROCKFACE, the boys picked up speed. It was wide enough now for them to move abreast, and Lee ran, pulling Mitch by the hand. As the way rose, exposing them to gunfire, he looked fearfully back, but the men were nowhere in sight. Lee slowed, breathing hard.

Overhead, the storm was thickening; the thunder was closer and louder. Lee looked up as the first drops began to pelt down, steaming on the hot granite. Now, as the first crackling filament of lightning arced through the soot-black thunderheads, the storm descended with a roar.

Rainfall whipped the boys in wind-blown sheets. Bolt after bolt of sizzling lightning flashed past them, and cracking thunder echoed, booming, down the gorge. The granite trembled under their bare feet, and loosened by the vibration, rocks floated by from above.

Mitch leaned against the cliff-face and put his head all the way back, drinking in the rain. The brothers giggled insanely, glorying in the sudden abundance of water. Within minutes, they were spotlessly clean, their water-darkened hair plastered to their heads.

The boys were out on the rockface when lightning struck the ledge above. With the underpinning blasted away, great boulders hurtled past on either side, as they flattened themselves to the wall. The boulders smashed hugely into the river below, sending discolored geysers high in the air.

Now, through the driving rain, Lee saw the men come into sight below them. He pushed Mitch ahead, and they started off with a quickened pace, slipping and sliding on the wet granite.

THE THUNDERSTORM CAUGHT THE MEN IN THE OPEN. The rain was so intense, the stragglers soon lost sight of Tony, fifty feet ahead. At the front of the column again, Eggar raised his good arm, and the men held up, huddling against the cliff. All along the cliff-face, rain ran down it like sheets of dirty glass. As they waited, shivering, the others joined them one by one. Buttafuco was the last to waddle up. His blubbery love-handles quaked from his chill.

It was then that a bolt of lightning struck the cliff above, filling the air with a crackling fireball that showered them with splintered rock. With a scream, Piscopo bolted, arms over his head. Where the ledge suddenly dipped down, he lost traction and began to slide. Shoved by the wind, he skated over the lip and dropped from sight, his scream lost in the downpour. His green cap marked the point of his departure. The men stared at it, gulping, as the rain pounded it out of shape.

THE BROTHERS CONTINUED DOWN THE LEDGE, making little headway in the sheeting rain. Trapped in the gorge, the storm wind whirled tornadically. Once, the boys saw a tree limb rise past them from below. A moment later, an eagle whirled past, wings beating furiously, but moving backward. Buffeted, off-balance, they carefully placed each step. The rain had washed lichen from the cliffside, and saturated, it was slick as overcooked spinach; the ledge slippery as glare ice.

Again, they skated to a stop and examined the way ahead. Lee's gaze traveled down the stinging rain … down the glistening cliff … to the tiny rivulet-river far below.

With a yell, he drew back, pulling Mitchell with him. For the second time, the ledge had come to a dead end!

The boys embraced at the drop-off, teeth chattering, and searched the rockface for shelter. Run-off fell in discolored cascades, large and small, all down the cliffside. Now Lee looked back down the ledge, saw a cleft in the rockface, and dragged Mitchell toward it.

Inside, they huddled together, shivering, and stared out at the storm. From the shelf above the cleft, rain fell in a muddy waterfall. With each thunderclap, the granite shuddered. Again and again, lightning struck the escarpment. Through the waterfall, they watched as rock and moss and bits of shrub rained past them like debris from a bomb blast.

Now lightning struck the pinnacle in another explosion of rock, and seconds later, a tree floated by dreamlike in a rush of foliaged limbs, clods raining from its roots.

Again, the lightning struck, and this time, there was the rumble of major movement from above. The boys scrambled deeper into the cleft to avoid the falling boulders that struck the ledge before them, gouging the granite white and spraying them with stinging slivers of stone. The chemical smell of cloven rock was strong.

It was then that Lee looked over his shoulder and saw that the cleft had no back. Staring deeper into the crevice, squinting, he saw the serpentine corridor that disappeared into the

127

blackness.

30

THE SUMMER THUNDERSTORM DIDN'T LAST FOR LONG. Soon the thunder was rumbling far down the river gorge, and a pale shaft of sunlight broke through the ravelling thunderheads. With the rainfall slackened, the men ventured out on the ledge. They were a bedraggled-looking lot; three were delirious with snakebite. A rainbow had formed between the walls of the gorge, arching over the river in a palpable, prismatic bridge that mirrored the Interstate bridge beyond, but they hardly gave it a glance.

"Okay, let's go! Guiliani, D'Amato, on your feet! Georgie, help him up. Move it! *Now!* Roselli, you gone make it?"

"I don't know, Tony. Check it out."

Roselli lifted his pants leg. Running on the granite had retarded the circulation and magnified the swelling. His swollen foot had engulfed his toes, visible now only as yellowed toenails. His leg was as big at the ankle as at the thigh and had split the seam of his pegged pants. Roselli had seen pictures of Africans with elephantiasis, and he remarked the similarity. The only difference was his foot and calf were bright purple. And there was a worrisome blackening above his ankle around the two punctures. He felt a twinge of fear as the others gathered in learned consultation.

"Oh, wow, man! That looks *bad,* Roselli!"

"Frigging A!"

"Looks like gangrene. Sure hope you don't lose it."

"How could it be gangrene? The sumbitch is purple."

"Jesus! How'd you get outta high school? A handgun?"

"Yo mama!"

"All right, all right, enough already! You can make it till dark," Tony told Roselli, looking away with distaste. "We'll make camp soon."

"Sure, Tony, sure."

"Okay, let's go. Eggar, lead off."

With Eggar on point, the men set off along the ledge. Roselli carried his wingtip in his left hand, his pistol in his right. Beyond the rainbow, he saw the Interstate bridge. In the evening light, a few cars already rode their parking lights, and atop the central spire, the aviation light was faintly visible.

He looked at the bridge wistfully; then, shaking his head, crossing himself with the pistol's two-inch barrel, he picked up his clubfoot's humping gait. There was no going back now. Tony was locked on. When he was like this, it didn't do to cross him. For the first time, Roselli looked forward to the killing of the boys. It was, after all, the only way home.

AT A CROUCH, LEE MOVED CAUTIOUSLY down the narrow passageway. Mitch followed closely, gripping his brother's shirttail. Twice, the roof dipped so low the boys had to crawl on hands and knees. Moments later, the passage narrowed vertically, and as Lee walked through, he noted with unease animal hair on the outcrops there. It was too dark to make out its color, but the passage was wide enough that it had to be something bigger than a boy. Lee was careful to keep the discovery to himself: His little brother had had enough for one day.

For a time, they could see the sunlit entrance behind them; but then they made a right-angling turn and were plunged into blackness.

Lee stopped, winded. Beyond the turn, the air was foul. He felt the walls on either side. They were foursquare as a hallway, and wet to the touch.

"Man, it's dark! Cain't see nothing. Jist hope they ain't no snakes."

"Me too, Lee." Mitch's voice trembled. "I cain't take no more snakes."

"*Huh!* You and me both. Jist watch a old big she-bear with cubs be denned up in here. That'd be something, wouldn't it? You'd think snakes! Ain't no room to turn around."

Again, they started off, and deeper in the cave, their words acquired an echo.

Mitchell wrinkled his nose. "Pew, it stinks in here."

"Yeh, bats, most likely."

On hands and knees again, they crawled deeper and deeper

130

into the mountainside, negotiating the square-walled fault-line entirely by feel. Deep in the mountain, the heat of day was gone, and the granite sweated icy condensation. Beneath the stench, there was the mossy, mildewed fragrance of a springhouse, and somewhere, Mitch heard the cistern *clicking* of water. Then, like a wind, he heard the creaking rustle of bats waking for a night on the town, and a rabbit ran over his grave.

Trapped behind Lee, in a passage no larger than a three-foot culvert pipe, Mitch was fighting a rising panic ... when gradually the tunnel's clammy walls began to widen ... the ceiling began to rise. Another fifty feet and the boys were walking at a crouch, legs cramping. Mitch held tight to his brother's back pocket.

Five minutes later, Lee bumped into a wall. Slowly, feeling above him, he stood to his full height and sighed with relief.

"It's some kinda room, feels like. Must be seven, eight foot high."

Reaching out in the blackness, he touched Mitchell's face—and, startled, Mitch shrieked.

Lee giggled. "Velcome to my home," he said in a Bela Lugosi voice.

"Funny," Mitch told his brother. "Hilarious."

Releasing Lee's shirt, he groped toward the back of the cave. Where the floor dipped down, he stumbled and recoiled at a dry rattle. He kicked it and felt it give way.

"Here's some wood and stuff, Lee."

"Good. Rake you up a pile. Watch where you put your hands."

MITCH WAS AT WORK WITH THE FIRE-DRILL. Though Lee could see little, he could hear the rhythmic rumble of the drill. The rumble decreased as friction smoothed the rough wood. Soon it was replaced with a shrill creaking as the drill bit deeper into the dry-rotted wood.

"I'm real thirsty, Lee." Mitchell's voice echoed in the granite chamber.

"I know. Me too."

131

"I'm hungry too."

"Me too, Mitch. Don't think about it. Maybe we'll find something in the morning. Oughta be some blackberries on the sunny side of these cliffs. Up top."

Now Lee saw a soft red glow as the punk began to warm. In the eerie light, he saw a wisp of smoke drifting up, and for the first time, he could make out his brother, kneeling barefoot, tending the spark. Mitchell's laceless tennis shoe lay nearby.

On and on, the fire-drill creaked. While Mitch bowed the drill, Lee knelt over the punk, blowing gently, fanning the fragile spark with his cupped hand. Sitting back, he smiled as he watched his little brother expertly bow the drill. Looking up, Mitch saw the smile and basked in his brother's approval.

All around them now bats answered the creaking drill. In the faint red light, the very walls and ceiling seemed to move. And now, in a rush, almost as one, the bats funneled, screeching, into the passageway.

The brothers hit the floor. For nearly a minute, the shrill exit went on. Flattened on the damp cave floor, the boys felt a urine-smelling wind at their passage.

TONY HAD JOINED EGGAR IN THE LEAD AS THE MEN shuffled down the ledge. At the end of the column, Buttafuco's asthmatic wheezing was loud as a punctured squeezebox. The sun was down in the gorge now, and far downriver, the Interstate bridge was a black cut-out pasted against the forest-fire sunset. The great center parabola bestrode a river of fire; the blinking Cyclops eye one color with the blazing sky. Already, a river chill was in the air, and to the men, sunburned and dehydrated, it seemed wintry after the heat of day.

They stopped, breathing hard, when they came to the dead end. Whirling, Tony looked high and low; looked up the sheer cliff-face with an open mouth.

"Where the hell!" he said, blowing. "Where the *hell!*"

Chest heaving, Eggar leaned against the cliffside, cradling his arm. Sweat filmed his gray face, and the blue shirt clung to his meatless frame. He watched as the bats snaked across the sunset and disappeared over the far mountain.

"Beats the hell outta me," he told Tony.

He pretended to examine his enormous arm as he looked at the crevice in the cliff. With the sun down, it lay in shadow.

Tony looked up the vertical rockface. "Could you climb up there?"

Eggar's gaze followed. "Nah," he said and spat. "But I ain't twelve years old."

At Eggar's response, Tony gave him a long look.

"Hey," Messina said, looking toward the crevice.

"Hey what?"

"I heard something."

"Screw you! 'Tony, I heard something.'"

"Nah, man, I did! *Listen!*" He held up his hand. "You didn't hear that? Hold it, Eggar!"

"I don't hear jack," Tony told him.

"They musta went higher," Eggar said, indicating the summit with his bristly chin. "Only way they coulda. Old game trail up there."

"'Less they frigging flew," Giordano said with a chuckle. "Wouldn't put it past 'em neither."

Tony gave him a dark look. "You ain't funny worth a damn."

Abruptly, the men's laughter died.

Tony removed his flask and took a drink, head back, Adam's apple chugging. He capped the flask and wiped his mouth with the palm of his hand.

"Dammit, I had about enough of this! Hear me? These kids is making monkeys outta us!"

Messina was still looking at the crevice. "And I tell you I heard—"

"It's getting night," Eggar said, looking up at the purpling sky. "Don't know 'bout y'all, but I ain't wanting to get my tail caught out here attar dark." He spat. "I say we go back a ways to 'at shelf yonder and make camp. Them little punks ain't going nowheres—not 'less they got wings, they ain't."

Tired and hungry, the men nodded their assent. With a final look around, they stumbled back down the ledge. Messina was last in line. He stood at the crevice, eyeing it suspiciously. Now, frowning, he turned and fell into step with the others.

INSIDE THE CAVE, THE BROTHERS HAD THE PUNK AFIRE and were feeding it dead leaves. Kneeling over the smoldering leaves, blowing softly, tousled heads touching in the smoke, they began to feed the sudden flame pencil-size sticks of wood. Mitchell's nose was still wrinkled with distaste. The stench in the cave was terrific.

"It sure stinks in here."

"I know. Cain't be me. I lost both tennis shoes."

The boys got a giggle out of that.

Now the wood took flame, and they added larger sticks. Crackling, it flared up, and in the sudden light, they saw they were burning an abandoned eagles' nest. It still held shards of tan eggshell. The nest burned with a foul, uric reek.

Carefully, the boys fed the fire larger and larger wood, and the flames grew higher and higher, illuminating the cold, granite dimensions of the chamber—the high ceiling with white guano streaks below the cornice ledges; the sandy, animal-tracked floor. Fox and raccoon scats near the fire contained bits of undigested fur, splintered bone, persimmon seeds and crayfish shell.

Nearby, a bear had purged its hibernal bowels in four pancake stools that held blades of grass and bits of elderberry. They were not yet dry, and Lee noted with unease the saucer-size tracks. The claws scored the sand a full three inches in front of the pads. It was a big solitary male, but unlikely to return if they kept the fire going.

With relief, he saw that, unaccountably, a quantity of driftwood had been brought to the cave, piled against the back wall. An algae fan of ground-water seepage stained the wall high above it. In summer, the dry season, the algae was blistered and brown.

Looking at the wall, Mitch absently noted a figure on it. As his eyes moved along the wall, he saw that the granite was adorned with drawings—a mural of stick buffalo and deer and

134

panthers; stick men with feathered headdresses and bows and arrows rode canoes through a river gorge. The drawings were done in vivid reds and blues and yellows, and somehow, the flickering firelight seemed to animate them. Even so, they barely registered on his perception. More immediate concerns possessed him.

When the biggest logs had taken flame, the boys sat back, smiling wanly at their success.

Suddenly, Mitchell looked across the room, his eyes widened, and he let go a piercing scream. Lee whirled and a look of mortal terror came over his ashen face.

Wide-eyed and trembling, the boys stared together at the far wall—where a human mummy—a grinning near-skeleton in gallused overalls and a red-plaid shirt—sat against the granite.

Staring at the shrivelled, yellow-toothed face, Mitch let go another echoing scream and leaped into his brother's arms. Lee hung on for dear life.

31

IT WAS DINNERTIME AGAIN IN THE HOUSEHOLD, and Mr. and Mrs. Rainey sat alone at the kitchen table. Tonight, they were really worried. Mr. Rainey picked at his hamburger steak and pushed his yellow squash around, clearly preoccupied. Mrs. Rainey made no pretense of eating. Her silverware sat undisturbed beside her empty plate. Again, the wall clock ticked loudly. For the umpteenth time since dark, she looked up at it and saw that it was nearly ten—and for the umpteenth time, she told her husband, "Cleve, we oughta call the sheriff."

Mr. Rainey opened his mouth to speak when the phone rang. Mrs. Rainey shrieked as her husband jumped to answer it.

"Hello?"

FIVE MILES AWAY, IN A WHITE-CLAPBOARD HOUSE on Elm Street, Jennifer Holt, dressed for a night on the town, paced around her pink-quilted bed, a pink phone to her ear. Her eyes were red from crying, and her face ran mascara. An army of stuffed animals—a goodly number of pinkish pigmentation—eavesdropped on the call.

"Mr. Rainey?"

"Speaking."

"Mr. Rainey, this is Jennifer Holt. Could I please speak to Lee?"

As she talked, she wound and unwound the phone cord around a pink-nailed hand.

"I'm 'fraid he ain't here."

"Well, do you know where he is?" she said. She began to cry.

"I wisht to blazes I did. What's wrong, honey?"

"Well, we were suppose to go to the movies tonight and—"

"Tonight?"

"Yes sir."

"You're sure it were tonight?"

"Yes sir, Saturday night."

Mr. Rainey looked at his wife. "I'm sorry, girl. I'll have him to call you jist soon as he comes in. I promise. 'At's right. Don't you worry none. Bye."

Mr. Rainey hung up. Slowly, he took his seat, a troubled look on his face.

Mrs. Rainey watched him until she could stand it no longer. "Cleve?"

"Well now, 'at's mighty strange," he said, surfacing.

"What, Cleve?"

"It were 'at Holt girl, Jenny. According to her, she and Lee was 'posed to go to the pitcher show tonight."

Mrs. Rainey stood abruptly. "That done it."

"Jist hold your damn horses fer two seconds."

"Are you gone call the sheriff or am I?"

"Hold on, I said."

Mrs. Rainey plumped down, muttering, tears welling.

Now, as they sat in the silence, a faint sound came from outside. It sounded like—it was—the whine of an animal in pain.

Mr. Rainey held up his hand. "Shh! Hold it a minute!"

Mrs. Rainey's hand went to her throat. "What is it?"

"Hush, I said!"

And clearly now, she could hear it to—the sound of a dog whining at the kitchen door. In one motion, husband and wife ran to the door. Mr. Rainey grabbed a flashlight off the refrigerator as he passed.

And out on the back porch, they found Suellen, shot through the stomach and close to death. She lay on her side, whining, her flanks heaving, a bloody froth at her nose and mouth.

When Mr. Rainey shone the light on the dog, his wife screamed.

"What is it, Cleve?"

"She been shot!"

Back inside, Mr. Rainey went straight to the phone. His wife stood behind him, sobbing, wringing her hands.

"I knowed it, I knowed it!"

"Hush, woman, cain't hardly hear myself think! Find me the sheriff's number! *Quick!*"

137

THE DISPATCHER, A THIRTY-ISH DEPUTY named Tommy Bennett, answered the phone—after swallowing a bite of cheeseburger and turning down the volume on *America's Most Wanted*. (No matter: His wife would be taping the show at home. Deputy Bennett was convinced that his life's ambition—working with the G-men in Washington, DC—lay in the apprehension of one of the celebrity fugitives profiled on the show.)

"Green River Sheriff's Department, Deputy Bennett speaking."

"Tommy, Cleve Rainey."

"Evening, Mr. Rainey."

"Sheriff in?"

"Yes sir, hang on a minute." Tommy covered the phone and called into the adjoining office, "Sheriff, Cleve Rainey. Sounds important."

And Sheriff Bo Rasmussen appeared. He was a big man, paunchy but far from fat, bald as a cue ball with strands of iron-gray hair—his "vanity," his wife called it—combed across his shining pate. Dinner done, there was a toothpick in the corner of his mouth. He rolled it to the other side as he took the phone from his deputy.

"Cleve?"

"Evening, Bo. 'Fraid we got some trouble out our way."

"How's 'at, Cleve?"

"Well, my boys left outta here yestiddy evening, gone fishing, and we ain't heared a word since. Anyways, one of my hounds come in tonight, shot through the gut."

"Whadaya make of it, Cleve?"

"Nothing good, I'm 'fraid."

"Where 'bouts was they aheaded to?"

"Green River."

"Lordy Lord, 'at's a sight of ground to cover." The sheriff sighed. "Well, I'll deputize a bunch of the boys."

"I can make some calls."

"'Course we cain't do nothing till attar church. What say we meet at the firehouse."

"Sounds good, Bo."

"Make it noon or thereabouts. Bring something another of their'n. I'll send over to Asheville fer some hounds."

"Okay, Bo. Thanks. I appreciate it."

"Glad to do it. What I'm here fer. Them boys'll turn up. Tell yer missus not to worry none. Like as not, they jist got turned around somewheres. Busted a ankle or somelike. Happens all the time. Prob'ly come adragging in 'fore we can get attar 'em."

"I hope so, Bo. I surely do. See you tomorrow."

Mr. Rainey hung up and turned to his wife, and they exchanged a frantic look. Now she burst into tears and threw herself into her husband's arms. He hugged her and patted her trembling shoulders, but above her unravelling bouffante, there was no reassurance in his troubled face.

32

IN THE CAVE, THE BROTHERS WERE STILL FLATTENED against the wall, staring at the mummy with wide eyes. With a terrible fascination, they took in the leathery skin and patchy blond beard; the black eyesockets and blond, shoulder-length hair. In places on the face, the skullbone showed through where the cave rats had gnawed on it. The long yellow teeth of the lipless death's-head grinned back at them.

It was then that Lee saw the rusty Winchester at the mummy's side. He pushed Mitch from his lap and crossed quickly to it. When he lifted the rifle, the skeletal fingers that gripped it broke off and fell to the granite with a dry rattle. Watching, Mitchell's eyes went wide.

Lee tried to work the corroded lever, but it was stuck fast. With the stock under one thigh, pulling with both hands, he got the action to creak open. Empty. Nose wrinkled with distaste, he searched the musty coat pockets, gagging at the smell of the dust he raised. Empty. Now, looking at the floor, he saw the tarnished 30/30 brasses strewn everywhere around the moldy boots.

Holding the useless rifle, Lee looked over the mummy's red-plaid shoulder and saw the inscription on the granite there: GOD FORGIV ME. I AINT NEVER MENT NO HARM. Below it, days, in crosshatched fives, had been marked off with a soft-nosed bullet. There was a good three week's worth.

Lee's dejected face lit up with revelation.

"Hell's bells, Mitchell, that ain't no deer hunter! You know who that is?"

With big eyes, Mitch gulped and shook his head.

"That's Bill Robinson!" Mitch drew a blank. "You know! Remember? Man what robbed the FCX 'bout five years back? Got a bundle!"

"Oh, yeh! Now I remember! Daddy said he lifted the safe out with a backhoe. Covered it up with hay bales and drove right down Main Street. Blowed her out in Mason's cornfield."

"That's the one! Looked ever'wheres for him. Gub'ment

men, *in*surance people. Most folks figgered he got clean away. Living it up somewheres, down in Mexico."

Mitch regarded the skeleton … the hideous grin … the tales-from-the-crypt hairdo … the freeze-dried skin. In the upstreaming firelight, the eyesockets were black holes. The shriveled, sunken cheeks and disordered hair gave the corpse the look of a demonic grandmother.

He shuddered and looked away. "He didn't."

"You got that right. Hey, wanna hear something funny?"

Mitch looked at his brother like he was crazy.

"He used to coach me in Little League."

"That explains a lot, Lee."

Lee laughed. "Bite my butt!"

Now the boys exchanged the same excited look at exactly the same instant. Whirling, kneeling, with trembling hands, Lee tore open the knapsack at the mummy's feet. Beneath the moldy flaps, the pack was filled with banded blocks the size of bricks! The denomination was $100!

Lee pulled out two bricks and screamed with joy. "We rich, Mitchell! We rich! Look! Man oh man oh man oh man! Jist *look!*"

Mitch gave his brother a here-we-go-again look. "Lee," he said softly.

"Oh, wow!" Lee broke a band and began to count. "They must be—two, four, six, eight, nine—they must be—two, four, six, eight, nine—fifty thousand here! At least! Maybe more! Corvette, here we come!"

"Lee."

"We can come back for it later! Put it in a safety deposit box down at the bank! I read about it! Take her out a little bit at a time! Won't nobody never know—"

"Lee!" Lee looked up. "It ain't ours."

"Sure, it is, Mitchell! I mean, who's gone know? Huh? Finders keepers … right?"

Mitch shook his head. With a sigh, Lee sat back and gave his brother a grin.

"It don't belong to us, Lee. We gotta turn it in. Else we ain't no better'n 'em. Look, maybe they's a *re*-ward or something.

Never know."

"Yeh. *Yeh!*"

Lee nodded and threw the bills toward the open pack, and they scattered limply on the damp cave floor. He shook his head, and his tattered bandage waved, blood-stiffened, a pennant of defeat.

"What?"

Lee sighed. "Jist thinking. 'Bout the mess I landed you in."

"It was jist as much my doing."

"Nah, I was the oldest. I shoulda knowed better."

"We both shoulda knowed better." Mitch smiled at his brother. "We do now ... right?" Lee nodded. "We both knowed that money belonged to somebody else. Didn't grow on that tree."

Laughing, Lee threw the knapsack at Mitch, and bricks of $100's flew out. There was an effort to laugh, to see the lighter side of their dismal situation, but it didn't take.

"Mitch, you know what I cain't stand?"

Mitch shook his head.

"At school. Them rich townie creeps with they new clothes and they new cars and they new albums. You know? And the girls drooling all over 'em." Lee sighed. "It weren't so bad at the little school. All them kids was like us. You know—country people. But ever since high school ... I don't know ... I guess the money made me feel like ... like I fit in ... like I was in. You know?"

Mitch nodded. "Yeh, but it didn't really. Me, I'll stick with Mica and Suellen. Don't give a care if'n I'm rich—like me jist the same."

Lee smiled at his brother and nodded. "Ain't no excuse to steal no ways ... is it?"

"Nope."

"You little punk! You oughta be a tent-preacher!"

Looking stern, Mitch raised a stubby forefinger in Mosaic admonition. Now, deepening his voice to maybe tenor, he told Lee, "'And the Lord God sayeth unto Moses, "Thou shalt not steal."' That's right, brothers 'n' sisters. Hellfire 'n' brimstone is set by fer 'em what takes the propitty of anothern."

142

Again, the laughter died in their parched throats.

It was then that Lee looked at the skeleton and his face blanched. Mitch caught the look and whirled fearfully, half-expecting a reanimated zombie with a palate for boy's brain. But Bill Robinson hadn't moved. He still favored the brothers with his horsey smile.

"What, Lee?"

"Look! His leg! It's broke clear through! He musta busted it on the ledge out yonder and dragged hisself in here. That's how come they ain't no cartridges! He fired 'em all up calling for help! Jesus, Mitchell! The sumbitch *starved* to death!"

Mitch gulped. "I surely do hope we don't end up that way."

"Or worse."

"Nah, Lee, cain't be no worse. I'm so hungry, my guts—"

Lee held up his hand and looked toward the mouth of the cave. And now Mitch heard it too!

Men's voices coming faintly from outside! The words acquired an inhuman hollowness as they found their way down the serpentine passage and reached the granite chamber with echo clarity.

33

TWENTY MINUTES LATER, THE BROTHERS LAY in the mouth of the cave, side by side, pressed to the ground. The voices were louder now, just outside the entrance, and now there was the flare of a lighter, and two profiled faces appeared in the little circle of illumination. Barely ten feet away, Mitch saw uncallused hands cupping the flame, as one man lit a cigarette, drew deeply on it, and passed it over. When he exhaled, they smelled marijuana.

The men were sitting in the same crevice the boys had used to get out of the storm, heads and shoulders framed in the rough granite arch. Their faces in profile were clearly visible as they drew, first one, then the other, on the joint. The red light gave their stubbly faces an evil look. The boys watched with terrified eyes, and the joint reflected in them like red sparks.

"I wonder where them little punks is got to? Swear to God, I heard something. This afternoon." When the man looked over his shoulder, the brothers hugged the ground. "Sounded like from over here."

He drew on the joint, the light brightened, and the boys could see that his eyes were blue. He wore a cap that read BUNCOMBE COUNTY LITTLE LEAGUE - COACH. The other man wore a gold earring and a red bandana in the pirate style. (Mentally, Mitch added the eye patch and missing teeth.)

"Who knows, man?" the pirate said. "Who the hell *cares?* Jesus! I ain't getting paid enough for this! I mean, snakes, man! Frigging *snakes!*"

"Yeh, yeh, life's a bitch and then you die. Quit your crying. They seen who we was, okay? You heard what Tony said. You wanna end up in the gas chamber? Way I see it, it's either them or us."

"I know. Still. Killing kids …"

"We ain't killed no kids yet—in case you ain't noticed. It's kids nine, grownups zip."

"Messina, you got kids."

"Shut up, I said!"

"I still don't like it."

"Hey, nobody *likes* it, Roselli." Again, he looked into the cave mouth. "Tell you what—them little punks is right around here somewheres. I know it."

"Feel it in your bones?" Roselli thumped his ash and tiny tracers streamed downwind.

"Screw you. Tell you what—I'm gonna have a little look-see in the morning. When it gets light."

Beyond the men, framed by their heads, the boys saw the Interstate bridge. Suspended in the blackness, cars sped across in both directions, headlights and taillights haloed in the river fog. The summer traffic was heavy – tourists bound for the Blue Ridge Parkway -- and the four lanes seemed ropes of light, white for the oncoming lanes, red for the southbound. In the southbound lanes, the amber-reflectored guard-rails blossomed in the headlights. From this distance, the lights looked like bars on a neon sign.

Now, as they watched, a semi crossed in the passing lane, a red-and-yellow constellation of itself. High above it all, the red lodestar of the warning light blinked in the blackness, the brightest star in a glittering, summer firmament.

Now the man called Messina looked up and sniffed the night air. "You smell something?"

"Just your frigging feet."

"Pinhead—you smell smoke?"

In response, the one called Roselli looked at the joint he was holding.

"No, butt-breath, woodsmoke."

The boys watched in terror as, sniffing, Roselli told him, "Hell, probably ours. These cliffs here are full of updrafts, downdrafts, *side*friggindrafts—Jesus, man! This high-wire crap's for the frigging *birds!* I mean, we're frigging *bar*tenders, for Chrissakes!"

"Bitch, bitch, bitch." Messina stood up. "Come on, let's go. You want any more of this?"

"Nah, man, *I* might start hearing things."

"Funny man, frigging comedian."

Messina took a final drag on the joint and tossed it away, streaking into the gorge.

The men stood then, Roselli groaning and stretching, rubbing the small of his back. Messina snapped on his flashlight and led the way. When the light played across the cave mouth, the boys flattened.

Grumbling—"Hey, man, how 'bout some light back here"— the one named Roselli followed. He walked with a deep limp.

Quickly, quietly, the brothers back-peddled into the cave.

THERE WAS PANIC IN THEIR FACES as they banked the fire. Now they sat shoulder to shoulder in the eerie, red glow of the embers, shivering, regarding the black hole of the entrance with big eyes. Bill Robinson sat between them and the entry, and wearing a black-cowled monk's robe of trembling shadow, he fixed them with his terrible stare. With his skeletal fingers pointing downward, he looked like an allegorical figure in a medieval tapestry, illustrating the path of death and damnation. All he required was a scythe.

There was hysteria in Lee's voice as, "Dammit, we trapped in here! We trapped! We gotta make a plan!"

"What, Lee?

"Dunno yet! Lemme think! Gotta think of something!"

"Lee?"

"What?"

"Let's rock 'em again. That was good. Or maybe we can find us some more rattlers. Or, I been thinking, we could get above 'em, start a rockslide ..."

In the dying firelight, Lee looked at his little brother's frowning face, studiously analyzing their problem, fearlessly proposing solutions, and took heart. Now he managed a faint smile, and leaning close, he put his arm around Mitch and gave him a hug.

"Don't you worry none, Mitchell. We figger something out. I reckon we ain't ready to roll over jist yet. Not by a long shot, we ain't."

But in the faint firelight, Lee looked far from sure.

146

THE BOYS WOKE IN THE NIGHT AS THEY HEARD the flumewater roaring through the gorge. The tidal wave echoed up the cliff-face and entered the cave with the faraway sound of breaking surf.

Mitch rolled toward his brother. "Lee?" he whispered. "Lee, you 'wake?"

"Yeh."

"Me too. You hear it?"

"Yeh, they driving the logs. What time is it?"

Mitch rolled toward the embers and took in Mickey's smiling face. He looked ridiculous with an arm growing out of his head – like one of those show-offs who could dislocate his shoulder.

"Twenty after twelve. About it." He rolled back and looked at his brother. "What we gone do, Lee?"

Lee sighed. "Dunno. We'll think of something. They ain't caught us yet. What'd he say? 'Kids nine, grownups zip.'"

The boys got a giggle out of that.

Now Lee reached out in the darkness and touched his brother's head. "Mitch?"

"What, Lee?"

"I'm sorry I hit you today. At the snakes? Weren't no call for that. None atall. It were mean."

Mitch smiled. "Yeh, they was. You was right—I was a chicken."

34

ON A NARROW LEDGE HIGH ABOVE THE RIVER, A WOODS RAT fed beneath the rockface, picking at the wind-borne seeds. Suddenly, it sat up, nose twitching, and disappeared into a crevice. Moments later, a rattlesnake crawled after it along the ledge. It oozed into the hole in a viscous filling, and shortly, there came muffled squeals. They were quickly cut short.

Higher up the cliff-face, a woodchuck ventured out of its den and hurried along a ledge, waddling with its weight of summer fat. Now, with a whoosh of wingbeats, a Great Horned Owl plucked it cleanly from the cliff, still on the run, and dropped into the inky gorge. The 'chuck's screams echoed down the gorge, growing fainter and fainter and fainter.

THERE WAS ANOTHER NARROW PASSAGE at the base of the cliff, a walkway along the river made up of fallen boulders and fault-line outcrops, and around two that morning, the bear returned along it. He knew the way well for it was prime fishing during the spring spawn, when the rapids collected roe trout in the stillwater against the cliff. Now, as he lumbered along it, he sniffed the fissured rockface, waiting for his nose to tell him the path of his descent.

He was, as Lee suspected, a solitary male. Though hibernation was short in those southerly latitudes, he was gaunt, emaciated after his winter sleep, and his heavy black coat, mud-matted, hung on him in rolls. Now it was the third day of his thirty-mile range from the cave, and the return leg had brought him back along the river, where he'd gorged on blackberries in the morning and chased an eagle from its trout in the afternoon.

The night before he'd unearthed a muskrats' den and supped on a whole family of half-grown kits. It was his first solid food since he'd emerged from hibernation, and though the pungent flesh of muskrat was far from his favorite – not like, for instance, the hamburgers and carrot cake he found in the green-painted garbage cans at the girls camp below the bridge -- he'd eaten his fill. With solid food, his disposition had improved, and a scent of estrus in the afternoon had put courtship on his mind.

Now he stood at the base of the cliff, nose up, tasting the currents of air that swirled about the gorge. A downdraft brought him a whiff of smoke, and he stirred uneasily, nostrils flaring. Smoke carried with it the double threat of man and forest fire, both lethal, though man, with his carrot cake and 30/30's, was the more treacherous of the two.

Again, the wind gusted and this time, the current delivered an acrid whiff of man. He started with a snort, *whuffing* to clear his nasal passages, and waddled rapidly down the river. Where he leaped an interruption in the ledge, the slack skin on his broad back rolled like a bag of sand.

There, he stopped and reared up, forefeet on the cliff. He growled, nostrils flaring, and the trout scales on his muzzle glittered in the moonlight. But the wind had changed, and the fearsome scent was gone.

Even so, he stood a long moment, head back like a circus bear drinking sasparilla, nose working, but the man-smell did not come again. At length, he dropped to four feet and began his ponderous, switchback climb.

TWO-HUNDRED FEET ABOVE, EGGAR HELD A STAND-TO, hunkered on the cliff-side, staring into the moonlit gorge. He had bummed a cigarette from Messina – his first in nearly five years – and he smoked it slowly, inhaling shallowly, for the harsh smoke hurt his lungs. As he smoked, he contemplated his and the boys' dilemmas. All during supper, Messina had held forth volubly on his intention to search the cliff-face in the morning. With a flashlight, the entrance to the cave would be obvious even to these men.

The campfire, built of wet wood with much cursing and white gas, burned down behind him. It was a ring of ember-tipped hardwood now, though here and there, a breath of night wind stirred the tips to blue flame.

Eggar glanced beyond the fire. Though widened, the ledge was still barely eight feet in breadth, and the men slept in a row.

Beyond them all, Buttafuco snored, and from his mountainous bulk came a granite-shaking rumble on the inhale and an adenoidal whistling as he breathed out. Eggar smiled. Rhythmic, the snore sounded like some kind of a load-bearing steam machine with a release valve. Twice already, two of the others had wakened and cursed him; kicked him to silence.

Eggar glanced at Tony's bag. Tony slept facing him, and sunburn, alcohol, hypertension and firelight combined to give him a complexion almost crimson. Though considered handsome – at least Tony said so – Eggar stared at the heavy-browed, Italianate visage with distaste.

Eggar looked back into the gorge and took a drag on his cigarette. What would he do if the men cornered the boys in the cave? He couldn't take them all on with his rifle. Would he want to? How could he face Cleve Rainey if he didn't? How could he face Reverend Stevens? Surely there were sins too great even for Jesus Christ to forgive, and the killing of children had to be greatest among them. Why had he gotten himself tangled up with Tony and his gang? Was being poor so bad it brought you to this? But if the boys got away, he would go to prison. Who would take care *his* boys then? And with a murderer for a father, how could they ever face the town again? They would come to hate him.

Eggar groaned and slumped forward, forearms on his thighs. Under a fresh rain of kicks, Buttafuco had rolled over, and in the silence, a sound, low and repetitive, intruded on Eggar's thoughts. It was coming from below, a sound like labored breathing. Eggar slid forward till both legs overhung the ledge. He leaned over from the waist.

There was a black shape a hundred feet below, clear against the white water and moonlit granite. At first, he took it to be a new shadow of the declining moon -- until it moved. Now it stopped, elongated, and in silhouette against the river, resolved itself into a bear, neck extended, head up. Eggar saw the glint of moonlight on the black, wet snout.

Eggar sat back, scooted back on his hands until he was within reach of the fire. There, he picked up a flaming brand and made as if to light his cigarette. He puffed up a cloud of smoke, then dropped the firebrand over the side, and watched, as end over end, it tumbled down the cliff-face in a fireworks of sparks. Now the slipstream ignited it, and the log fell on in a *whooshing* meteor of flame.

The bear looked up at the sudden light and saw the ball of fire falling out of the night. Startled, he rushed backward with a *whuff*, lost his footing, and in a scrabbling of claws, half-fell, half-surfed the dewy cliff-face to the river.

Eggar smiled, chuckled to himself when he heard it hit the river. Below, the darkness blossomed with the splash. Moments later, out of the shadow of the cliff, he saw the black bulk quartering across the white water. Eggar watched it onto the rocks on the other side, where it shook itself like an enormous dog, the water sparking in the moonlight.

Eggar smiled and shook his head. At least the boys would sleep tonight. Rain-damp like everything else, the cigarette had gone out, and he dug in his pocket for Messina's lighter.

Behind him, Tony watched with a frown.

35

A SHAFT OF GOLDEN SUNLIGHT FELL ON MITCHELL'S sleeping face. The light was so intense that he blinked, once, twice, waking up. Slowly, he came full awake, squinting into the brightness with puffy eyes. Now, looking up at the light, Mitch broke into wondering smile.

High above was a gaping hole in the cave roof, filled with streaming sunlight. The radiant light poured down in a palpable, dust-defined column like light through a rose window in the apse of a cathedral. Mitch stared at it as though it were a vision of the Virgin.

HALF AN HOUR LATER, STANDING BELOW THE HOLE, preparing to climb out, Lee looked longingly at Bill Robinson's backpack. Beside him, Mitch plotted their ascent, his eyes mapping each crevice and handhold. Now, turning to Lee, he picked up on his brother's stare.

"Lee, you promised!"

"Jesus, Mitchell, I was jist looking, okay? I can look, cain't I? No harm in looking."

"You promised!"

"Okay, okay, let the rats have it. I guess they got expenses. Living up here in the penthouse."

Still staring at the mouth-watering pack, Lee sighed. "Hey, Mitch? What if we was to jist take ... a couple twenties? You know? For emergencies?"

"*Emergencies?* Ain't like we gone have a flat tire."

"Well, hell, Mitchell, you never know! I mean, in another month, it'll be a rat's nest."

Mitch wavered. "I reckon it's okay. Ain't like we stole it."

"There you go! Let's say fifty, okay? Nice round number, easy to keep account of? Okay?"

Mitch smiled. "Okay."

"Apiece?"

Mitch laughed. "Okay!"

"Mitch? A hundred? Long as we here? Waste not, want not? God helps them what helps theirselves?"

Mitchell sighed and nodded. "Okay."

"Then help yourself, brother! Thanks, don't mind if I do!"

Mitch laughed as Lee stuffed half a dozen blocks in his shirt ... but the boys grew deadly serious as they began their climb toward daylight.

Lee led off, feeling out the handholds in the vertical granite. The bats had returned, and here and there, they hung in squirming, squeaking clusters on the cave walls. There was fresh guano on the ledges, and Lee gagged as he put his hands in it. Climbing higher, he stepped in it and lost his footing, hanging momentarily by his arms, legs bicycling. Finally, he regained his feet and looked down at the granite floor far below. He sighed with relief.

"Careful, Mitch," he whispered down. "These ledges are slicker'n owl doo. Literally."

The brothers sputtered with suppressed laughter.

At the top, as slowly as a woodchuck leaves its burrow, Lee stuck his head through the hole. He froze there a long time with only his head out, periscoping The Wall in every direction.

Mitch was below him, at eye-level with his brother's lacerated feet. There was guano between his toes. The smell was foul.

"See anything?"

"Nah."

"You reckon they give up on us?"

"Nah."

"Me neither."

Slowly, Lee ventured out, and from the higher vantage, again he scanned the cliffside. The dewy ledges ran far upriver, gleaming in the morning light. Looking downriver, he saw the river go into shadow, the green of the water darkening as the facing cliffs constricted for The Narrows. At the end of it all, the Interstate bridge leaped the chasm, the concrete like ice in the morning sun. A column of river mist hung below the center span, dense as smoke in the beam of sunlight.

Lee completed his circuit by looking back upriver. There was no one in sight. Kneeling, he pulled Mitch by both arms up through the hole. It was a tight fit, but he made it.

The boys were crouched together at the opening, when Mitchell saw Lee's smile fade and his face blanch. Mitch whirled and his eyes grew wide.

Eggar was leaning against a boulder across the ledge, gun folded into his arms, watching the boys' exertions with a smile. On his unshaven face there was again the look of undisguised admiration—and something like sadness. Now he shook his head and spat.

Slowly, he raised the rifle and leveled it at Lee ... and for a long moment, they faced each other in silence ... faced each other down over the gunsights. Lee's face was pale and his hand shook as he wiped the sweat from his face. Beside him, Mitch gripped Lee's filthy teeshirt, trembling. He regarded Eggar with his wide brown eyes.

Abruptly, Eggar raised the rifle and fired it into the air. "Yonder they go!"

And the brothers took off, limping down the ledge toward the glimmering Interstate bridge in the distance. Their legs were rubbery from the close call, and the fright had left Lee nauseous. Mitchell's back, at the thought of Eggar's rifle, felt a yard wide. Sweat poured off him as he passed Lee on the narrow ledge.

MOMENTS LATER, THE MEN JOINED EGGAR ABOVE. Some were still shrugging into their shirts and jackets. Others held steaming mugs of coffee. Buttafuco was eating a fried-egg sandwich, and grease glistened on his bristly face. When Eggar pointed in the direction of the vanished boys, Tony screamed like a drill sergeant.

"Move it, move it, move it, move it!"

The men milled about in confusion. Coffee spilled and men yelped, scalded. Roselli stepped on Buttafuco's egg and went down, arms waving, with all the panache of a vaudeville pratfall artist. He was wearing his knapsack, and he hit the granite with a body-shop clang. Now he lay on the ledge, moaning, tenderly holding his gigantic foot.

Buttafuco belched forlornly as he examined his ruined egg.

36

BUOYED BY THE ADRENALINE OF THEIR NARROW ESCAPE, the boys flew down the ledge. Here, the ledge ran flat as a city sidewalk, and Lee kept his eyes well ahead, sweeping the path. He didn't want to come on rattlesnakes at this speed. Far below, the river roared through the gorge, echoing up. It was louder now as they approached The Narrows. The sun was well up; the dew was gone; the granite incandescent. Already, the lizards made their whispery escape.

Lee stopped now, breathing hard. Hands on his knees, he waited for Mitchell to catch up. For the first time, he noticed the pain in his feet, and looking down, saw bloody footprints on the granite. He looked back down the ledge, squinting against the blinding sunlight, and a motion beyond his brother caught his eye: A flash of red and a splinter of sun, and shortly, Eggar materialized down the ledge, wobbling in the heat waves. Red and blue, he floated above the granite like a big balloon.

Lee smiled. He understood Eggar's poor marksmanship now, and what it would cost him. If they got out of this, the sheriff would have to know. *If* they got out.

Now Mitch staggered up, red-faced, gasping, his hair sweat-plastered to his head, and the brothers took off again.

A HUNDRED YARDS BACK, TONY HAD TAKEN POINT, and Buttafuco brought up the rear of the straggling column.

"Hey, yous guys, wait up!"

Already, the men were breathless. In their haste, they ran with untied shoes and unzipped pants. Messina's shirt was buttoned wrong. Gritting his teeth, Roselli ran with the swirling limp of a clubfoot, swinging his huge leg before him like a walking cast.

Hanging back, Eggar ran with his snakebitten arm held away from him as though the movement hurt him. He had freshened the tobacco poultice, and it glistened in the sun. At times, he could see the boys' heads as they leaped the boulders. The moment truth was fast approaching. As a kid, Eggar had trapped these ledges for fox and bobcat, and no one knew them better. He knew there was no way out.

THE LEDGE WIDENED AS IT ROSE TO FOLLOW THE FAULT-LINE, and the boys picked up speed. Lee was fifty feet in front when Mitch saw him stop suddenly and look down at something on the ledge. His face lit up with a devilish grin. Coming up, Mitch saw the old and rusty can of motor oil, green-and-silver Quaker State.

Lee picked it up. "I reckon the loggers left it. Must of rolled down from up top." He grinned at his brother.

"What, Lee?"

"I gotta idea."

"Oh, no!" But this time, Mitchell broke into a wide grin.

With his pocketknife, Lee made two jagged punctures in the can and poured the oil, thick and bluish, along the ledge. Emptied, he threw the can over the cliff, and the brothers watched it float toward the river, crawling along the gorge like a white snake. Now Lee took Mitchell's hand, and they hustled off down the ledge.

MOMENTS LATER, THE MEN CAME INTO SIGHT, and Eggar saw the boys. "Yonder they are!" He threw up his gun, but held his fire.

The brothers ducked behind a boulder as the gunfire began. Again, the rounds left long, leaden streaks, the buckshot showed in silver splatters on the light granite. Echoes turned the gunshots into a barrage, and bullets seemed to ricochet endlessly down the gorge until they were faint as the whines of mosquitoes.

Tony smiled as he stared at the boulder. Kneeling, he reloaded.

"Oh, yeh," he told the others, "*Now* we got the little punks."

The pause had allowed the stragglers time to catch up – even Buttafuco wheezed among them -- and now the men took off in a group.

157

Fifty feet ahead, they hit the motor oil at a dead run.

Immediately, they began to skate, arms windmilling, legs churning. Now Roselli, unable to check his momentum, skated across the cliff and into midair. He hung there, wide-eyed, screaming, legs pumping, and slipped from sight. Guiliani quickly followed. Now Messina, in a classic, banana-peel pratfall, sat down hard and bobsledded backward over the edge, screaming.

And now, near the end of the pack, Eggar tried to check his speed—but bumped from behind by Buttafuco, he hit the oil and fell hard, momentarily stunned--and his rifle banged down, the forearm snapping off, clattering over the rocks, slipping over the edge—and now Eggar followed it, clawing frantically at the slippery granite, digging with his heels, wall-eyed terror on his bloodless face—and, screaming, he slipped over the edge—but caught a crevice at the last minute and hung there by his fingertips over the tiny river.

Eggar looked up, dripping with perspiration, and saw the others standing by, arms folded, watching without expression.

"Tony, help me! Tony? Tony, please! Help me!"

"Sorry, Egg, can't help you none. Maybe them kids'll help you out. They owe you one. Or is it two?"

"Tony, come on now! You're talking crazy! Tony? *Tony!* I ain't gone make it! Please, God, Tony! I cain't hang on much longer! *Help me!*"

Of the original fifteen, only two of Tony's men now remained, Giordano and Buttafuco, and they had drawn back, afraid to venture out on the oil.

Slowly, Eggar began to crawl back up the cliff-face. Workboots scrabbling for a purchase, leaving rubber marks on the cliff. Tendons standing out in his rawbone neck. The bill of his cap was comically over one ear, above a face scarlet with exertion. His snakebitten arm bled afresh and spasmed as it took his weight.

Finally, at full reach, he gripped the ledge with his good arm and, smiling, pulled his eyes level with Tony's feet—when the exfoliated rock scaled off—and Eggar disappeared backward, screaming, still embracing the granite flagstone, bouncing down the cliff-face, heels over head, arms and legs windmilling, blue shirttail flapping, passing his sailing red cap en route to the river.

UP AHEAD, HAND IN HAND ON THE WIDENED LEDGE, the brothers hurried along. They stopped when they heard the terrible scream behind them. Listened to the soprano echo dying down the river gorge. They smiled, slapped hands and broke into a run, following the ribbon of granite, as now, for the first time, the way began to descend.

THE MEN HAD GOTTEN AROUND THE OIL, and though he was blowing and sweating and still weak from his close call, there was a look of vengeful fury on Tony's sunburned face. Cursing, he pushed Giordano and Buttafuco hard. Now he glimpsed the boys' heads as they hurdled the fallen rocks, and picked up his pace. It wouldn't be long now. Tony felt the weight of his loaded revolver. Forget making like hillbilly birds. This time he would be sure.

THE BOYS SCALED A LOW WALL AND CAME OUT onto a higher ledge. The ledge was wider, easier going, and they were picking up speed—when suddenly, Lee stopped and looked ahead with an expression of horror—and coming up beside him, Mitchell screamed as though hit.

For the third time, the ledge had come to an abrupt end! The boys looked above and below, but this time, there was no way out.

"Lee? Lee, what we gone do?"

37

IN RESPONSE, LEE LEANED OUT AND LOOKED OVER THE EDGE. He saw the river, green and white, crawling minutely along the gorge floor. They were below the rapids now; above the headrace of The Narrows. Bracketed by white water upstream and down, the river ran deep and green as it widened into a lakelike pool. Sawlogs had jammed in the shallow headrace, damming the river to an even greater depth. The sound of white water filtered faintly up, softened by distance, hardened by echo.

Now, as the boys watched, an eagle sailed by below them, the white primaries at its wingtips flared like fingers. Circling, it soared on an updraft and rose by them, yellow-eyed, at arm's length. When it detected the boys, it flared away with a startled squawk.

With horror, Mitch divined his brother's intention. "Unh-unh, Lee! No way!"

Lee opened his mouth to argue when bullets smoked off the cliff-face behind them; rock splinters filled the air. The brothers flattened. Sweat ran off Lee in rivulets, and all the blood had run out of Mitchell's puffy face. His eyes were glazed with the enormity of it.

"You ready?"

"I cain't, Lee!"

"We got to, dammit! I'm fresh outta good ideas, Mitchell!"

"No, Lee! We'll give 'em the money in the cave!"

"On three!"

Mitchell shook his head—and Lee grabbed him by the hand.

"One—"

"No, Lee! We'll promise not to tell!"

"Two—"

"Please, Lee! We'll start a rockslide!"

"THREEEEE!!!"

WHEN THE BOYS HADN'T RUN, TONY HAD LOOKED beyond them

and seen the sheer lip. Now he crouched down to reload, smiling sweatily, breathing deeply, savoring a moment he'd long anticipated. (Giordano and Buttafuco wheezed on either side.) Tony thumbed the release, and the big revolver's cylinder fell open. He pushed the plunger, and the spent brasses rang on the granite. His hands shook as he took a handful of cartridges from his jacket pocket and began to fill the cylinder.

"Oh, yes," he told himself, smiling. "Now we got the little—"

"Tony! *Look!*"

As Tony watched with an open mouth, the boys ran across the ledge, holding hands, and went over in a flying leap, the little one screaming at the top of his lungs. Down, down, down, they plummeted, both boys screaming now, arms and legs pinwheeling! Down, down, down, what looked like money streaming up, buoyed by the updrafts, fluttering like upscale confetti!

Tony's mouth was still open, the half-loaded gun still hung limply from his hand, when the boys landed, sending a geyser of green river twenty feet into the air. His mouth closed as he swallowed, gulping.

"Ain't no way! No possible way!"

"Jesus Christ!" Giordano said. His eyes held the glitter of a psychopath at a car wreck. "Could you do that? I couldn't do that. Could you?"

"Able to leave tall buildings in a single bound," Buttafuco said, belching sweetly. Clearly, he was glad it was over.

UNDERWATER, THE BOYS STREAKED DOWNWARD in a column of boiling bubbles. Lee hit the scoured river-bottom with enough force to buckle his knees. The force of the landing had torn Mitch from his grasp, and far beneath the surface, he rotated, searching for his brother. He saw him then in among a tangled, green-slimed rick of waterlogged timbers. Swimming with the current, Lee reached him in two kicks, and gripping his suspenders, started for the surface.

SMILING, TONY POCKETED HIS GUN, took out the flask and—
"Tony! *Look!*"
Again, Tony's mouth dropped open.

WHEN THE BROTHERS SURFACED, GUNFIRE BEGAN from high atop The Wall. The angle of fire was nearly vertical now, and the bullets *whocked* into the water, making craters the size of coffee cans. The air was filled with stinging spray. Mitch was groaning, holding his ankle, as again, the boys dove, and underwater, looking up, they saw bullets crater the surface and *whiz* toward them in short white lines. Mushroomed, the spent leads sank past them toward the river bottom.

Surfacing at the tail of the pool, Lee saw another of the sawlogs adrift in the current. He pointed, and quickly the brothers swam to it. Straining, kicking their feet, they forced the log out into the current, trying to keep the log between them and the gunfire as they crossed to the opposite bank. Bullets *whocked* into the water; *thudded* into the log, bark and splinters flying, forcing them down again.

They were halfway across, halfway to the sycamores standing tall on the far shore, when out in the whitening current of midstream, the river grabbed the log. Seconds later, the green-glass headrace bent and, before they could react, boys and log were swept into the thundering white water of The Narrows.

Astride the log, the brothers went through The Narrows like two cowboys on a bucking bronco. Left hands gripping limb stubs, right arms waving free, they rode the lunging log down the rapids, veering right, veering left; now airborne, now submarine; the thunder of white water in their ears. The river shuddered from the force of falling water, and driven spray stung their faces.

The Narrows ended in a long cataract, half-rapids, half-waterfall, that shot downriver like spray from a hose. Now the brothers reached the chute, and the waterfall launched boys and log in a long parabolic arc downriver—the boys' screaming high-pitched as girls'—Mitchell's eyes shut tight—Lee's eyes open wide in terror.

Their screams ended as they disappeared beneath the frothing white water.

AS TONY WATCHED FROM HIGH ABOVE, THE LOG SURFACED, splintered white. This time, he sighed as he put away his gun and turned toward—

"Tony! *Look!*"

LEE SURFACED FIRST, GASPING, COUGHING UP WATER, and looked fearfully around for his brother. When he saw Mitchell's sleek seal-head break the surface downstream, coughing the seal-bark of swallowed water, he broke into a victory cry. He swam over to him then, and treading water in the wide inland lake of the tailrace pool, they gave each other a high five.

"Aw-right!" Lee screamed to be heard. "We done it, Mitchell! We made it!" Now he saw his brother's face. "You okay?"

"I don't know, Lee." Mitch gritted his teeth. "My ankle hurts awful bad."

Now bullets *buzzed* into the water around them; glanced off, *ringing,* smoking on the granite wall; streaking it with soft-nosed lead. The boys began to kick toward shore when Lee saw the log. He pointed to it, and the boys changed directions. Kicking hard, they reached it in a dozen strokes.

Straining, they swung the big log against the current, across the current to make a shield. Still, the gunfire continued. Bullets *ripped* into the log with bursts of bark and sap. The brothers ducked behind it. Quickly, the current took them out of range.

Safely downstream, the boys looked back and saw the men high above them, three silhouettes now; refracted stick-figures pasted against the cobalt sky. Squinting against the brightness, Lee smiled and waved to Tony and gave him the finger. Watching his big brother, Mitch shot them a bird. They whooped and slapped hands over the log. Now, struggling astride the log to free his hands, Lee fired double-barrel birds at the men, and Mitch broke up with crazy laughter.

"DAMMIT!" FROM HIS VANTAGE HIGH ATOP THE WALL, high above the river, Tony watched the boys' escape; watched their bobbing heads as they rode the log out of sight down the glittering white water. "Dammit to *hell!*"

Now the boys disappeared around the sheer-walled riverbend, wet heads glistening, arms raised above their heads.

Tony stood a little in front of the others, and they didn't see the look of admiration on his face. Smiling, he sighed and shook his head ruefully, then snapped the brothers a smart salute.

Now he took a cellphone from his pack and punched an autodialer button.

"Geno! Yo! You there?" He turned up the volume on the staticky voice that answered. "Yeh, they got by us, Geno. Sorry 'bout that. They headed your way."

38

FAR DOWNRIVER, AT THE BASE OF THE INTERSTATE BRIDGE, a silver-haired man of fifty leaned against the concrete with a cellphone to his ear. Behind him, twenty men lounged around the immense, graffiti-marked foundations. There was a festive air to the whole enterprise. As with their brethren two days before, they looked as though they were dressed for a corporate golf outing, and their shotguns and rifles leaned against the concrete like golf bags at a bag-drop.

But though golfwear did seem the fashion of the day, Geno wore foil warm-ups and jogging shoes with inch-thick, waffle soles. Mirror sunglasses reflected the white water below, distorted as through a fisheye lens. His jacket was partially unzipped, revealing silver chest hair and ten feet of gold chain. (A crucifix hung from one of them.) A big revolver was holstered on one hip, low-slung Western-style.

There was fatigue now in Geno's suntanned face. It was a seven-hour drive from Atlanta, the last three over switchback county roads. This was not how Geno spent his weekends, and he was not a happy camper.

Behind him, a boom-box played rock 'n' roll—Michael Jagger couldn't get no satisfaction—and the music echoed off the underside of the concrete, drowning out the sound of white water below. Now one man broke out a thermos and flask, and the others importuned him to pass it around.

"Yo, Battaglia," Demarco said. "Come on, man, be a pal. Didn't yo' mama teach you to share?"

"Yeh, Battaglia," Luciano told him. "Don't be selfish."

"I never took you to raise," Battaglia told them, before handing over the silver thermos and leather flask. "Do I look like your mother?"

"Hell no, man!" Demarco said. "My mama got a better 'stache than that raggledy-ass thing on yo' harelip."

Demarco and Luciano howled at this and high-fived each other over Battaglia's head.

"Roger, Tony," Geno said, stepping away from the others with a finger in his ear. "I copy—Hey, yous guys, I'm talking here! Shut up!—We're headed your way. How many are there?"

"Two."

"Two?" Geno stared hard upriver, his eyes in the glasses cold and insectine. "What kind of firepower?"

"They unarmed, Geno."

"Unarmed?" Geno looked at the army he had raised. He would never hear the end of this. "What size are they?"

BACK ON THE CLIFF ABOVE THE NARROWS, Tony was looking more than a little chagrinned, more than a little sheepish. There was definite fear in his face as he told Geno, "They a couple kids, Geno."

"You're screwing with me, right?"

Tony gulped. "Negatory."

"My aching back! *Two kids?*"

"They ain't 'xactly your average kids, Geno. You'll see."

Tony's face was fearful as Geno told him, "'Ain't your average kids, Geno.' We'll talk about this later, Tony. You hear me? Atlanta'll hear about this. If you can't handle a simple little thing … I'll find somebody who can!"

Abruptly, Geno hung up.

Tony handed the phone to Buttafuco and took the flask from his hip pocket. As he regarded the empty river, he mumbled something to himself, inaudible to his exhausted companions.

"What's that, Tony?" Buttafuco said.

"Vietnam."

Behind him, the men exchanged a look of confusion. "Huh?"

Head back, Tony finished the contents in one swallow, and with an animal cry of rage, of impotent fury, he completed the motion by throwing the flask off the ledge, far downriver, in the direction of the vanished boys.

Flashing end over end, the flask landed with an innocuous splash and started downriver as though in pursuit. Slowly, it filled with water and sank, wobbling, flashing toward the riverbed like a fisherman's silver spoon.

39

LATE IN THE DAY, A MILE DOWNRIVER, THE BOYS HEARD the sound of white water, faint at first but growing steadily. Lee rode the front of the log, and as they barged around a riverbend, current quickening, the sound grew to a sudden roar.

Fifty yards downstream, he saw the green river go glassy as it bent over the waterfall. Beyond the lip, spray steamed into the sunlight. Summer-sere on both banks up to now, beyond the falls, the weeping foliage was sleek and hothouse lush with mist.

The boys abandoned the log then and swam to shore. Exhausted, shivering, their lips blue, they crawled on water-pruned hands and knees through the shallows and onto the sandbar. There, they collapsed and lay on their backs, absorbing the warmth of the sand. Slowly, their shivering subsided.

At length they stood—but the first time Mitch put weight on his ankle, he collapsed with a scream of pain. Gripping his knee, he lay back on the sand, grimacing, moaning, while Lee knelt to examine the swollen and discolored little foot.

"I reckon the water helped the swelling some. Can you walk on it, Mitch? Best not to let her stiffen up. Nothing ain't broke—looks like—jist real bad sprained."

Mitch nodded, and Lee helped him to his feet. Tentatively, Mitch placed his weight on the ankle and groaned, gritting his teeth. He limped in a small circle, testing the leg, and it seemed to bear his weight. Trying to smile, trying to maintain the euphoria of their escape, he looked doubtfully at Lee.

Lee supported him as they climbed through the log-scarred sycamores and started along the riverbank footpath. Mitch hopped on one leg, his arm draped over Lee's shoulder. At the first curve, they stopped and looked back. Here, river and trail were straight as a runway, and the virgin forest had shaded out the understory. They could see three-hundred yards down their backtrail. The path was clear. Lee grinned at his brother. In spite of the ankle, their spirits were high.

"We done it, Mitchell! Dammit, we *done* it!" Lee extended his hand. "Gimme five, baby bro! High five! On the side! Skin it!"

Again, the brothers shouted and slapped hands. Laughing, whooping it up, they limped on down the trail. Hand in hand, the brothers soon vanished in the perpetual twilight of the towering evergreens. In their ragged clothes and bare feet, they looked like little boys lost in an enchanted forest.

TWO MILES BELOW THE NARROWS, GREEN RIVER took another breather as it slowed and widened into a lakelike expanse of green water that ran back into a canyon of towering riverbank spruce. There, a ramshackle hunter's cabin with deer antlers and a sign over the door—TARLETON'S DEER CAMP—sat on a bluff overlooking the river. As though misunderstanding, a family of whitetails, two does and four spotted fawns, stood in the shallows, eating wild watercress, waiting to check in.

A red canoe with a broken keel lay half-submerged on the sandy beach. It was chained to a spruce, and the violence of the flumewater had worn the rusty chain halfway through the trunk. Sap ran from the wound in amber ropes.

There was a sawbuck and woodpile in the backyard, and a picnic table and red gas can on the front porch. The bank across the river held a sheet of splintered plywood where city hunters sat on the porch, guns braced on the sapling rail, and sighted in their rifles. It was the only shooting many of them did, for deer camp held other, wifeless pleasures.

IT WAS NEARLY DARK, THE SUN DOWN behind the purple mountains, when the boys came upon the log cabin at the end of the footpath. For nearly a mile, they'd seen litter along the trail and had taken heart from sign—any sign—of Civilization. Now they stood at the clearing's edge, behind a screen of limbs, and checked out the cabin. Their eyes took in the woodpile ... the sawbuck ... the sunken canoe. Below the bluff, near the river, there was a second canoe wedged high in the crotch of a tree.

Mitch looked at the canoe and gulped. At least on The Wall they had been safe from the water—so safe they'd nearly died of thirst. He felt vulnerable now down on the river. Nervously, he looked over his shoulder. Behind Lee's back, he glanced at his watch. With the white mitts showing ten after seven, Mickey looked like he was trying to fly.

Mitch looked up the riverbank. There was a big spruce on the flank of the mountain, and he noted with satisfaction the tightly spaced limbs. Like Jack's beanstalk, it soared out of sight above him.

"Who lives here, Lee?" he whispered.

"Don't nobody—'cept in season. It's Old Man Tarleton's deer camp."

"Lee?"

"Hm?"

"You reckon they's any food?"

Cautiously, using the cover of the big spruce, the boys approached the cabin. Near the woodpile, Lee saw a rusty camp-axe sticking in the chopping block and took it as they passed. Up on the low porch, he smashed the padlock with a single stroke, and the brothers stepped in.

They stood in the door, looking warily around the dark room. It was a basic hunter's cabin. Potbellied stove for a centerpiece. (A blackened percolator sat atop it.) Bunk-beds along the walls. A glass-fronted gun cabinet of knotty pine. A *Playboy* calendar from last year with darts sticking in Miss November's pubic hair. There was a knocked-together table with jar-lid ashtrays, stacks of red and blue poker chips, and decks of cards. Some were still in their blue Bicycle boxes; others fanned out on the rough-cut planking.

Oddments of clothing—mostly red or yellow or camouflage—hung from dowel gun racks and deer antlers along the log walls. Copies of *Field & Stream*, *Outdoor Life* and *Playboy* lay on table and bunks and chairs. One section of wall was covered with fading Polaroids of successful hunters. In the night pictures taken with a flash, the hunters' eyes were red, the deer's green.

In the kitchen, a yellow drain-rack supported blue ironware

169

pots and dishes. Looking toward the kitchen, Mitch saw the cabinets over the stove and made a beeline for them. On tiptoes, he threw open the pantry and his face broke into a radiant smile. The cupboard was filled with canned goods, row upon row, stacked nearly to the ceiling. But Mitchell's smile quickly faded as he saw that the larder was stocked with cooked carrots, broccoli, English peas and spinach. He gulped queasily.

Now, from across the room, Lee let out a whoop, and Mitch whirled, startled. With a stick of firewood from the woodbox beside the stove, Lee smashed the glass front of the gun cabinet, reached past the spearheads of glass and took out a rifle, a bolt-action 22.

With trembling hands, he worked the silken action, and the smell of gun oil filled the room. Now he threw up the rifle and took aim out the window, then drew a bead on Miss November.

He leaned the gun against a chair and began to rummage wildly through the cabinet drawers, pitching aside oily rags and hunting gloves, whetstones, sheath knives and cleaning rods, until with a yell, smiling wide, he came up with a box of ammunition. He shook the yellow-and-green box and it rattled.

"Yes! *Hell,* yes! We in business, baby bro!"

Immediately, Lee began loading the gun.

40

A GREAT FIRE ROARED IN THE POTBELLIED STOVE with a strength that rattled the rusty stove lids. From the open damper grating, a flickering red light set the rough-hewn room atremble. A dozen jagged, knife-opened cans sat empty on the floor around the boys. Other cans simmered on top of the red-hot stove. The brothers sat in their underpants on the floor before the open grate, eating from steaming cans, the labels scorched, they held with leather-fingered shooter's gloves.

Their damp clothes, over chairbacks before the fire, still steamed slightly, and as they dried, sand from the clothes had collected on the floor beneath them. Lee had the rifle leaning against a chair within easy reach, and the open box of ammunition—the little brass cartridges gleaming redly in the firelight—was on the seat of the chair. The bandage was off his head—lost in the leap—and his wound was healing nicely. Mitchell's mileage—his swollen ankle; his scaling, scabby arms and legs and face—was much more visible.

Otherwise, full bellies and their narrow escape had worked wonders on them. The tension was gone from their faces; the pinched look from around their eyes. Even the river had conspired in the transformation, washing three days' road dust from their faces. But basic hunger satisfied, their distaste for cooked carrots was reasserting itself, and they picked at the cans halfheartedly, taking smaller and smaller bites that they somehow chewed longer and longer.

From beyond the closed windows came the shrill chirrup of cicadas, rainpeepers and crickets, piercing, pulsating, like rotary machinery with the bearings going bad. Somewhere back of the cabin, a whippoorwill warbled, and down on the river a bullfrog sang bass. On the mountain across the river, a fox yipped coyote-like, then tailed it off in a mournful, lupine howl.

Lee put down his can of English peas and burped, and monkey-see-monkey-do, Mitch put aside his broccoli and brought up an imitative croak of his own. He sat back and sighed happily.

"You reckon they still after us?"

Burp. "Nah."

Croak. "Me neither."

Lee smiled as he remembered. "Ain't but one way through The Narrows and we took it!" He whooped. "Oh, man, that was something else, wudn't it? What a ride! Won't nobody believe us!" He held out his hand. "Gimme five, baby bro!"

The brothers shouted and slapped hands. Mitch smiled and took another ginger sip of the steaming coffee. Lee stood and yawned and collapsed backward on a bunk behind the stove. There, he extracted the wrinkled picture of Jennifer from his wallet and studied it in the firelight.

"Lee, how much further to the bridge, you reckon?"

"Dunno for sure, Mitch. Two miles maybe. Maybe a tad more. She's real rough going though. We still gotta climb a mile out The Gorge. Get an early start, I reckon we oughta hit the bridge by noon. Hard part's behind us."

"God, will I be glad to get home!"

"That makes two of us."

"I'm gone eat till my guts hurt."

"You jist did."

"I know. Hey, Lee?"

"Hm?"

"Broccoli ain't half-bad," Mitch told him with amazement. "It ain't a cheeseburger, of course, but it ain't half-bad neither."

Lee pointed to Mitchell's board-stiff overalls. "Them overhauls ain't half-bad neither—if'n you're hungry enough— and got some ketchup."

Mitch laughed. "I know one thing—I'll never carry on 'bout mama's cooking again. Swear to God! I'll even eat eggs. And liver. And English peas."

Lee smiled fondly at his little brother. "Well, that's worth something, I reckon."

The boys grew silent. Mitch hugged his knees, staring into the flames.

At length, he said dreamily—speaking as much to himself as to his brother—"Waffles … with loads of butter and sourwood honey … and bacon—no, sausage—no, country ham!"

"Would you please shut up?" Lee told him, laughing.

Mitch smiled and sank back into his food fantasy.

After a time, Lee said wistfully, "A cheeseburger, all the way … and fries … and onion rings … and a gigantic cherry Coke."

"Nah, a chocolate milkshake."

"There you go!"

"Baked chicken and dressing … with cranberry sauce … and stuffed celery … and giblet gravy … and yeast rolls … and peach cobbler … and …"

On his bunk, Lee just sighed and rolled over to face the wall. He pulled the moth-eaten Army blanket tighter around his shoulders.

OUTSIDE, THE FOREST PULSED WITH THE SOUNDS of a summer's night. Rainfrogs, bullfrogs, crickets and cicadas sent up a chorus of peeps, croaks, grunts and chirps. The backwater river roared softly between its wide, sandy banks. The night wind sighed through the great spruce and fir, and their massive trunks creaked and groaned as they bent and twisted. On the mountain behind the cabin, an owl hooted, and across the river, the fox barked, high-pitched and piping, at a full moon rising above the mountain, its orange face snared in a net of limbs. The bark crossed the water with echo-clarity. From the river, a bullfrog added a baseline to the shrill chorus, and downstream, the rapids were softly audible between gusts of the wind.

On the riverbank, a black snake spiralled slowly up a small fir toward a nest of robin fledglings in the treetop. The adult birds flew in excited circles, squawking, dive-bombing the snake … as now it reached the nest and began to feed.

A mink slithered snake-like along the riverbank, in and out of the culvert creeks, sniffing out the burrows in the undercut rootage. At the eroded base of a great sycamore, its root-system a congeries of caves, it came upon a muskrats' burrow and slunk silently in. Shortly, there came the squeals of its terrified occupants.

Below the cabin, the family of deer had returned to feed in the watercress shallows. They stood withers-deep, tails twitching, ears moving, tearing the pale, peppery stalks from the river bottom. Slowly, one of the fawns fed upstream beneath the overarching boughs of a streamside spruce.

Now, as it dipped its head to feed, a bobcat leaped from the tree onto its back, and the other deer scattered in a confusion of splashing, whitetailed leaps. The little deer bleated pitifully as the cat dragged it by its nape out of the river and onto the riverbank.

There, it bit through the neck, and the fawn's cries and exertions ceased. For a moment, the cat groomed the carcass like one of its own kits; then, with a yellow-eyed look up the river and down, it bit through the tiny paunch and began to feed.

41

A QUARTER-MILE ABOVE THE INTERSTATE BRIDGE, barely a mile below Tarleton's old cabin, the river took its lead from the gentling topography and returned fitfully to its nominal green. A sagging cable footbridge crossed the river there, spanning a final stretch of halfhearted rapids; a footbridge known thereabouts with the functional simplicity of mountaineers as The Cables. There, two heavy steel ropes strung five feet apart, one for the feet, an upper one for the hands, were anchored on either bank by great spruce trees. The metal had cut deeply into the trunks, raising bulbous welts where the bark had overgrown the stainless steel.

On one shore, the downstream access, the footpath widened and took on the dimensions of the logging road it once was. Bulldozer tracks and the deep wheel-ruts of logging trucks were still visible in the mossed-over roadbed. Rusty motor oil cans, sardine tins and soft drink bottles with obsolete trademarks littered the roadsides. It was the terminus in the old days of mechanized travel, and the last attempt before the Interstate to span the river. Since construction of the dam, no bridge could withstand the sawlogs and flumewater.

JUST AFTER DARK THAT NIGHT, JUST DOWNSTREAM of the footbridge, Geno's army came stumbling along the old road. The mountain had been logged off on that side of the river, and the moon was patchy in the cut-over. The barrels of their rifles and shotguns gleamed, and here and there along the shuffling defile, there was the spark of eyeglass and wrist watch. Star-bright, the beacon on the Interstate bridge winked through the windy treetops. It was high in the sky now.

Below them, as they passed, the river moved beneath the moon with a ponderous beauty. Swaying between grass-tussocked banks. Lapping at midstream boulders silvery with spray. Sighing like a soft summer wind.

But as they walked, by talking twos and threes, their bobbing cigarettes like drunken fireflies in the thickening second-growth, the river's volume slowly increased, until finally, in the darkness beneath the great, anchoring spruce, they arrived at The Cables.

Battaglia gulped. "What the hell...?"

"Oh, man!" said Demarco. "*This* wudn't in the brochure."

"I hear that!" Luciano said. "I got enough of this weirdness at Parris Island."

There was a landing where the road ended, wide enough in the old days to U-turn a timber truck, and there the men stood, breathing hard, staring across the river down cables silver with dew. Spray smoked into the moonlight, wind-swirled as it topped the gorge.

Inching closer, they checked out the white water fifty feet below. The rapids looked glacial, and beyond the lip, they thundered up, amplified by the facing cliffs. Though tame by comparison with what lay upstream, it was the river's first white water, and the men were impressed. They drew back in lockstep, gripping each other by the clothes. Luciano had Battaglia's sleeve in a death grip.

"Yo, Geno, what say we make camp—for a week. Chopper in the T-bones."

"Get moving, Luciano."

"I don't know, Geno. What's my motivation?" As Luciano talked, the tip of his cigarette bobbed, streaking the darkness. "I need to feel good about this. My shrink's concerned with my poor self-esteem."

"I'm going to yawn now," Demarco said.

"Hey, you go first, Geno," Battaglia told him.

Demarco lowered his beer and let go a thundering belch. "Yeh, Geno, show us the way."

"Yeh," said Battaglia. "You the leader, Geno, we the mindless followers."

"Hey -- speak for yourself, Nicko."

"Then who'd speak for you?"

Geno cursed and stepped out on the swaying base cable, weaving from the waist. The men snickered as he slipped and lost his footing. Hanging from the hand-cable, legs bicycling, he looked like a high-wire artist who had lost his ride. Now he regained the cable and began to cross with a slow step-and-slide, knapsack banging, rubber soles squeaking. Out from under the spruce, the moonlight fell full upon him, a Space Invader in his foil jumpsuit.

When Geno was over the river, Demarco tossed away his cigarette, streaking like a meteor into the gorge, and stepped up onto the cable. He slung his pumpgun to free his hands, crossed himself and started across. He kept his eyes fixed on Geno.

FIVE MINUTES LATER, BITCHING AND MOANING, the whole queue was strung out on the swaying, seesawing base cable. Silhouetted against the moon, they looked like dancing marionettes strung from a wire. At the end of the line, laughing Luciano urinated a glittering, quicksilver stream fifty feet to the river below.

"Man, this water's cold," he told them. "And *deep* too!"

This was greeted by the others with howls of derision.

42

Mitch was tidying up the cabin. He collected the empty cans, limped to the front door and flung them into the yard. (The bears, he knew, would smell them in the garbage and gnaw their way in.) Beside the pantry, he found a broom and began to sweep. The broom was so old, the yellow straw was worn nearly to its red threadwork.

Lee lay on the bunk, hands behind his head, and watched his little brother with amusement and affection. Jennifer, momentarily forgotten, lay smiling on his chest.

"Mitchell? What the hell you doing?"

"Thought I'd pick up a little. Didn't wanna leave no mess behind."

Mitch limped to the stove. Ashes had fallen from the open grate, and he swept them onto the roofing tin beneath it. He stood at the red-bellied stove, leaning on the broom.

"You want this last cup of coffee? I'm gone wash the pot. For in the morning."

"Nah, you can take it."

"I'm done. Won't sleep none as it is."

"Okay, thanks."

By its jagged top, Mitch lifted a can off the stove. "They's a little bit more of this broccoli," he told Lee with a wince. "And carrots too. And peas."

"Nah, that's okay. Had enough." Lee laughed. "Had more'n enough."

"You and me both."

Mitch leaned heavily on the broom as he crossed the room to rinse his brother's cup, and Lee watched his deep and painful limp. Mitch gritted his teeth each time his weight came down on the ankle. Lee watched his little brother limp awkwardly along. He looked like a little old man with arthritis. In only his underpants, the full extent of his injuries was visible. His arms, legs and face were scaling, scabby, red-welted masses from the bee stings and poison ivy. There were nicks and cuts—stone abrasions on his chest, chin and back; split knees and elbows—all over his little body. The ankle was hugely swollen now, and ankle and foot were purple as a plum.

Back at the stove, Mitch picked up the coffee pot and turned to Lee, and Lee saw his face, swollen and lopsided from bee stings. In spite of it all, Mitch grinned, and with the hand that held the white enamelled mug, he gave Lee a thumbs-up.

And now remorse and guilt hit Lee like a body-blow! Without warning, his eyes filled up, his face crumpled, and he began to sob. Bitter tears poured down his anguished face. With a cry, he flung Jennifer's picture from him.

Mitch looked on in horror, coffee pot poised over the cup. Now, setting them on the stove-top, he came quickly to his brother's side. He kneeled at the bed and placed a hand on Lee's trembling shoulder.

"Lee? Lee, what is it? What's wrong? What?"

"Mitch!" Lee sobbed. "Mitch! I'm real sorry what I done to you! *Real* sorry!"

Mitchell shook his head in bewilderment. "What, Lee? You never done nothing."

"Yeh, I did! Yeh, I *did!* I'm sorry, Mitch! I'm real sorry what I got you into! I don't *think!* I never *think!*"

Mitch patted his brother's back, comforting him, and his sobbing slowly subsided. Tears tracked his flushed face.

"It's okay, Lee, I'm okay. Look—my ankle's all better now. You was right—the water helped the swelling."

And Mitch extended his stubby leg and rotated his foot, showing Lee his complete recovery. But at the sight of the swollen and discolored little ankle, Lee's sobs began anew, redoubled.

"No, it ain't! No, it ain't! It *ain't!*"

"It's okay, Lee. We be home soon. Ever'thing'll work out. Like you said—hard part's behind us now."

But shaking his head, biting his lip, Lee sobbed on and on, inconsolable; deep, soulful sobs that wracked his body with shudders.

Now, inhaling sharply, wiping his nose with the back of his hand, he told his brother, "I'm jist no good! Daddy's right! I'm

179

jist mean and no-account! Always me, me, me!"

Mitch patted his back. "Shh!" he crooned. "No, you ain't, Lee. You ain't. You jist rest easy. I'm gone get you that coffee now, okay? You'll feel a whole lots better in the morning."

Lee sniffled and nodded. Looking down, Mitch saw Jennifer on the floor at his feet, still smiling.

AN HOUR LATER, THE BOYS WERE GETTING READY FOR BED. Lee lay on the bunk, his face red and swollen from crying, tear-tracks shining in the firelight, and Mitch covered him with the blanket. Smiling, he picked up Jenny's picture and put it back in the wallet, then placed the wallet on the chairseat beside the ammunition.

The river-chill was off the boys now, and the heat of the stove had gotten intense. Before turning in, Mitch limped to the window and opened it. The night-sounds increased as though he had turned up the volume. Down on the river, a second bullfrog, smaller, his groan higher pitched, had joined the chorus, and the two frogs dueled on with a sound like a heartbeat.

As he swung the window wide, Mitchell looked up through the trees and smiled at the star-bright sky; then looked down through the spruce at the river. The moon was high in the sky now, and through the windy trees, the infall at the pool's headrace glittered.

Mitch sighed happily. They would be home soon. Tomorrow night, he would be sleeping in his own bed, feeling it shiver as Suellen got at a rambunctious flea. Though he missed his mother sorely, it was his hounds he could hardly wait to see.

43

GENO STOPPED AND STEPPED OFF THE TRAIL, counting the men as they passed him in the darkness. They were in single-file now as the path curved through the trees. Geno had a Forest Service map—one that showed the new access trail—and an hour before, after consulting it, he had made them put out their cigarettes and flashlights. In the blackness beneath the spruce, the men stumbled, following each other closely as circus elephants, a hand gripping the shirttail of the fellow ahead. Disturbed by their clumsy passage, the rank must of rain-wet humus filled the night, an alien smell to these men of the city.

A quarter-mile above The Cables, the new footpath had left the river and gone steeply over the mountain to circumvent Green River Gorge. (The men weren't aware of what happened to the river there.) Then, following the fishermen who made it, the path came back to the river and paralleled it pool by pool into a canyon of towering, riverbank spruce.

The river was off to the left now, through the trees, and where it curved into the moonlight, it had widened into a lakelike body of water. Out over the river, the moon was bright as day, and Geno could see the glittering headrace and above it, the great spruce silvering in a breath of night wind. For the first time since the path had left the river, he heard upstream and down, the sound of white water.

Now, squinting, Geno saw what looked like a sign on the opposite bank. Closer, he saw that it was a target, the backstop bullet-splintered. Now the wind shifted, and he smelled woodsmoke. Quickly, he stepped back into the column of stumbling men, hands on their shoulders to pass them in the night.

It was then that one of the men, Demarco, stopped and whispered to the others, "Hey, yous guys, wait up! Gotta take a leak! 'Bout to frigging bust. Yo! Battaglia! Wait up, man!"

But driven by Geno, they ignored him and continued up the dark footpath. Stepping off the trail, Demarco looked after them, cursing.

"Wait'll you gotta pee, man. I hope you frigging *explode,* man!"

Hurriedly, he unzipped and started to urinate, his heavy stream spattering the forest floor, sparking in the moonlight. There was a blissful sigh as, back bowed, he leaned into the task at hand.

IN THE UPPER BUNK, MITCH SNORED SOFTLY, lips fluttering on the exhale. Below, Lee whimpered in his sleep and tossed in the grip of a nightmare. Crying out, he struggled against ropes of twisted bedding.

With the damper closed, a flickering red light leaked from the stove lids, and Dali-esque chairs and table and coffee pot trembled on the beamed ceiling. The deer antlers threw massive, Boone & Crockett racks on the firelit walls, and the deer head over the door glared at the sleeping boys with red catchlights in his glassy eyes.

Suddenly, the rainfrogs, crickets and cicadas ceased on a single chirp. Only the bullfrogs, down on the river, kept up their booming heartbeat. Now it died; bass first, then baritone. A seamless silence followed.

Moments later, Mitch stirred in his sleep and opened his wide brown eyes. He lay completely still for a long moment, blinking, listening. The pulsing creak of a single cicada rose for a dozen notes ... then died. Kicking free of the covers, he rolled to the edge of the bunk.

"Lee!" he whispered down. "Lee!"

"Shh! I hear it."

The boys lay still, listening. In the deep silence, they heard only the night wind in the big spruce. The limbs creaked and groaned, whitening in the moonlight beyond the open windows, tapping politely at windows and walls as though requesting admission. Now the roar of the river was momentarily lost in another rush of wind, and Mitch shuddered at the memory of the flood.

Quickly, Lee rolled out of bed. From the chair before the stove, he began to pull on his clothes. In one motion, Mitch jumped down and stepped into his overalls. The fire-hot buttons and rivets burned his legs and back, but he hardly noticed.

OUTSIDE, IN THE DIM PENUMBRA OF THE CLEARING, where the moon broke in silver patches through the windy spruce, Geno and company stood beneath the trees staring at the dark cabin. Against the moonlit sky, they saw smoke issuing from the stove pipe. The moon's grinning, gray-eyed face wobbled in the heat waves above the chimney cap.

Geno smiled a malignant smile. "Oh, yes indeed," he said. "*Now* we've got the little creeps."

ASHES HAD SIFTED DOWN AT THE BASE OF THE STOVE, and kneeling at the open grate, the boys smeared their faces with soot. Standing, Lee looked at Mitchell's ragged teeshirt. After a day in the river, it was white again. He saw the shirts hanging from the antlers and unhooked two of the darker ones. He threw one, a red-and-black wool check, to his brother and put the other one, a turkey hunter's camouflage chamois, on over his suspenders.

As Mitch buttoned the shirt—and it hung to his knees—he whispered, "How'd they get down here so fast?"

"It ain't them. I reckon they got telephones."

Dressed, Lee dumped the box of ammunition into his pants pocket. Shirt buttoned, Mitch found a knapsack hanging from a gun rack and dropped in several cans of food. The short-handled camp-axe was leaning against the woodbox, and Mitch put it in the pack. The warped handle stuck out around the flap.

Now Lee picked up the rifle and slowly swung the back window wide. It creaked softly and thudded against the outside wall. The sound of white water was suddenly louder. Lee boosted Mitch up, and he squeezed through, grimacing at the touch of rough wood on his chest. Now Lee handed out the rifle and pack, and followed him, dropping with a thud to the ground outside.

44

SLOWLY, THEY SCANNED THE DARK WOODS. Only their eyes moved; only their eyewhites were visible in their soot-blackened faces. In the perfect blackness beneath the trees, the boys could see only a few feet in any direction. For the first time, Mitch noticed the heat from his overalls. The crouch had brought the metal parts in contact with his back, and it was on fire in a dozen places. The smell of woodsmoke somehow made it worse.

Lee looked down through the trees at the glittering river. The way was clear. At a crouch, the brothers started across the clearing, heading toward the riverbank footpath.

They were halfway across when they heard a twig snap behind them. The boys froze in the shadow of the sawbuck. As one, their eyes slid left. A man was coming toward them, rifle at port-arms. The boys crouched by the sawbuck, caught out in the open.

But in the blackness beneath the trees, the man walked by, an arm's length distant. His corduroy pants trilled, and they could hear his pocket change and smell his aftershave. The Walkman on his belt was on, and they saw the lighted dial and the red "on" dot. With the indelible clarity that comes of perfect fear, Mitch noted that it was tuned to his favorite country station.

Now, with the man safely past, the boys slunk out of the clearing and made for the treeline. Behind them, they heard the crash of the forced door.

"Geno, they ain't here!"

"Dammit, spread out! Find 'em! They can't have gone far!"

In the trees now, they picked up their pace.

A hundred feet farther on, they intersected the riverbank trail and started quickly down it. The footpath was sandy from flooding and swept clean of leaves; the curves were washes of ankle-deep sand that still held the day's warmth. Moonstruck, it glimmered in the black forest, and their bare feet moved soundlessly as they followed it. Below, the moonlit river glittered, silhouetting the dark trees.

A FIFTY YARDS DOWN THE DARK FOOTPATH, Demarco had completed his urgent business and came up the trail, zipping his pants. He stumbled along, humming, his shotgun under one arm, his other arm up to catch the limbs. He was still pissed off at being abandoned, but, as he noted with a wry smile, it was better to be pissed off than pissed on. He had just witnessed the palpable truth of that truism.

THE BOYS FOLLOWED THE PATH AS NOW IT APPROACHED the river, slowly turning up the volume on the white water. Another fifty yards, and they saw its gun-metal sheen through the windy understory. Lee was in the lead, and Mitch followed closely, gripping the tail of his brother's too-large shirt.

Bracketed by the treetops, they could see the Interstate bridge. From this low angle, the bridge's five parabolas were darkly silhouetted against the moonlit sky. Above the waving treetops, the warning light blinked like a dying star. It was much nearer now, much larger, and as the boys moved down the footpath, they gazed at the red light hopefully.

DEMARCO WAS BETWEEN VERSES OF HIS SONG, listening for sound of his fellows, when he heard the soft footfalls beneath the trees. He stopped and stood, frowning, squinting into the darkness. Now, as the moon broke through the windy canopy, he glimpsed movement, and two figures passed through a patch of moonlight. He walked toward them, gun up.

"Geno? Battaglia? That you, man?"

Slowly, the boys sank to their knees. Fearfully, they watched the man's approach. Another fifty feet and he would stumble over them. There was a circle of moonlight that struck the trail midway between them. Hands shaking, Lee raised the rifle, took a bead on the man and just when the moon spotlit the moustached face, he pulled the trigger.

The rifle misfired with a sickening *snick*.

185

Demarco saw them then. He threw up the shotgun, racked the pump and fired. The charge caught Lee high in the chest and shoulder, blasting him completely off his feet. He spun to the ground in a broken pirouette, crumpled up, groaning, crying out.

"Geno, I got 'em, I got 'em!"

Gun up, Demarco started toward Lee's writhing body.

Mitch watched his approach with terrified eyes. At the last moment, he picked up the rifle and frantically worked the bolt. With the man only yards away, he raised the gun and, eyes shut tight, pulled the trigger.

This time, the rifle fired, and a red star appeared between Demarco's eyes. He raised a hand to his forehead, regarded his bloody fingertips with an expression of utter stupefaction, blinked twice and collapsed backward, stone-dead.

"There they are!"

"I see 'em!"

"Move it! Let's go!"

With their position revealed, gunfire ripped through the trees, limbs and leaves raining, and the boys stumbled headlong, panic-stricken, toward the river. Lee was barely conscious and bleeding freely. With the rifle in his free hand, Mitch supported him as best he could. They staggered heavily, noisily through the woods. Off the trail, the trees grew thickly, and limbs slapped at their faces. They fell again and again, and Lee moaned at each fall.

Mitch looked back toward the sound of the oncoming men, crashing, cursing through the trees. He wrestled Lee to his feet, picked up the rifle and stumbled on toward the roar of white water. Behind them now, he could see the beams of flashlights darting wildly through the treetops. Now the ear-ringing blast of a high-powered rifle toppled a sapling on them.

At the river, Mitch dropped the rifle to free his hands, and the brothers staggered into the river. Out of the trees, the roar of white water was thunder now. Mitch pushed off and began to swim. He had Lee in a cross-chest carry, trying to hold his head above the water. The shock of the cold water stunned him, and he let the current take them, angling toward the far shore. Already, he could feel the shuddering roar of the rapids downstream.

FLASHLIGHTS WAVING, THE MEN ARRIVED AT THE RIVER. They coursed along the mossy bank like hounds on a scent. Almost immediately, Geno found the bloodtrail, the scarlet spatter vivid in the intense beam of his flashlight. He smiled when he found the blood-stained rifle. Lifting it by the barrel, he threw it into the river, and without hesitation, he waded in and began to swim.

The others followed, grumbling, rifles and shotguns above their heads. When they stepped off the shoal into the channel, the water reached to their armpits, and they cursed its icy embrace.

45

THE BROTHERS MADE SHORE WELL DOWNSTREAM of the cabin. Mitch waded toward shore, Lee's uninjured arm draped over his shoulder, stumbling and splashing through the moonlit shallows.

Nearing the bank, he stepped up on what appeared to be a boulder, but it gave way under his weight, and both boys went down with a splash. As he fell onto the rock, Mitchell's arms went out to break his fall—but as he hit, the rock rolled over, and Mitch found himself in an embrace with his dog, Mica, bloated with death, lips pulled back in a snarl, a bullet hole in his side.

Mitchell screamed and burst into tears. "Mica!" he cried, holding the dog in his arms. "Oh, Mica!"

The brown eyes had been leached white by the icy water, and Mitchell's heart broke at the sight of the red collar. Now he looked back across the river.

"Murderers!" he screamed. "Murderers! I'll kill you! I'll kill you!"

Mitch looked back into the dog's cold eyes and *Pet Sematary* crossed his mind. He dropped Mica with a shudder. With his foot, he pushed him out into the current and sat chest-deep, sobbing, watching him float away. Hugely swollen, the dog's ribs showed like barrel staves, and hair had been worn away in patches by the violence of the floodwater. The collar had shrunk and cut deeply into the swollen neck.

Mitch looked away. Bitter tears streamed down his anguished face. Beside him, Lee lay on his back in the shallows, moaning.

"Lee? Lee, can you stand up? Help me, Lee. We gotta go now."

The cold water had revived Lee, and he splashed to his knees with a groan. Mitch kneeled beside him and pulled his arm over his shoulder. Grunting, he stood, and Lee rose slowly, then toppled against Mitch. Though the water had slowed the bleeding, watery blood still dripped off the fingertips of his right hand.

Stumbling, the boys splashed out of the river and onto the sandbar. There, they knelt, gasping for breath. On hands and knees, they climbed to the riverbank trail.

Mitch was still crying as the brothers staggered along the mossy footpath. Tears tracked his sooty face, and an occasional choked sob escaped him. Twice, they fell hard, and Lee cried out. With dwindling energy, Mitch struggled each time to get him to his feet.

Now, looking upstream, Mitch saw the men straggle ashore, their splashings quicksilver in the moonlight. As he watched, they regrouped and sloshed through the shallows, using their guns for staffs. Slipping and sliding, they made the riverbank trail. One of them wore some kind of metal clothing, and he gleamed in the moonlight. As he waved the men ashore, Mitch saw the revolver.

"Let's go, Lee! You gotta help me! You gotta get up!"

With Lee's arm around his neck, gripping Lee by his wrist and waist, Mitch started along the trail. They were near the tail of the pool now, and the river curved left back into the trees and dropped away.

Mitch stopped to take a new purchase on Lee, renewing his grip, and the brothers stumbled on, legs tangling, sending them down again and again in a tangled heap. At each fall, Lee cried out, and his wound bled afresh. The front of the camo-print shirt was scarlet with blood.

At one fall, Lee drove the axe handle sharply against Mitchell's head, and for several minutes afterward, brass gnats swarmed in his vision, and his legs would hardly support him.

When Mitch paused again, gasping for breath, the river was much louder, and looking downstream, he saw the first of the white water leaping into sight. Under the moon, the rapids were so bright they hurt his dark-adapted eyes.

Mitch looked back upstream. The men were much closer now, and he experienced an ammonia wash of fear as he saw their number. The two dozen flashlights were spread out along the river for fifty yards. He watched as the powerful beams spotlit circles of green river, a red shirt, gray-lichened granite, white-blooming laurel, a bearded face beneath a green cap. In silhouette against the lights, the column bristled with rifles and shotguns. Some had slings and telescopic sights. Faintly now, he heard yelling, cursing, and for a moment, his murderous hatred was slaked. Boosting Lee up, he started off again.

TEN MINUTES LATER, THE FOOTPATH ENDED in a granite wall, and looking up, Mitch saw, glimmering in the moonlight, the high granite cliffs of Green River Gorge.

The current had increased as the boys moved along the riverbank, and now a chute of wild white water roared at their feet. Between square banks of fault-line granite, the river looked like molten aluminum in a foundry sluiceway. Moonstruck spray hung above the rapids like smoke. The cliff-faces towered over them on both sides of the river, sheer as skyscrapers in a midtown block. Looking downstream, Mitch saw the river vanish as into a great aqueduct. The line of illumination was just that sharp.

Carefully, he lowered Lee to the sandbar. With his hand, he cupped water from the river and wiped his brother's face. The water revived him, and he came to, groaning, opening his eyes, now squinting with pain.

"Lee? Lee, can you hear me?"

Lee nodded feebly. "Mitch, I'm ... sorry I ..."

"Shh! We at The Gorge, Lee. Listen! We gotta go through. Ain't no other way. They right behind us. You gotta help me all you can, okay? Lee? *Lee!*"

Faintly, Lee managed, "What ...time is...?"

Mitch pushed back the enormous sleeve. In the moonlight, Mickey grinned back at him, oblivious of the danger, his white-mitted hands raised in the semaphore of an idiot cheerleader. Just once that weekend Mitchell had wanted to look at Mickey and find him saucer-eyed with fear; like in the cartoons when he shivered and sweat jumped off of him. In one cartoon, he sweated bullets. Now the hands were superimposed as one, a single arm growing out of his clap-eared head.

"Midnight," he told Lee. "About it."

"Never make ... it with me ... gotta ... leave me ... the

190

woods … go for help …"

"No!"

"Got …to …"

"I ain't gone leave you, Lee! Now get up!"

With surprising strength, Lee gripped him by the sodden front of the red-plaid shirt.

"Got to … Mitch … won't make it … never make … it!" Lee began to cry. "Hurts real bad … real bad …"

"Get up, Lee! You gotta get up! They be coming soon!"

Three rough steps rose to a narrow ledge. Painfully, Mitch got Lee to his feet, and pushing him ahead, the boys climbed up and stepped out onto the ledge. It was only a few feet above the river here, and the algaed granite was slick with spray. The boys were quickly drenched in a fine cold mist.

Lee leaned against the cliff-face, his wound leaving a bloody smear, as the boys stumbled slowly along the ledge. Lee hung on the edge of consciousness, and Mitch was exhausted with the effort of supporting him. The ledge was so narrow they could barely walk abreast.

Resting now, leaning Lee weakly against the wall, pinning him there with his shoulder, Mitch looked upriver at the waving line of lights. He tasted fear again as he saw that the men were closing.

Changing hands, he pushed back the foot of excess sleeve and looked at his watch. His wrist trembled so violently from his spasming muscles, it required his other hand to steady it. Safe behind the starburst crystal, Mickey found ten after twelve hilarious. Mitch shivered as he looked down the cliff-face. Curving gently to the right, it stretched out of sight in the blackness.

Mitch boosted Lee up started off on rubbery legs. Lee moaned each time his shoulder bumped the rockface. Only the pain kept him conscious.

46

WITH THE AID OF THEIR FLASHLIGHTS, THE MEN moved quickly along the footpath. Geno pushed them hard from the rear. A hundred yards downstream of their landing, Luciano, at the head of the column, came upon the scuffled footprints. Looking closer, he saw the blood. On the monochrome sand, it seemed incredibly red in the beam of the powerful light.

"Yo, Geno! Check it out, man! One of 'em's bleeding bad!"

Coming up, Geno examined the blood with a smile.

"Okay, let's keep the pressure on. Lead off, Lucie."

Luciano took the point, following the bloodtrail in the beam of his light. He saw how the droplets increased in size where the boys had fallen. At one fall, the light revealed half a dozen .22 cartridges. At another, there was, mysteriously, a can of broccoli.

Another hundred yards, the footprints and blood ended abruptly as the men arrived at Green River Gorge. The sound of white water was everywhere now. The rapids boomed back out of the gorge like thunder. White water smoked in the moonlight.

Luciano gulped as he looked at the powerful rapids. He mounted the first step and shone his light down the ledge.

"Unh-unh," he said. "I don't think so. I never signed on for this weirdness."

Like the others, his enthusiasm was rapidly waning. Had he liked Demarco better, he might have been more motivated.

"What's that, Lucie?" Geno said, shoving his way to the front. "What's the hold-up?"

Benelli belched. "He wants to know his motivation, Geno."

"I *said* it's a glorious night for an invigorating stroll through the wilderness, Geno. That's all."

"Well, then, stroll your candyass up there."

"Right. Somebody hold my light."

"Hey, Lucie, can I have your 'Vette?"

"In your dreams."

"Can I have your wife?"

"I done had her," Battaglia told Licata. "Take the 'Vette. At least it starts."

192

"Funny man."

"All right, all right, break it up!"

"Hey, Geno?" said Sciortino. "What say we go around the way we come in. Head 'em off downriver." He was nervously flicking his flashlight on and off. "Or like half could go—catch 'em in a trap. I'll volunteer."

"That's what you get for thinking."

"Well, somebody needs to."

This earned a snicker from the others.

"All right, move it! You too, Disanti. We don't have all night. Let's close it up and stay together. I wanna go home too."

"Tell us how you really feel, Geno."

"Dammit, let's go! *Now!*"

"That's more like it. That's the kind of take-charge executive action we like to see."

Luciano climbed up and stepped gingerly onto the ledge. His eyes were fixed on the rapids, on where they vanished into the inky gorge. Now he started down the ledge, and three steps later, his penny loafers hit a patch of algae.

Luciano's arms windmilled wildly as he tried to keep his balance, backward, forward, backward, the leather soles slapping rhythmically. The beam of his flashlight streaked as his arms described giant circles.

Finally, he regained his equilibrium and leaned against the cliff-face, breathless. His heart pounded, and his legs had turned to water.

"Jesus Louise!" he said, eyes like saucers in his bloodless face. "Oh, man! No way, Jose! No possible way!"

On the sandbar below, his confederates expressed their appreciation with polite applause.

"Far out!"

"John Revolta!"

"Nice move, man!"

"Let's see that badness again!"

"Lucie, my man, I didn't know you had it in you!"

"*Move it!*"

Luciano leaned against the cliff-face, carefully removed his shoes and put them in the pockets of his leather flight jacket. His hands trembled violently as he rolled down his socks, wrung them out and stuffed them in the shoes. Somehow, he had cracked the lens on his light, and it projected a spider's web on the lichened granite near his head.

Barefoot now, he moved off with confidence, picking up speed. One hand was on the cliff-face for support, the other held his flashlight. His rifle was slung from his shoulder.

Battaglia was next to shed his shoes, knotting the strings of his wingtips to hang them around his neck, and join Luciano on the ledge.

47

HALF AN HOUR LATER, THE MEN HAD MADE it only a couple hundred yards down the ledge. They were together now for the ledge had served to equalize their various speeds. Geno had passed Luciano and taken the point. In the heavy river mist, the yellow cones of their failing lights seemed substantial as the stone around them. Disembodied, they hung in the blackness of the gorge like great-blooming flowers. Only Geno's light stabbed ahead—and now the beam spotlit the brothers, clinging to the cliff-face.

"There, they are! Let's go! Move it!"

The men broke into a wild scramble, and from fifty yards, they opened fire. The gunshots echoed down the gorge, booming.

Mitch flattened himself to the cliff-face, shielding Lee, as bullets glanced off the granite. Rock chips stung his face, and streamers of moss and bits of lichen rained from above.

When the gunfire suddenly ceased, he looked back. The men were humping it down the ledge, following the man in metal clothes. Though they were slipping and stumbling, already they had closed half the distance. As he watched, one of the men lost his footing and instinctively grabbed the man in front. Both men belly-flopped into the water, and seconds later, they flew past Mitchell's feet, arms up, screaming.

Mitch drew back. As he watched, the current slammed one man into a midstream boulder and his cries ceased. The river sucked him under. The other man raced, screaming, into the night.

Looking down, Mitch saw another of the sawlogs trapped against the base of the cliff, held fast by the current against a boulder. There was an eddying deadwater upstream of the boulder, and embracing Lee from behind, he jumped stiff-backed into it.

Again, the cold water revived Lee, and he cried out as the current slammed him into the cliff. With painful slowness, Mitch pulled Lee astride the log. Then pushing from the front, pushing away from the cliff with both feet, rocking the log, Mitch got it free of the boulder, and out in the current, it shot away. Gripping a limb stub, Mitch swung astride the log as it rocketed past.

Once again, the brothers rode a bucking log through the rapids. Lee sat in front, slumped over like a wounded Indian-fighter. With one hand, Mitch steadied him from behind, gripping the collar of his shirt.

Running, cursing, firing wild, Geno watched as the boys flew down the river, quickly outdistancing them.

"Let's go, dammit! Move it! Battaglia, get outta the way!"

In a knot, the men bolted down the ledge. Colliding, feet tangled, two more pitched into the white water. They surfaced, screaming, trying to cling to the algaed cliff-face, as the current bounced them along it.

When the others stopped to help, Geno screamed, "To hell with them! Go, go, go!"

The boys raced down the rapids. Now a midstream boulder sluiced the log against the cliff, slamming Mitchell's injured ankle, and he screamed in pain. He pushed off with his hand, and back in the current, the log accelerated. It bucked over a small waterfall, the nose submerged, bulldozing through the water, half-unseating Lee, then surfaced and rocked on through, accelerating. Gripping Lee's collar, Mitch managed to right him.

Mitch glanced back at the waving flashlights. The clothes they illumined were the only colors in the blackness of the gorge, and they seemed vivid as neon. There was a hundred yards now between boys and the men, and the gap was rapidly widening.

Smiling, Mitch turned back in time to see the two monolithic boulders loom ghostly out of the dark. Before he could react, the log jammed hard between them and wedged tight. The sudden stop launched Lee from the log. Mitch dove behind him, and the rapids sucked them under.

IN THE BEAM OF THE FLASHLIGHT, GENO SAW THE LOG JAM. Screaming, cursing, he drove the men along the ledge at a wild scramble. Now Benelli stepped on the heel of the man in front,

196

and both men pitched into the river. The current tore them from the cliff-face and swept them along, screaming, wet heads bobbing. A hundred feet downstream, they went under, arms waving.

The boys surfaced, and the current slammed them into the cliff. Mitch hung there by his fingertips, holding Lee's head above water.

"Lee, grab on! Help me, Lee! Grab ahold!"

Weakly, Lee gripped the crevice with his good hand. By now, not even the icy water could revive Lee fully.

Slowly, crevice by crevice, Mitch climbed toward the ledge three feet above. Finally, he reached it and hung there by his elbows, his feet in the water, trying to find the strength to lift himself.

Mitch looked upriver and saw the men coming, their flashlights a wild, waving queue that projected colossal, many-armed shadows high up the towering cliff. As they ran, the looming shadows ran, waving giant pistols and club-like flashlights. In the echoing acoustics of the gorge, their screams had a clarity that cut through the thunder of white water.

Mitch gasped as he hauled himself onto the ledge. On his knees now, he reached down and took Lee by the suspenders.

"Help me, Lee! You gotta help! Use your feet!"

Mitch leaned back, straining, lifting with his legs, and hauled Lee up beside him. Lee cried out with each movement.

Upstream, the ledge had narrowed to little more than a crevice, and Geno and his men moved slowly, heel-and-toe, step-and-slide, carefully feeling out each foothold on the algaed granite.

Now, bumped from behind, Fusco dropped his flashlight. Cursing, he watched it to the bottom, where still burning, it showed like a reflection of the moon.

Downstream, the ledge had widened, and the brothers stumbled along. Supported by the wall, Lee was keeping up. Now the way began to climb, and they followed it breathlessly. At a grotto in the cliff, Mitch stopped, pinned Lee with his shoulder, and consulted Mickey. With hands pointing due north and south, he looked like a tent-preacher illustrating sin and redemption: 12:30. Already quaky, Mitchell's legs nearly failed him then. They weren't going to make it.

It was then that Mitch looked hopelessly up, looked blearily down the ledge, and saw the tree.

QUICKLY, THE MEN CLOSED ON THE BOYS. Now their flashlights, stabbing through the river mist like lasers, spotlit the red-plaid shirt, and the men opened fire. The heavy magnums and shotguns boomed in the gorge, and ricochets whined off the granite, sharpened and redoubled by echo. Again, moss and lichen rained on the boys, and pulverized rock stung like bees. They flattened behind an outcrop in the cliff, and the gunfire ceased.

There was nowhere to go but ahead, and so the brothers struggled on. Repeatedly, Lee fell and cried out -- but now Mitch could see the end of the gorge, abrupt as the last building in a city block, only a hundred feet ahead. In the moonlight beyond the gorge, Mitch could see the footpath recommence and gully up the mountain into the dark rhododendrons. He could make out the tree now, an oak.

"Lee, come on! We nearly there! Get up! You gotta help me, Lee! I'm give out!"

He boosted Lee up, pinning him to the rockface to renew his grip, and the brothers stumbled on.

And now they heard it coming! Faint at first, a faraway freight train coming to a crossing. Mitchell's hand was on the rockface, and it detected the faint tremor. Mitch stared at his hand with dread. Steadily, the roar increased; the tremor hardened to a shudder. Mitch looked back, looked upriver with terrified eyes. The growing thunder seemed to revive even Lee. There was a feverish intensity as, moaning, he passed Mitch on the ledge and scrambled on hands and knees, sobbing for breath, crying out each time his shoulder bumped the cliff.

Only hundred feet back now, Geno and the men also heard the oceanic roar. They stopped and looked upriver. Two dozen cones of light probed the mist, and it kicked back the light, dazzling. Frowning, they stared at each other with a wild surmise.

Even Geno seemed nonplussed as he stared at the growing thunder behind them. From far upriver, a roar like a hurricane tide echoed down the gorge. He looked up at the strip of starry sky; leaned out and squinted into the luminous mist. He wiped the spray from his eyes.

"What the hell...?"

Luciano was leaning against the rockface, and he felt it tremble all along his body.

"Geno, man," he said, crossing himself. "I gotta bad feeling about this."

THE BOYS RAN AND STUMBLED AND CRAWLED with every ounce of energy, every remaining drop of adrenaline. Fear and adrenaline had revived even Lee, and he was on his feet now, lurching along, gasping, leaning heavily on Mitch and the cliff-face, going down, getting up, sprawling headlong. The camouflage chamois had come open, the buttons popped, and his undershirt was black with blood. Now he stumbled and tripped Mitch, and both boys went down in a tangled, sobbing heap.

"I'm sorry ... Mitch ... I'm sorry ... what I ..."

"Get up, Lee! Get up!"

The echoing thunder was deafening now, and the men bolted headlong. Running over each other. Scrambling to pass on the narrow ledge. Knocking one and now another into the rapids. The boys were forgotten as they stumbled along the ledge, looking fearfully back at the shuddering thunder that chased them down the cavernous gorge. The granite trembled as from an earthquake.

The brothers were nearly there—the end of the cliff-face only twenty feet ahead—when Mitch looked back and saw the tidal wave roar into sight. The leading edge glittered in the moonlight, thirty vertical feet of white water, filling the gorge like a canal lock, tumbling a booming, cracking flotsam of rock-scarred sawlogs before it. The wall of water towered over the stumbling, screaming men. As Mitch watched, the wall engulfed them and tumbled them under.

199

With one last adrenal effort, Mitch reached the end of the cliff. He grabbed Lee, pushed him over and leaped after him, as with a jetport roar, the tidal wave swept thundering by.

Now, in a surging backwash, it flooded the pocket at the end of the cliff with a powerful, eddying whirlpool, and caught in the vortical backwater, the boys were spun quickly away; spun back toward the thundering mainstream. Round and round they whirled, clockwise, the star-punctuated sky spinning giddily above them.

Now a revolution slammed them into the wall, and Mitch reached high and grabbed a laurel that grew from a crevice in the cliff-face there. The power of the water was such that it yanked them nearly horizontal. Mitch held on with one hand as he gripped Lee's suspenders with the other, scissoring Lee's body with his legs, trying with his last strength to hold Lee's head above the glassy water—when the shallow rootage gave way, and he and Lee were sucked, spinning, screaming, down into the whirlpool, down into the pit-shaped maelstrom of whirling, roaring, suffocating water.

48

IT WAS DAYBREAK AND MITCHELL'S SCREAM had been replaced by the shrill chirping of birds; the roar of rapids by the gentle splash and gurgle of green water. Downstream of the white water, the river slowed and widened luxuriously into a lakelike pool, as though stretching from the back-breaking labor of The Gorge. In the cut-over, in the absence of the great spruce, hardwoods grew to the very margins of the river, their root bolls humped in trolls' nests of moss.

The trees nearest the shore bore scars on their trunks from impacts with the sawlogs, and flotsam, natural and manmade, streamed from high in the skeletal branches. Water-killed, bleached bone-white, they leaned with the same downstream cant as though frozen in the grip of a gale-force wind. Back through the denuded floodplain, the repetition of the graceful, long-bow curves had a beautiful and abstract symmetry.

Now a butterfly, an orange-and-black swallowtail, floated gently into the pool. Caught in the current, wings fluttering, it surfed through the ripples. Twirled in the eddies downstream of the mossy boulders. Finally, out in the green depths of mid-pool, a trout rose and struck at it, once, twice, thrice, reducing it quickly to an iridescent smear of wing-dust .

The fragments floated on, and safely in the shallow tailout, an encircling school of minnows rushed in to finish it off. Seconds later, there was no evidence that the butterfly had ever existed..

JUST UPSTREAM OF THE DYING RIPPLES and dissipating wing-dust, Mitchell Rainey lay sprawled, face-down on the sandbar. From long immersion in the icy water, his skin was waxen, corpselike. Dead fir needles clung to his matted hair, and his visible ear was filled with sand. He still wore the backpack, and the protruding axe handle was half-buried in the sand. One arm was flung outward, and the pale, water-pruned hand gripped the suspenders of the tall boy in denim overalls beside him.

Now he moaned and rolled over, grains of sand sticking to

one colorless cheek, and opened his eyes. Slowly, his eyes widened, and he broke into a radiant smile.

He was staring into the towering girders of the Interstate bridge! Mitch fairly beamed as he took in the intricate trusswork of the bridge's I-beam underpinning.

Beside him, Lee moaned, and Mitch came full awake. He started up and looked fearfully around. Then, remembering, he settled back on both elbows with a smile and took in the flawless June morning. The birds singing in the streamside trees. The river gurgling between its wide, sandy banks. As Mitch watched, a great rainbow trout arched out of the river to intercept a yellowjacket, and in the morning sun, the big trout flashed silver as a sea-run salmon.

Mitch looked back at the bridge. It seemed close enough almost to touch; for the first time, more above them than downriver.

Now Lee moaned again and, slipping the pack, Mitch rolled to his knees. He woke his brother gently, smiling.

"Lee! Lee, we done it! We made it!"

Lee opened his eyes, smiled faintly and winced in pain. His skin was waxen from the frigid water and loss of blood. Now he closed his eyes with a groan and slipped toward unconsciousness—but Mitch shook him awake.

"Lee, wake up! The bridge ain't no more'n quarter-mile downriver. Can you make it?"

Almost imperceptibly, Lee shook his head.

"Yeh, you can! You'll feel better afterwhile. I seen some 'sang once up that little feeder crick back yonder. I'll make you a poultice." Mitch jumped up. "I'll be back directly."

Lee smiled weakly and passed out. Thinking the worst, Mitch knelt by his brother and shook him.

"Lee? Lee!"

When Lee groaned, Mitch smiled with relief. With a final look upriver, with a glance at Lee's reddening teeshirt, he hurried away, back up the river toward the tributary creek.

A HUNDRED YARDS UPRIVER, GENO ROUSED HIMSELF from the

same exhausted sleep. He looked bad, unshaven, sand in the roots of his thin gray hair, and moved stiffly, painfully, as he climbed down from the bank of driftwood.

Now he stood unsteadily over the other men. His warmup suit was a castaway tatter, and somewhere, his gold chains adorned the river bottom. The holster on his gunbelt hung between his legs like a codpiece, but somehow, it still gripped the big revolver. Groaning, he limped among the sleeping forms, kicking them awake.

"Hey, yous guys, get up! Luciano, Battaglia, get your butts up! Hear me? Disanti, Licata, on your feet. *Now!* I'm not gonna tell you again."

The men groaned and bestirred themselves. They moved with the arthritic creakiness of old men as they struggled to their knees, to their feet. Of the twenty men, barely half had survived the night.

Disanti's arm was broken above the elbow, and the jagged bone protruded through livid flesh. When Geno kicked him awake, he sat up, screaming, holding his splintered arm, then passed out, falling backwards.

MITCH SPLASHED UP THE CREEK UNTIL HE FOUND the ginseng patch. It was in the first boggy terrace of the stream's stepping-down descent. Quickly, he pulled up handfuls the medicinal herb. He was washing the pale, tuberous roots in the fast-flowing brook when he looked upstream and his eyes grew wide.

One of the men hung by his armpits from the high crotch of a tree. His bare feet and face were corpse-white, and his city clothes were streaming tatters. His contortionist posture suggested a broken back—and legs and arms. Sand ran from his staring eyes and gaping, toothless mouth. Even his pockets had been turned out by the force of the water. Mitch gulped and backed away.

BACK AT THE RIVER, HE KNELT BESIDE LEE and cut away the shredded, bloodstained teeshirt. Lee moaned as Mitch pulled the shirt away. The shotgun wound was wide and shallow; the skin around it bruised and blackened. Flattened birdshot fell away with the shirt. Mitch crushed the root and packed it on the wound by the handfuls. When he touched it, Lee's moaning redoubled. Now he passed the shirt under his brother's arms and bound the poultice in place with a square knot.

Standing, he looked at the already reddening bandage, then glanced nervously upriver. "Lee, can you stand up?"

Faintly, Lee shook his head.

"Try, Lee! We cain't stay here! It's jist a little ways yet!"

As Mitch looked on in fear and frustration, Lee began to cry.

"We gotta get you to the hospital! You're still bleeding!"

In response, Lee slipped toward unconsciousness. Gripping him by the shirtfront, Mitch began to slap him across the face. "Wake up, Lee! Dammit, wake up! *Wake up!*"

"I … cain't, Mitch!" Lee sobbed. "I … cain't! Leave me … alone! Leave me …"

But Mitch continued to slap and shake him. "We nearly there! You hear me, Lee? We nearly there! We cross The Cables and we home! Get up! *Get up!*"

"Okay, okay, don't hit … me no more! Please … Mitch! Don't … hit me …"

"Then get up!"

With Mitchell's help, Lee staggered to his feet.

There was a muddy fisherman's path that climbed through the dead timber to the riverbank trail. Lee leaned heavily on his brother as the boys struggled up the path. Lee sobbed with pain at every misstep. Finally, they reached the trail and turned downstream. Already, the poultice was crimson with blood.

GENO AND THE MEN CAME ALONG THE TRAIL with a vengeance. Though they had lost their rifles and shotguns, some still carried their tarnished sidearms. From the end of the column, Geno pushed them hard, cursed them, shoved them when they faltered.

Luciano had again taken the point, and now they came into an area of dead timber, the trees along the river bleached and bent. His ears still ringing from the constant sound of white

204

water, Luciano found the sudden silence and the dead forest spooky. In his jacket pocket, he gripped the revolver with a sweaty palm.

When they arrived on the trail above the big pool, he saw the tracks in the sandy wash.

"Yo, Geno! Here we go!"

Geno pushed his way to the front and saw the small footprints and the man-size ones. He saw the scuff marks where the big boy had stumbled. A few feet farther on, there were deep knee-prints where the boys had gone down. Between two of the prints, he saw blood. He knelt in the path then and blotted it up with his fingertips, smiling as he noted its freshness.

Standing, he stared down the trail. "Oh, yes," he said. "*Now* we've got the little creeps."

49

THE FOOTPATH ENDED ABRUPTLY AS THE BOYS arrived at The Cables. They stood, Lee leaning weakly against Mitch, in the shade of the big spruce. Mitch looked up the trunk and took in the welted bark and riverward cant. Years of tension had pulled the spruce twenty degrees off of vertical. The cables had cut deeply into the tree, and the welted bark had overgrown the stainless steel to a depth of five or six inches. Mitch saw the rusty turnbuckles that were used to keep the cables taut. There was a TROUT WATER sign below the top cable. Fine print gave the seasons and limits and size restrictions. Mitch was amazed to find himself reading them.

Inching closer, careful to avoid Lee's feet, he looked into the gorge. The rapids thundered through fifty feet below. Trapped between vertical rockfaces, spray rose as from a chimney. Mitch gulped. He had crossed The Cables once before, years earlier, riding his father's back, and now he remembered the utter terror of it. Anticipation of the return passage had ruined the day's fishing. As he looked down at the white water, fear knotted his stomach, and his legs seemed to lose their bones. He looked back down the trail, and the phrase "between a rock and a hard place" crossed his mind. For the first time, he knew its full import.

Now, swallowing hard, he pushed Lee up on the base cable and climbed up behind him. By sheer act of will, he kept his eyes off the river below.

"Lee, you ready?"

"Gotta leave … me, Mitch … catch you if …"

"Shh! I ain't gone leave you. Wake up! We gotta go now, Lee. Stand up! You gotta help me all you can, okay? Here we go, Lee. *Lee!* Here we go!"

Taking a deep breath, Mitch gave Lee a shove, and the boys started across. Lee hung from the cable by his good arm, and Mitch supported him from behind. On the abraded wire, the cuts on Lee's feet quickly reopened, and soon the cable was slippery with blood. They moved inch by painful inch in a slow step-and-slide. Several times, Lee misstepped and nearly fell. But each time, Mitch caught him with his legs and righted him. At each misstep, Lee cried out.

Over the river now, clear of the riverbank trees, the bridge towered over them like a skyscraper. Mitch could see graffiti painted on the bridge railing. The words were illegible at this distance, but he could make out an orange tiger paw print of Clemson University.

They were halfway across, and Mitch looked up and saw down the shining cables clear sailing and the wide landing where the footpath continued on the opposite bank—when the men broke out of the woods and into the clearing behind them. They quickly raised their pistols and took aim at the boys—sitting ducks on the swaying base cable—but Geno put up his hand.

"Hold it! I got a better idea. These careless boys are gonna have a little fishing mishap. Tragic—but happens all the time."

Geno holstered his revolver, climbed out on the cable and began to jump, sending a vicious seesawing down it. The brothers immediately lost their footing, but hung by their arms, legs pinwheeling, trying to regain their feet. Mitch gripped Lee in his scissoring legs.

Finally, they found their footing and, inspired by fear, buoyed by adrenaline, they moved rapidly across. Mitch hung to the upper cable by his fingertips, and hand over hand, gripping Lee around the waist with his legs, he made it across the river.

They had made the far shore -- were above the ledge on the other side -- when Geno saw the dead limb lying by the trail. He picked it up, and with a powerful, two-handed swing, he whacked the hand cable.

With a cry, Mitch lost his grip, and the boys fell ten feet to the shelf below. On impact, Mitch rolled around in agony, screaming, holding his ankle. Lee lay unconscious beside him.

Groaning, Mitch struggled to his feet and looked back across the river. The first of the men were out over the river now. Mitch took the axe from the pack and, grimacing with pain, using the axe as a crutch, he climbed the rockface to the old road.

He was out of breath when he arrived at the spruce. From behind the tree, Mitch looked across the river. The men were out over the gorge now. The cable was slick with spray, and in their city shoes, they were making wary progress. As Mitch watched, they looked fearfully below.

"What's the hold-up?" The man in foil was at the end of the line. "Come, on, Lucie! Pick it up!"

"I'm going, Geno. Godalmighty! This ain't easy."

Now Mitch went to work! Chips flew as he chopped at the hand cable, deeply embedded in the welted trunk. Out of sight behind the tree, he could stand, and he put his back into it. In twenty strokes, he cut through the bark and reached bare metal, and the big cable *thrummed* with each stroke of the axe.

When the men felt the vibration, they tried to pick up their pace, but it only served to panic them. Now one man misstepped and dropped, screaming, into the gorge. Frozen with fear, the others watched as he disappeared beneath the white water, arms waving.

"Dammit, let's go! Move it!"

Mitch returned to his task with new energy. Sparks flew as metal met metal! Again, the men tried to speed up. Two tried to shoot, but on the swaying base cable, their gunshots missed widely, dirt spurting on the embankment behind him.

They had passed the halfway point when, with a mighty, ringing *thwack,* Mitch cut through the cable, and it let go with a *twang,* shooting like a silver arrow back across the river. The first man took the cable full in the face, and with a shriek, he cartwheeled backward into the gorge.

Incredibly, the others kept their footing momentarily and stood on the shivering base cable in open-mouthed disbelief. They looked like a whole family of wide-eyed Wallendas, arms out for balance -- and they did manage to keep their footing for four or five seconds—until one of them lurched, and the slack cable seesawed, and the whole family pitched, screaming, into the gorge.

Gripping the axe, Mitch stood and stared into the gorge. He smiled as he watched the rapids suck them under, silencing their screams.

50

THEY WERE ON THE OLD LOGGING ROAD NOW as it ran back into the deep shade of the hardwood second-growth. Blowing, the brothers staggered along the road as now it began to climb. The footpath ran like a centerline down the roadbed, worn between the mossed-over bulldozer tracks and gullied wheel-ruts of the logging trucks. The green-water river ran below, silent and slow as an estuary.

There was a sandy wash at the crest of the incline, and there, the boys collapsed in the road, chests heaving, the shade a welcome relief from the sun. Retrieving Lee from the shelf below The Cables had almost undone them, and Mitchell was beyond exhaustion. Lee slipped in and out of shock, revived periodically by fear and his terrible pain. The fall from The Cables had re-opened his wound, and the camouflage shirt clung wetly to it. The poultice had slipped down around his waist and sagged there like a bloody fanny pack. He was delirious, barely coherent, his voice barely a whisper, as he grabbed his brother by the bib of his overalls.

"Mitch … Mitch, I'm sorry I … I'm …"

"Shh! Rest easy, Lee. Don't try to talk none."

As he spoke, Mitch watched their backtrail. Like the river, the old road ran straight and flat, tunneling through the cut-over in hardwood arcade. From the crest, he had an unobstructed view of nearly two-hundred yards. The trail was clear.

"Gotta leave … me, Mitch … gotta lead …"

"I ain't gone leave you, Lee! Don't give up on me now! We nearly there!"

"Got … to Mitch … slowing you …down …"

"*No,* I said! I ain't gone leave you! Now jist shut up about it!"

With a groan, Lee lay back and closed his eyes. Mitch knelt beside him and covered his shivering body with the red shirt. He pillowed his head with the knapsack, trying to make him more comfortable.

Mitch sat back and looked down the trail ahead. Behind the heavy canopy, the bridge was no longer visible, but Mitch could almost sense its soaring presence. It could be no more than a hundred yards ahead. With rising spirits, he noted fresh wader tracks in the muddy footpath. On the embankment, he saw a Vienna sausage can with its blue label still unfaded.

As he looked at the bank, he saw the sapling that overhung the roadbed. Mitch smiled.

Lee was watching him intently. "What...?" he managed.

Mitch nodded at the tree. With painful effort, Lee turned his head. When he saw the sapling, he gave Mitchell a quizzical look.

"I gotta idea."

Lee managed a smile. Faintly, he told his brother, "Oh ... no!" then lay back and closed his eyes, exhausted with the effort.

Mitch grinned at his brother, and at the sight of his ashen face felt hot tears burn against the backs of his eyes. Blinking them back, he stood and pulled the camp-axe from the pack. He used the axe as a crutch, the head under one arm, as he hobbled to the sapling.

Sitting astride the tree, choking up on the axe nearly to the head, he went to work. There was an ugly smile on his swollen, scabby face, utterly devoid of humor, as he lopped off the limbs and honed the stubs to a razor point.

Lee watched his little brother sadly.

NOT FAR BELOW THE CABLES, THE WALLS of the gorge opened, and the river funneled out into a long, vertical-walled pool. There, the white water ended as though running into a great vat of green dye. At the tail of the pool, the river deposited all the sand collected from a mile of rapids in a broad alluvial fan. This was the Blue Hole, much-loved by area flyfishermen, for the tailout sandbar made the head of the pool reachable to those with chest waders and a double-haul cast, bringing the biggest brown trout into range of a Ted's Stonefly in spring and a Female Adams in summer. Below the bar, beneath the willow canopy, the river ran green and flat as an irrigation ditch. Close inspection would reveal the willows aswarm with trout flies.

It was on that sandbar that Geno and his seven surviving men—wholly unenlightened in the finer points of caddisfly presentation—grounded some moments later. Raising clouds of sand, they sloshed through the shallows toward shore. Three favored injured legs, and a fourth had the hand of a broken arm thrust in his shirt in the sling position.

Battaglia waded ashore dragging Fusco by the collar, but thigh-deep in the river, he looked down, saw the lifeless eyes, and recoiling, dropped him. The corpse landed with a splash and started downstream. Head-first, face-down, arms out, he looked like a snorkeler.

Up on the sandbar, the men sprawled around Geno, gasping for breath, coughing up river. They eyed their fearful leader with hatred.

Geno picked up on the stony stares and stood uncomfortably.

"All right, let's go! This isn't girls camp." His wooden laughter was met with silence.

"Too frigging bad," said Urato. The fall had knocked his front teeth out, and his tipped tongue explored the bloody gumline. "Girlth camp would be okay. Girlth camp I could get inta."

"Marcello, Benelli, on your feet!"

"Jesus, Geno!" said Benelli. "Give it a rest. You need to get more fun outta life."

"Yeh, Geno, chill out, man." Marcello groaned as he sat up and massaged the small of his back. "My D.I. at boot camp wudn't this bad. And *he* was a *she*."

"Geno, man, I gotta be straight with you, okay?" Battaglia said. He was still watching the snorkeler. "I'm like having trouble maintaining my enthusiasm for this. I mean—what the hell—so's the kids stole a couple grand. Big deal. Vendetti'll make it up."

"They saw Tony kill a supplier."

"Hey, screw Tony!" said Benelli. "Sounds like a personal problem to me."

He wrung out his Braves cap and put it on. The cap was so

shrunken it fit his bald head like a beanie.

"Tony has got a problem," Geno admitted, thinking of Atlanta. "There's no denying that."

Luciano snorted. "Our *Anthony* has got *multiple* problems. Damn lush!"

"Ain't the first time he's gone postal," Battaglia said. "Brought the heat down on all of us."

"Tony tries. Okay, come on, let's go! Move it! *Now!*"

The men made it to their feet, grumbling, and climbed wearily through the log-scarred sycamores. There was a TROUT WATER sign on the one nearest the road. Battaglia showed his interest by tearing it down and dropping it in the path. Trout water had just kicked his ass.

At the muddy intersection of the trails, they turned downriver and started along the old road. By unspoken agreement, Luciano took the point. (A former Marine and a great fan of Western movies, he was enjoying his role as Indian scout.) They were a dispirited lot and moved entirely by rote, putting one tenderfoot in front of the other. From the rear of the foot-dragging column, Geno kept up a steady stream of abuse. He had a tireless ability to work fresh combinations of four-letter words.

Almost immediately, they came upon the boys' footprints, and fifty yards down the road, at the crest of a little incline, Luciano saw where they had stopped and rested. Kneeling, he saw the deep prints their elbows had made in the sand. The imprints were on either side of long depressions where they had lain down. The sand of one depression was bloodstained, and a blood-sodden lump of teeshirt lay beside it. Greenbottle flies the size of bees crawled on the teeshirt. With the barrel of his pistol, Luciano turned it over, and the flies started loudly. One landed on his mouth, and he waved it away with distaste, sputtering.

Luciano stood and looked down the road. Ahead, a length of dead tree ran from the rocky roadbed up the embankment. It leaned at an impossible angle. Though he had been in the deep woods less than a day, it registered on his innate paranoia. He was about to give it closer inspection when Geno yelled from the end of the column.

"Hey, Kit Carson, pick it up! We know where they're

headed."

Luciano started down the old road. "Come on, Geno, man," he said, looking back. "I'm going as fast as I—"

When Luciano stumbled over the cairn of stones, he released the dead tree, and it dropped to the embankment. With a whiplike whistle, the sapling rebounded to its place across the road, and the sharpened limb stubs stabbed into his chest.

Luciano fell to the roadbed with a bubbling scream, mouth and nose frothing blood. For a moment, he thrashed, trying to free himself; then grew deathly still. His wide eyes glazed over, and he stretched luxuriously, shuddering. As he exhaled his final breath, his mouth and nose blew an enormous bloody bubble that popped with a scarlet spatter.

He was still stuck to the tree, and under his weight, the limbs released with a sucking sound, and the tree whipped back to its place across the road. There, it appeared to be running red sap. Now, with a long release of wind, Luciano flopped over on his back, and blood began to soak the sand around him. His dirty fingers trembled with the delicacy of a safecracker.

"Oh, man!" Sciortino said. "You see that? Jeez-*us!*" His eyes were fixed on the twitching fingers. "This *sucks!*"

Benelli crossed himself. "Christ on a crutch!"

"Oh, man!" said Licata. "I ain't seen that since 'Nam."

Geno saw that he was losing them. "All right, let's move it!" He stepped to the front and gave Baggio a shove down the trail. "Charley, take the point."

"Don't say that word," Licata said.

"No way, man!" said Baggio. He dropped his shotgun on the embankment and sat down beside it, head between his knees. "I had enough of this weirdness. I want my mama. Though I'd settle for Julia Roberts. In a pinch. Which this definitely is."

"Yeh, time out, Geno."

"Yeh, Geno, we can whack them kids anytime. On *our* turf."

"Not if they go to the feds. Now, dammit, get up! I'm not paying you to lie around!"

"I quit."

"Me too."

"I hate to be indelicate -- but has anyone mentioned

overtime?"

"Overtime."

"Hell with that," said Marcello. "I'm putting in for Workman's Comp." Again, his hands found the small of his back. "I screwed up my back last night. Big time. Hurts like a hell."

"Yeh, Geno, my lawyer will be in touch—by 30/06."

"You move it, Geno," Battaglia said. He was staring at the spreading stain around Luciano's body. He looked at the tortured face—where already the greenbottles had found the blood—and looked away with a shudder. He dated Lucie's kid sister, Marcelline, and dreaded breaking the news. Also, Luciano owed—had owed—him sixteen-hundred dollars. "We'll follow."

"Overtime."

Cursing, Geno took the point. As he followed the footprints, he noted the scuffed sand where the boys had stumbled. Knee-prints marked the places where they'd gone down. Between the big boy's prints, there were bright droplets of blood. As he regarded the blood, the smile returned to Geno's weary face.

51

JUST DOWNSTREAM OF THE CABLES, juxtaposed like a museum display charting the state-of-the-art, the Interstate bridge spanned the gorge. The concrete parabolas gleamed in the morning sun, high above the great, windy spruce in the valley floor. It was Monday morning, and the highway was thick with commuters. Semis crossed, downshifting, starting the nesting swallows in the steel-strutted underpinning, and the birds dropped into the gorge, wheeling, screaming like seagulls. From far below came the muted roar of white water, drowned out now by a louder roar as another convoy of tractor-trailers crossed the span, gearing up for the steep run up the other side. Above the bridge, Green River, in fits and starts of white water, bisected a hundred square miles of virgin forest. Bridge and highway were like a razor slash in a Tintoretto.

BENEATH THE HEAVY CANOPY OF THE CUT-OVER, the boys hobbled along the old road. There was something wrong with Mitchell's ankle now, he had felt something give in the fall from The Cables, and the pain he felt when he stepped on it in a certain way was like nothing he'd ever experienced. Now he walked almost on the side of his foot, and that way, curiously, the pain was manageable.

The road grew swampy as it descended to the river, and algaed water stood in the wheel-ruts, full of tadpoles and working with mosquitoes. Water striders raced away at their approach. The boys stayed clear of the central footpath for it was deeply cut in the muck and not wide enough for them to walk abreast. It had taken twenty minutes to cover the hundred yards, but ahead now as at the end of a tunnel, Mitch could see a brightening; see the shimmering summer's day beyond.

"There it is, Lee! We nearly there!"

There was a fisherman on the river below who raised a hand in greeting. When the boys stumbled by, unresponsive, he looked after them incuriously and returned to his fly. He knew the end of school was often celebrated in drunken camping trips. There was a twinge of worry as he considered his own son. That morning, his bed had been unslept in. Not that he went fishing with his father anymore.

Now the roadbed turned to gravel causeway, built up across a length of silver culvert pipe to drain the boggy springhead above the road. Pink lady slippers and white baby's breath grew in profusion. Crystalline springwater bubbled up in squat section of the same pipe, overflowing, and Mitch looked at it longingly as they stumbled past.

Fifty feet more, the boys hobbled from the trees as through a green archway, and found themselves on the great granite shield of the riverbed. Out of the trees, the granite kicked back the morning sun so brightly it hurt their eyes.

And there in front of them, big as buildings and impossibly white, were the bridge foundations, soaring topless through the spruce!

Mitch looked left at the double line of foundations, marching across the gorge. On the far wall, the last twin towers were thin as phone poles. Now he looked up, up, up, the foundation before him, eyes squinched, head swimming, and lost his balance. He and Lee collapsed to their knees. The flexure of his ankle brought the sickening pain and the hard yellow light against the backs of his eyes. Lee lay with his head in his brother's lap.

"We at the bridge, Lee! Get up! It's jist a little ways yet!"

"Gotta leave … me, Mitch ... Gotta go …"

"Get up, Lee!"

The boys struggled to their feet. Mitch pulled Lee's arm over his shoulder, took him around the waist, and together, they hobbled toward the bridge. Litter was everywhere now, thick as at a landfill. Hundreds of soft drink and beer cans. Enough paper to save a rainforest. Broken glass, green and clear and brown, bejewelled the bedrock, and they staggered through it barefoot. On the light granite, bloody footprints soon marked their crossing. Mitch saw a washing machine, trapezoidal from the force of the fall. Over there was the engine from a car and the green shutters from a house. A sofa, a sink and a microwave.

The plastic shards of a shattered TV. Now half a dozen bicycles with bent frames. Near the rivercourse, old campfires blackened the granite in a dozen places.

Now they were beneath the bridge, staggering through the foundations, drink cans crunching underfoot; and on through the deep cellar shade – JC + ML, ROCK RULES! ENKA 68 - ERWIN 51, LENNON LIVES! -- and finally out into the brilliant sunlight beyond.

They were beyond the bridge when Mitch looked right, looked up and saw the footpath, rising like a ladder to the highway above. His spasming legs nearly failed him then. There was no way. They had barely made it down the road.

"Let's go, Lee! You can make it! Lean on me, Lee! Lean all you can!"

"I'm sorry … Mitch I'm …sorry I …"

The boys entered the path and began to climb. Due to the grade, the path was deeply gullied by run-off, and only their heads were visible as they stumbled and crawled up the near-vertical wash. Lee was barely conscious, barely able to support his weight. Mitch was straining and blowing, his heat-mottled face streaked with grime and sweat.

GENO WAS FAR IN THE LEAD AS THE MEN LIMPED along the road. The punji stick had made them wary, and they had fallen well back. Twice, Geno stopped and waved them forward with the revolver, and reluctantly, they made a show of doubletime. But where the roadbed opened, the width of two timber trucks, their boldness returned, and together again, they hurried along it.

Geno started at the sight of the fisherman on the river, but after Mitchell's snub, the man didn't look up. Relieved, Geno holstered his revolver and hurried by. The man's unaccustomed rudeness had saved his life.

There was the gravel, they remembered that, and the spring above the road, but when they stopped to drink, Geno herded them on.

Now the roadbed dumped them out on the riverbed, and in the open again, on familiar terrain, they hurried across the outcrop. Though it had been barely twelve hours since their departure, it seemed like forever. With a wince, Battaglia remembered sharing his Irish coffee with Luciano and Demarco. "Hey, Battaglia, be a pal, man. Didn't yo' mama teach you to share?" Furtively, he crossed himself. He tried a *Hail Mary* but the words got tangled. An *Our Father* was out of the question.

Ahead, Geno stumbled for the trail, kicking through the cans, crunching across the glass, wading through the paper, and for once the others kept up. When he saw the bloody footprints, he did his best to run. He had done something to his hip in the fall from The Cables, and whenever the leg took his weight, there was an excruciating grinding of bone.

At the trailhead, he stood with the handgun, and as the men arrived, he directed them one by one into the gully. As they stared up the precipitous chute – where in places rain-uprooted saplings crisscrossed the gully – several balked at the memory of unlucky Luciano. Geno pressed his gun to their backs and shoved them into the wash like a bouncer dealing with unruly guests. There, they began to climb, stumbling and falling, sobbing for breath. They were cursing Geno openly by now. He cursed them back.

THE BROTHERS CLIMBED, SLIPPING AND SLIDING. The great bridge towered over them, skyscraper-tall. Mitch looked up and saw the complicated, cantilevered system of struts and undertrusses; the massive, monolithic bridge towers— WAYCROSS SUX! GO TARHEELS! JC + ML. And then, for the first time in three days, he could hear it—sounds of the 20th century! The whir of tires! The loud down-shifting of a big semi! The muted blare of car horns! Civilization!

The boys scrambled on hands and knees. Rootage held back erosion in a series of steps, and Mitch climbed ahead, hauling Lee up behind him. They were above the flank of the mountain now, and the grade steepened sharply. The leaves were wet; the red clay a muddy soup. They slipped back a foot for every two feet of progress. Both boys were quickly orange with mud.

Now Mitch slipped and went to his knees with a splash,

toppling Lee, who screamed in pain.

SLIPPING AND SLIDING, THE MEN SCRAMBLED after them. Geno had taken the lead and set a brutal pace. Though he was a thrice-weekly jogger, he gasped for breath in the thin mountain air. Below, the clay-coated men wallowed after him on hands and knees. Benelli and Sciortino, grossly overweight, looked like sumo mud-wrestlers.

Now, near the middle of the column, a root broke under the weight of Benelli, and he belly-flopped and sledded back down the mountain, taking down four of his fellows. They cursed him violently and kicked at his beached-whale form as he passed.

Finally, well downhill of the group, a boulder arrested his backward momentum. He rolled over and lay still, groaning, hands on his crotch.

On impact, a cheer went up from his cheerless colleagues.

A FALLEN TREE BLOCKED THE RAVINE. MITCH STRUGGLED over it and, sobbing with the effort, pulled Lee after him. Under his weight, the two splashed down in a tangled, moaning heap. Exhausted, Mitch hung on the edge of consciousness.

"Cain't stay … here, Lee. Got to ... go. Got to … *get up!*"

With monstrous effort, he rolled Lee off and stood. Wheezing, he wiped the clay from his eyes and mouth, and looked up the ever-steepening, ever-deepening gully. The ladderlike gradient was undiminished.

"Let's go, Lee! Get up! You gotta help me!"

As he got Lee to his feet, he saw the blood that already streaked the clay.

THE MEN FLOUNDERED WILDLY UP THE GULLY; wallowed on hands and knees up the muddy stairway. Though they too slipped and slid, they were clearly outpacing the boys. Still in the lead, Geno had put away his gun and was using both hands to pull himself up.

He stood now, blowing, and looked back at his men. They straggled halfway down the mountain. Only when he drew his gun did they show animation. He drew it now and saw that the muzzle was clogged with mud. Cursing, he dropped the cylinder and blew the barrel clear. The men nearest him, who knew Geno best, were inspired by that simple act to move faster.

THIS TIME, WHEN MITCH COLLAPSED, he could hear the men below. Clearly, he heard the older man cursing them and their breathless responses. With pain in his face, he knelt beside his brother.

"Lee?" he whispered. "Lee, can you hear me?" Lee's eyes fluttered. "Lee, I cain't go no further! I jist cain't!" Mitch sobbed. "Gotta hide you, Lee! Gonna hide you!"

There was no response. Lee, a clay-coated effigy, looked to be dead.

With his little remaining strength, Mitch dragged his brother over the gully bank. A great spruce grew on the mountainside there, its bottommost limbs brushing the ground in a low green tent. Mitch crawled under the limbs and dragged Lee after him.

There, he covered his brother with dead needles and branches and knelt beside him, orange tears running in his clay-covered face.

"Gotta leave you, Lee. I'm sorry! You gotta lie still, okay? You gotta lie real quiet. I be back, Lee. I be back! I promise!"

A HUNDRED YARDS BELOW, THE MEN were also on their last legs; on all-fours as they crawled up the steepening grade. Now, looking up the wash, they saw Mitch high above them, as he climbed out of the gully and scrambled over the ridgeline into the adjoining ravine. Sobbing for breath, they attacked the gully wall in a fury. There were ratlines of exposed roots, and they used them to scale the near-vertical wall.

Near the top, Sciortino, his face scarlet, grabbed his chest and fell back into the wash with a splash. His big body writhed in pain. As the others watched from the wall-face, his exertions

220

ceased, and his body began a slow sled back down the mountain.

Impassively, Geno and the others watched him go, feet-first, picking up speed, blubber aquiver. His bald, hypertense head was the last thing they saw as he bobsledded expertly through a curve en route to the river.

"Jesus!" gasped Battaglia. "Bruno's got high blood pressure. I guess he's on medication."

"Not now, he ain't," Geno wheezed. "*Now* he's on his ass."

AND NOW, LOOKING BACK, MITCH WENT over the ridgeline and scrambled madly, desperately through the trees. Halfway down the ravine wall, he stepped on a rock hidden in the leaves, and his ankle finally gave out. Collapsed beneath him with a pain so intense he blacked out for a second. With a cry, Mitch tumbled down the steep hillside. Cartwheeled toward the looming bridge abutment in the ravine floor.

There, he came to rest at the feet of a man! Fell at a pair of spit 'n' shined black combat boots! Mitch stared at the boots, eyes wide with terror!

52

SLOWLY, FEARFULLY, HE BEGAN TO LOOK UP the long, camo-print legs; to look up at his certain doom ... but when his saucer eyes had finally risen above the brass-buckled belt ... above the 'scope-sighted rifle ... above the twin flap pockets on the Army field jacket ... he saw the smiling, blackened face of an immense mountain man. His lower lip bulged with a dip of snuff.

"Mitch?" The man squinted through the blackening. "'At you?"

Mitchell broke into a radiant smile. "Mr. Cummings!"

Weaving, Mitch stood and looked blearily around, and his smile widened as he saw the small army gathered there -- a Rambo-esque People's Militia of tobacco-chewing, duly-deputized deer hunters, maybe twenty strong. They looked like a Vietnam-era platoon preparing to go out on patrol—and, in fact, most of the men were of 'Nam-vet age.

And they were armed to the teeth with state-of-the-art firepower. All wore camouflage coveralls, and their faces were rubbed with Camo-stik to near invisibility. Only when they smiled—when the green was broken by the line of good teeth—were they visible. And now they were all smiling down at Mitch and exchanging howdy-do's—and Mitch seemed to recognize most of them.

"Hey, Mr. Tarver!"

Another huge man in camouflage smiled and nodded to Mitchell. "You leave any fer us, Mitch?"

Mitch really laughed for the first time in three days. "Yes sir. A couple. Littl'uns."

And the men broke into uproarious laughter—as Mitch recognized another posse member.

"Hey, Mr. Blankenship!"

An immense black man with an AR-15, the civilian version of the M-16, nodded and smiled at the boy. He was the size and build of an NFL lineman. He held a brace of bloodhounds who strained at their leashes, leaping up, licking Mitchell's dirty face.

Changing hands on the leashes, the man took a thermos from his gamepocket and handed it to Mitch.

"Now don't drink it all," he told him with a wink.

"Yes sir! I mean, no sir! I mean, thanks a lot, Mr. Blankenship!"

Mitch uncapped the thermos and drank greedily, the iced tea running down his chin and throat. The hounds managed to capture most of what missed his mouth.

"Somebody go get the sheriff and Rainey," Cummings said. "Tell 'em we found the boys. One of 'em anyways. Mitch? Where's Lee got to?"

BACK DOWN THE MOUNTAIN, THE MEN HAD REVIVED and were sitting up. Most of them had made it out of the wash. Licata and Rizzo had lighted cigarettes, and LoCicero massaged his cramping calf muscles. Clay-covered, they looked like aboriginal mud-men. The clay had dried on them, and cracked at the joints when they moved. Their faces cracked when they spoke.

Geno stood and stared up the hillside over which Mitch had disappeared. "They're up that next hollow," he told them. "Come on, get up!"

Groaning, the men staggered to their feet. As he stared at the hilltop, Geno wiped the mud from his revolver. Now he smiled, and his clay-covered face crazed in a crow's-feet of hairlines.

"Oh, yes," he said, his smoker's smile yellow in his brick complexion. "*Now* we've got the little creeps."

THE PLATOON MOVED OUT SILENTLY, FANNING OUT skillfully, working off the point man, Jensen Cummings, like a well-practiced team. Working off his hand signals, they deployed left and right down the mountainside. Dissolved into the woods. Vanished without a trace into the heavy summer foliage. Without a sound.

Mitch, Mr. Rainey, Jennifer and the sheriff stood a little apart, watching them go. Mr. Rainey embraced his son from behind, his face working with emotion. Jennifer cried as she held

Mitchell's hand.

Breaking the embrace, Mitch turned to his father. "We gotta go get Lee!"

TEN MINUTES LATER, WITH MITCH AND JENNIFER following, holding hands, Mr. Rainey and the sheriff chair-carried Lee up the final few feet of mountainside. He had regained consciousness and groaned at each misstep. His father watched him with concern.

"You gone make it, boy?"

Lee managed to smile and nod—and passed out.

And now, blowing, they topped the path and broke out onto the windy, wide-open Interstate. After the deep woods, they seemed to be on top of the world, as turning the corner, stepping beyond the concrete guard rail, the mile-long bridge stretched before them like a jetport runway.

There was an ambulance on the shoulder of the bridge, red lights flashing, and traffic on the Interstate slowed to look. Several rubber-necking faces passed in the windows, and Deputy Bennett waved them impatiently on. Two paramedics in white coveralls, a man and a woman, rolled a gurney out to meet the party.

As they placed Lee on it, he revived. "Mitch? Mitch, I'm … sorry I …"

"Shh! I'm here, Lee. Jenny's here too!"

"You … okay?"

"Yeh, we made it, Lee! We made it!"

Lee smiled at his brother and began to speak … then groaned and passed out.

And now from down in the gorge came the first burst of automatic-weapons fire. Now another one. It sounded like the crack of dawn on Opening Day. Or perhaps the first day of the lunar New Year during the "Year of the Monkey"—the Tet Offensive.

The sheriff turned toward the sound. "Well, I reckon I best get back down there—'fore they ain't nothing left to handcuff." He spat over the guardrail. "'Course, they good, Christian boys,

224

most of 'em—but 'bout half was in *Veet*-nam, and they get a little strange 'round gunfire." He wiped his mouth and examined his palm critically. "Know what I mean?"

Mr. Rainey nodded and managed a smile, eyes brimming. "Thanks, Bo," he said, his voice choked with emotion. "I surely do appreciate it. Missus too."

"Don't mention it. What I'm here fer."

"I owe you one."

"One man, one vote."

As they shook hands, a look passed between them.

"Fair enough."

The sheriff turned and started back toward the trailhead, toward the roar of gunfire, as Mr. Rainey, Mitch and Jennifer walked toward the ambulance where Lee was being loaded.

INSIDE, FATHER AND SON CROUCHED ON EITHER SIDE OF LEE. (Jennifer knelt at the head of the gurney, crying.) As Mr. Rainey touched Lee's waxen forehead, wiping away the beaded sweat, his son regained consciousness with a groan.

"How you doing, boy?" his father said softly.

"Okay, I reckon. How's mama?"

Mr. Rainey raised his eyebrows. "Worried sick."

Lee winced. "I'm sorry, daddy. *Real* sorry!"

"Couldn't be helped."

"Yeh, it could."

His father smiled at him then. Already, he could see that his son had done a lot of growing up that weekend. For the first time, he detected what might be the makings of a good man. But sadly too, he had lost a certain innocence; boyhood was, in a very real sense, irrecoverably behind him, irrecoverably upriver of his life.

Still smiling, Mr. Rainey looked at his first-born and shook his head.

"Well, 'at's worth something, I reckon."

Now, looking across Lee, Mr. Rainey saw that Mitchell was crying silently; copious tears that literally dripped in a stream off his trembling chin. His little body fairly shook with silent sobbing.

"Mitch? What's wrong, son?"

"They kilt Mica, daddy!"

"I know, son."

"You do?" Mitch saw his father's expression. "Suellen?"

"I'm 'fraid so, Mitch."

And Mitchell fell into his father's arms and sobbed without shame! All of the pain and fear of the last three days was unleashed in a torrent of tears! Pain too much for a twelve-year-old to bear!

FROM THE END OF THE BRIDGE, THE SHERIFF WATCHED as the ambulance pulled out into the traffic and put on its siren. He watched it across the bridge, weaving in and out of the cars and pickups, until the flashing red light was lost in the distance; the siren as faint as the whine of a mosquito.

With a shake of his head, the sheriff turned and stared downriver. Below the bridge, Civilization had once again hung out her signs. Planted her telephone poles and billboards and big golden arches. There was the glint of roofing tin through the windy trees. The smell of woodsmoke. At riverbend, he saw dairy cows up to their muddy haunches in the streamside, tails lashing at fly-specked flanks.

Nearer, a flyfisherman baited up from a white can of yellow corn, and from the slack backwater below the riprap, he hooked another knothead. He slammed it, cursing, against a rock.

Bikinied girls sunned on a sandbar above Camp Tonawanda, flirting with, up against the cold flank of the Wilderness for $850 a week. Red canoes pulled up on sandy shores. Gunwales hung with teeshirts and cutoffs. On a radio, James Taylor, like a weatherman, sang of fire and rain.

But now, batteries failing, deep-river reception, his voice went staticky as a police dispatcher's. Now cockcrow, and somewhere, the sound of a chainsaw, whining and groaning, the pitch rising and sinking, biting and binding in wet wood.

The sheriff spat over the guardrail, and dodging the traffic, he crossed four lanes to the other side. He paused at the rail as he

226

cut a fresh chew from his plug. Upriver, the view was one of blue ridges, wave after wave of folded mountains, purpling toward a vanishing point in the morning light. And through the center of it all, the big white-water river ran through an endless evergreen forest. As far as the eye could see, there was no trace of human habitation.

The sheriff shook his head and with a sigh turned back toward the end of the bridge; toward, in the sudden silence, the sound of white water, softened by distance, hardened by echo, faint and faraway.

About the Author

Author of seven novels, 10 screenplays and four collections of nonfiction, Sam Mills has been a professional writer for nearly 30 years. Articles for publications like *The Saturday Evening Post, Motor Boating & Sailing, The Denver Post, Golf Magazine, Gray's Sporting Journal, The Atlanta Journal-Constitution, Home & Away* and *Southern Magazine,* have taken him to four continents and 22 foreign countries. Born in Brownsville, Texas, Mills grew up in the mountains of Western North Carolina. He attended UNC-Chapel Hill and graduate school at UW in Madison. He is a winner of the Ned Ramsaur Travel Writing Award, given annually by the South Carolina Department of Parks, Recreation and Tourism.